THE GAME MASTER'S BOOK OF
RANDOM
ENCOUNTERS

ILLUSTRATIONS
BY JASMINE
KALLE

FOREWORD
BY MICHAEL
SHEA

✳ JEFF ASHWORTH ✳

THE GAME MASTER'S BOOK OF
RANDOM
ENCOUNTERS
CONTENTS

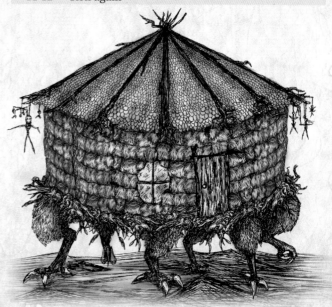

62
The Great Outdoors

86
Homes, Hideouts, Labs & Lairs

Random Tables & More

Random Location Generator

Is your party heading through a door but they (and you) don't have a clue where it leads? Are your adventurers diving through a portal to the unknown? Did they teleport without a sense of their destination? This book is here to help. Start by rolling 1d4 to select a section as outlined on the table below, then roll the requisite dice for that section to determine your random location.

1d4	Where Should You Begin?
1	Taverns, Inns, Shops & Guild Halls
2	Temples, Tombs & Crypts
3	The Great Outdoors
4	Homes, Hideouts, Labs & Lairs

"*The Game Master's Book of Random Encounters* is a toolbox packed with ready-to-use ideas, covering a wide variety of situations. You'll find something useful on every page. No matter what your Game-Mastering style is, this book will help add depth to your game."

—*The Kind GM*, thekindgm.wordpress.com

"This book is so useful! I'm definitely giving a copy to my DM."

—*Madeline Hale, author of* Arcane Artifacts and Curious Curios

FOREWORD

There's a reason most tabletop RPGs always have more players wanting to play than Game Masters able to run games for them. Game-Mastering is hard work. It takes time to prepare. It takes time to organize and schedule. It takes time to come up with all of these crazy stories that our players can fall into.

We GMs need help. We need tools to help us run these games. We need to fill in the infinite gaps in worlds that didn't exist until we thought them up while taking a shower.

This book is one such tool to help you run great roleplaying games. Within it you'll find a host of encounters you can run as-is or harvest for your own stories. Don't like the premises or NPCs? Fill them in with the ones your players already love. Every book like this is a ship out on the sea filled with precious booty just waiting for you to come aboard and take it.

And then there are the locations. This book is full of location descriptions, and every one of them includes a map you don't have to draw. Need an inn? There's one right here. Need a laboratory? This book has you covered. Each location includes seeds for your own adventures. Many of these locations include tables you can use to generate your own stories and seed your own ideas. Such tables are powerful; they shake our minds out of the ruts we often fall into and push us into new realms of creativity that couldn't exist without a random shock to the system.

This book is a wonderful tool to help you run games. Within it is the magic to help you bring entire worlds to life.

MICHAEL SHEA
Author of *Return of the Lazy Dungeon Master*

INTRODUCTION

WELCOME TO
THE GAME MASTER'S BOOK OF
RANDOM ENCOUNTERS...

*I*t's happened to the best of us: You're running an adventure with your party—an adventure for which you've spent countless hours prepping and planning and painting models. Maybe you spent the better part of three days perfecting the accent for a primary NPC you're absolutely certain your party will be desperate to follow into the unexplored abyss of a nearby cave system. You've run several mental simulations to game out the permutations of how each encounter will unfold—the spells they might cast, the strategy they'll employ and supplies they'll utilize to win (or lose) the day. "This session will be perfect," you think aloud as you reorder your note cards and exhale one last time before welcoming players into your world. And then they say those magic words for which there is no saving throw:

"Can we go shopping?"

Or, "Is there a tavern nearby?"

Or, "Should we not have killed that guy? He was just asking us to help him explore a cave, but his accent seemed evil, so...."

And just like that, all your plans go to ruin. Storytelling-by-the-seat-of-your-pants moments are often what make tabletop RPGs such an incredible communal experience. They are also the fastest way for the whole thing to fall apart. Now, maybe this hasn't happened to you because you are some kind of genius (or an actual wizard) and your players never force you to improvise entire adventures as a direct result of their endless supply of creativity. But you are likely the exception rather than the rule. For everyone else, this book is here to help. While it won't stop your players from being creative, or meta-gaming, or stabbing the only person who could have helped them solve that mysterious murder from two weeks ago, it will focus your efforts to put them on a new and exciting path—even if that path simply leads to more mayhem.*

---

*It will. It always does.

What This Book Is

The Game Master's Book of Random Encounters is primarily a collection of locations for your players to explore, complete with unique NPCs, randomly generated problems for them to tackle (or avoid) and optional hazards and triggers to keep your sessions exciting even when you don't exactly know where you plan to go next. Each location is presented on a 5-foot scale grid and includes detailed descriptions so you'll know exactly where you are, even when you're totally lost. The Table of Contents also doubles as a table that will help you choose a completely random location if you want a more chaotic experience.

This book was created using the System Resource Document for the Fifth Edition of the world's most popular TTRPG but is compatible with as many tabletop RPG systems as you're willing to translate it into. The license for the SRD is printed for your convenience on pg. 140.

What This Book Is Not

This book is not perfectly balanced. Because every party is different, I leave these locations and the encounters associated with them in your capable hands. If it seems like your party is about to be torn to shreds because of a random dice roll on a Variant Encounter table, adjust the necessary stats or motivations for the creatures in question in order to keep your players alive and carry on. Or kill them. The choice is yours. Just don't blame this book. It wouldn't be able to live with itself.**

This book is not a manual full of monsters, nor does it feature a list of spells and their various effects. There are creatures mentioned throughout this title that you'll find correspond with various ghouls, goblins, orcs and oozes that you likely know on a first name basis, and you'll find their stats in whatever standard resource you use for encounter building. They'll be marked bold. Spells and magical items will be italicized for easy reference.

This book is not as good as the one you could have written. No one knows your party as well as you do, and therefore no one can create adventure modules or random encounters that challenge and surprise them like you. It's why you're their GM, not me. This book's aim is to inspire you to tell better stories at your table. Part of that process is recognizing that if you think you can improve on what's written here, you absolutely should. That means changing not just the details of the encounters in this book, but the spirit in which you present them—if you choose to use them at all. Use your judgment. Follow your players. Or drag them somewhere unexpected. Let me know how it goes.

This book is not trapped.

How To Use This Book

FLAVOR TEXT: When you see text styled like this, it means you should read it out loud to your party to describe specific actions, relay important quotes or share pertinent details of the location or situation they find themselves in.

QUOTE TEXT: WHEN TEXT IS STYLED LIKE THIS, IT'S SUPPLEMENTARY AND SHOULD BE USED TO INFORM YOUR PRESENTATION OF A LOCATION OR NPC.

Maps

The maps detailed on these pages are presented on a grid, and each square represents a 5 foot x 5 foot space unless otherwise noted. If you'd prefer to use theater of the mind, feel free to adjust the sizes of different spaces to suit your needs as necessary (which you are also within your rights to do if you are planning to draw these locations out for your players).

Variant Encounters

At GM discretion, when a party enters one of the locations detailed in this book, roll on the Variant Encounters table associated with the location to determine which encounter to trigger, or select one for yourself. These encounters add flavor, urgency and variety to a given location and are one of the main features of this book—so put them to use! Or don't. It's your game.

Encounter Variants

Similar to Variant Encounters, these optional adjustments typically refer to a location's atmosphere, climate or clientele. If you choose to use them, it's a good idea to roll on the tables before describing the layout and features of a location to your party, as these options can have a drastic impact on the way players might approach an encounter. For example, a random pond could be "overgrown" or "frozen" or "teeming with undead." These are the types of things you'd want to know before your party's impulsive paladin shouts "CANNONBALL" and plunges into the shallow end. Of course, whether you share this information is entirely up to you.

**This book is not alive.

TAVERNS, INNS, SHOPS & GUILD HALLS

A COLLECTION OF STOREFRONTS, BARS, HOTELS AND MORE, SUITABLE FOR ANY TOWN OR CITY.

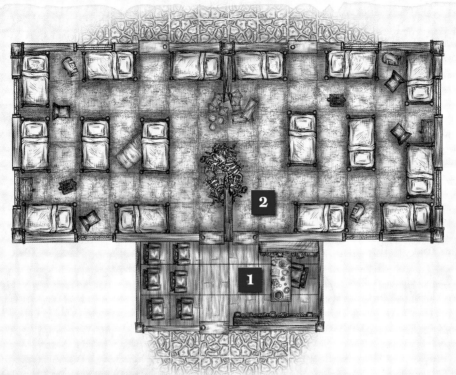

THE NOT HOSTEL

For cheap lodging, you could do worse than this rundown spot. But you'd have to try extremely hard.

RECEPTION

The front desk *(1)* at the Not Hostel is run by a stout dwarven woman named Millie Hunk. The foyer of the reception area is exquisitely appointed, and Millie works diligently to ensure her humble hostel looks presentable at all hours of the day or night. Rates are 2 cp for a bunk, which is a pittance compared to other places to stay but still feels a bit overpriced once guests are escorted to the sleeping quarters. Millie and the Not Hostel have a strict "no refunds" policy.

SLEEPING QUARTERS

Bunk beds stacked three high are the most prolific visual in this space *(2)*, and depending on the time of year, each might be home to more than one resident. The room, once divided into two parts by a now-busted wall, features a mix of stale breath, wet shoes and a patina of body odors from across the realm hanging in the air. Upon entering the room, each creature must succeed on a DC 10 Constitution save or suffer a bout of nausea, vomiting on a failed save.

RESIDENTS

Roll 1d4 to determine how many guests other than those in the party are staying at the Not Hostel.

1d4	The Not Hostel is...
1	**...nearly empty** but only because there's a dead half-orc rotting in one of the bunks.
2	**...full** with one body for each bed.
3	**...packed** with one body per bed plus a group of musicians sleeping beneath a few bunks.
4	**...overflowing** with an extra 3d10 gnomes and halflings buddying up with other bunkmates.

VARIANT ENCOUNTER (OPTIONAL)

Roll 1d6 to see what hostilities ensue at the Not Hostel.

1d6	The party...
1	...must contend with 3d4 drunk **goblins**.
2	...must endure the sounds of an angry half-orc dictating a letter for his ex to a terrified halfling.
3	...sees a trio of gnomes playing dice with a **berserker** who keeps losing, and isn't pleased.
4	...is confronted by a surly dwarf who says they are in his bunk.
5	...finds a hole in the floor, from which scamper 3d4 **swarms of rats**.
6	...walks in on an all out brawl between two gangs of 2d4 **bugbears** over who has to bunk with whom.

THE TWO DOORS TAVERN

A lively ale house where every evening promises only unpredictability, the main features of the Two Doors Tavern are its titular doors. They serve to separate the clientele into teams across a variety of random categories, and each night the tavern's bars are lowered several times for games of skill, chance and athletic prowess. The tavern's owner, a half-elf named **Noon Fantasia,** conceived of the idea to foster stronger relationships between strangers, and many patrons regularly return to the tavern to see if they'll be "Right-siders" or "Left-siders" the next time through the doors.

DIVIDING SIGN. Upon approaching the Two Doors Tavern, would-be patrons are met by a two-arrowed sign (*1*) directing them toward the proper entrance based on that day's stipulated manner of separation. The sign is updated at random (see Dividing Sign Table), though occasionally the division works so well it'll be repeated.

DIVIDING SIGN TABLE

Roll 1d6 to determine the sign's message.

1d6	Left-siders	Right-siders
1	The Pointy-Eared	All Others
2	5 feet or fewer	More than 5 feet
3	Locals	Out-of-towners
4	Wizards, Mages, Magicky-types	Blades, Bows, Brawlers
5	Devout	Depraved
6	What do they call you? A–M	What do they call you? N–Z

THE TAVERN. The Two Doors Tavern's defining physical features, apart from its entrance, are its two bars, which run parallel to one another, separating what would otherwise be the largest tavern in town into two smaller portions (*2*). Barkeeps sling ale to both sides of the room, scuttling around one another as necessary to cater to thirsty (and often a bit unruly) patrons. Left-siders and Right-siders are not permitted to switch sides, and a strict expulsion policy is enforced for those who don't abide by the Dividing Sign—typically by the patrons themselves. The space lacks much in the way of furnishings, but the few tables and chairs on either side are built to take a beating. Sawdust from a nearby mill lines the floor and is brought in fresh each morning. Several times per night, upon a signal from the Middle Man, the dividing bars sink into the floor and the tavern's two spaces merge into one—a sign that the games are about to begin.

THE MIDDLE MAN. Throughout the night, the Middle Man—effectively a master of ceremonies—rings a bell and announces the nature of the face-off (see Random Revels table). For years, Noon Fantasia served as the Middle Man every night of the week but has since relinquished the duties to his son Porter and his daughter Miriam. Noon occasionally will step back into his old role, especially if the tavern is particularly packed or has distinguished guests.

NPC PROFILE
NOON FANTASIA, THE ORIGINAL MIDDLE MAN

A half-elf who grew tired of the way citizens in the city were treating those who could be categorized as "different" from them, Noon is a showman who plans to leave the Two Doors Tavern to his children, Porter and Miriam. He is creative, charismatic and competitive.

VARIANT: BATTLE ROYALE

In the event of a double dice roll on the Random Revels table (or at GM discretion), the Middle Man announces the final Revel will be a Battle Royale—a no-holds-barred face-off between patrons. Last side standing wins. The Middle Man should also make it clear that it's frowned upon to intentionally maim or kill a member of the other side in combat. Still, the bar's relationship with a nearby temple ensures a cleric or two can step in to quickly revive or regenerate anyone who loses an arm, leg or life. The recently deceased drink for free for the rest of the night.

Random Revels

Roll 3d6 for three consecutive contests, which can play out in any order you choose. Each side of the bar should select competitors for each event, as necessary.

1d6   "Tonight's revels will be..."

1   **"...arm wrestling!"** Two challengers face off using consecutive contested Strength (Athletics) checks. A winner is determined after three high rolls in a row.

2   **"...dodging this ball!"** Three challengers from each side alternate throwing a stuffed sheep's bladder at one another (contested ranged attack vs. Dexterity save). A failed save is a hit, which eliminates that player. Last team standing wins.

3   **"...an ale guzzling contest!"** Each side chooses one challenger to consume five ales in a row, making five Constitution checks—highest total wins. At the end of the contest, both participants must make a DC 15 Constitution save to determine their level of inebriation for the rest of the night.

4   **"...trivia of the obscure!"** Three random questions are presented to both sides one at a time—and the side that determines the answer first (contested Intelligence (History) check) is declared the winner.

5   **"...giant boar taming!"** One representative from each side must face off against a **giant boar**—which magically appears in the center of the tavern room—and attempt to ride it. Longest time (consecutive Dexterity or Strength checks against DC 15) wins. A DC 17 Wisdom (Animal Handling) check offers advantage on the checks.

6   **"...a battle of instruments!"** Three representatives from each side must perform their favorite tune (contested group Charisma [Performance] check) using the lute, flute and shawm hanging on the wall.

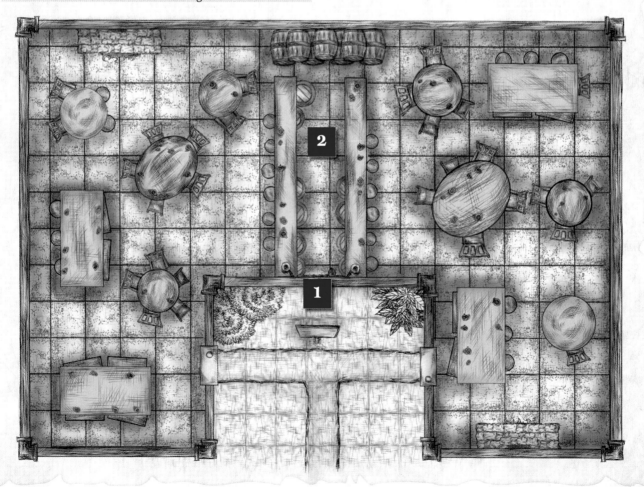

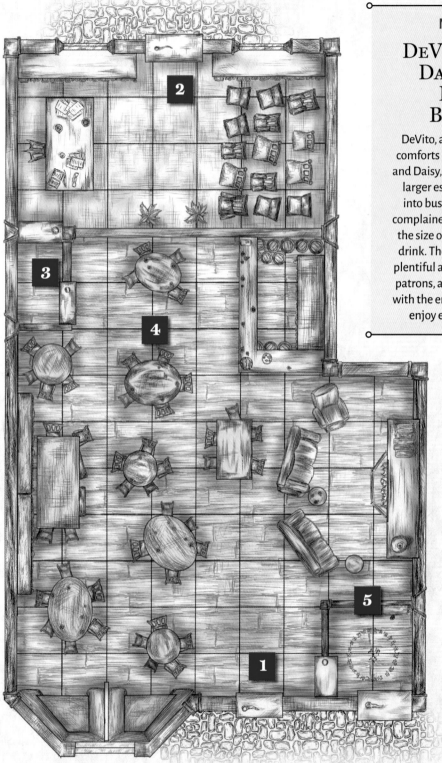

NPC Profiles

DeVito Fenwick & Daisy Flyfoot, Big Little Bar Owners

DeVito, a gnome who longed for the comforts (and scale) of his hometown, and Daisy, a halfling barmaid at a much larger establishment, decided to go into business together after DeVito complained of having to lift mugs of ale the size of his torso in order to enjoy a drink. The booze and banter is just as plentiful at their cozy bar for pint-sized patrons, and the duo carry themselves with the energy of platonic friends who enjoy each other and their work.

THE BIG LITTLE BAR

The Big Little Bar is a destination for many of the city's more diminutive dwellers to revel and relax in a space built with their size in mind. With a ceiling just under 5 feet high, any guest who can't easily walk through the 4-foot Big Small Door is immediately directed around the back to the Small Big Entrance, where a powerful *reduce* spell will temporarily transform them into pint-sized patrons.

GETTING IN

There are two entrances to the Big Little Bar, with those under 4 feet tall using the Big Small Door. All others must report to **DeVito Fenwick** through the Small Big Entrance.

THE BIG SMALL DOOR (1). A rather wide but still squat doorway leads in and out of the bar for those who can fit through the frame, which cuts off at 4 feet. This door serves as the main entrance for the Big Little Bar's target clientele, and woe to anyone who chooses to enter by ducking beneath it—a powerful glyph of warding is triggered by anyone who ignores the clear warning that states: *"4 Foot or Below Entrance Only—All Others Go Around. No Exceptions."* Those ignoring the sign are immediately hit with two doses of the *reduce* spell (Wisdom save, DC 20) which, if successful, doubly reduces their size—an effect that lasts until their next long rest.

THE SMALL BIG ENTRANCE (2). Upon entering the Big Little Bar's Small Big Entrance, adventurers find themselves in a compact but well-appointed space, not unlike a waiting room, with fine leather chairs facing a relatively small desk, where they're greeted by one of the bar's owners—DeVito Fenwick**,** a powerful gnomish wizard who explains the bar's concept to anyone who isn't on board. He minimizes any willing creatures who don't meet the bar's size ordinance (4 ft. or less) with the *reduce* spell by sending them through the Be Small Hall.

BE SMALL HALL (3). This narrow corridor connects the Small Big Entrance holding area to the bar proper, its walls adorned with artful silhouettes of taller figures that get progressively smaller as they get closer to the opposite end of the hallway. The ceiling shifts diagonally from roughly 9 feet down to 5. Most nights, music carries through the 4.5-foot tall door at the end of the hall, leading to the Big Little Bar Room.

INSIDE THE BIG LITTLE BAR

Upon entering the Big Little Bar Room (4), guests find themselves among a calm but high-spirited clientele, the majority of whom are halflings and gnomes seeking a cozy space to relax, share stories and drink ale out of mugs that don't require a two-handed grip to lift. The bar's other proprietor, a charming if occasionally foul-mouthed halfling named **Daisy Flyfoot,** manages the flow of half-pints and gossip from her post behind the bar. On any given night, the Big Little Bar hosts miniaturized humanoid creatures of various races, with its no-nonsense hospitality and particular aesthetic having helped build a constant stream of regulars over the years. Occasionally, dwarves or smaller humans who barely pass the height requirement forgo the *reduce* spell and fill out the space like a goliath might a more traditional establishment, their arms easily extending to the 5-foot ceiling.

GETTING OUT

There are two exits to the Big Little Bar, both clearly marked. Anyone under 4 feet or those wishing to remain reduced for the remainder of the day are free to leave through the Big Small Door. All others are directed to leave through the Big Again Byway, an exit that leads to a small chamber where one by one, guests can return to their normal size.

BIG AGAIN BYWAY (5). Upon entering the Big Again Byway, reduced guests will notice a glowing ring on the wooden floor, a clear marker for a magical enchantment. A sign in Common and Elvish just above the circle reads "Stand here, pull this, be big" and also indicates a lever that stands at 4.5 feet on the wall, nearly out of reach for smaller guests, a subtle reminder for each patron not to take their full size forms for granted. The lever also features a small coin slot labeled "5 sp." Should guests choose to insert 5 sp into the slot and pull the lever, they'll find themselves quickly restored to their normal size. Guests who forgo payment and choose to leave the bar will discover the *reduce* spell wears off after a long rest. Dropping a coin in the slot produces a satisfying "clink" but upon further investigation doesn't appear to lead to an accessible bank. The lever only works once per patron per day, a further testament to the proprietor's magical prowess.

VARIANT ENCOUNTER (OPTIONAL)

Roll 1d6 to see what small wonders and big trouble await the party at the Big Little Bar.

1d6	The party sees...
1	...a half-orc **berserker**, concerned by his suddenly small size, who goes into a rage and riots.
2	...a group of 2d4 rotund dwarves picking a fight with 1d4 newly small half-elves.
3	...a halfling wild magic sorcerer surges, causing everyone in the room to double in size before screaming like a woman possessed (note: she is).
4	...a miniature suit of armor adorning the wall springs to life as a small **helmed horror**.
5	...a trio of figures at the bar remove their hoods, revealing themselves to be miniaturized **scarecrows**.
6	...a tap behind the bar starts to seep a mysterious yellowish substance, the start of an **ochre jelly** assault.

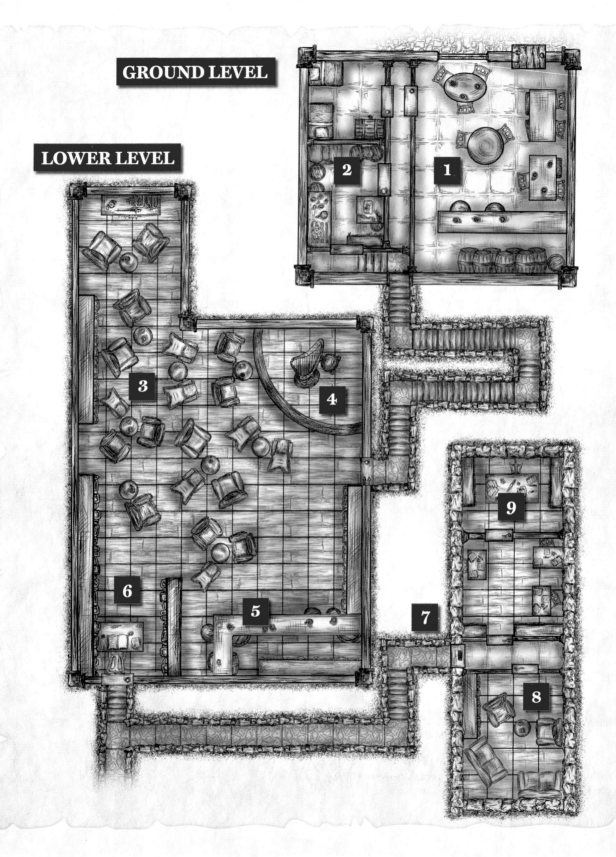

GROUND LEVEL

LOWER LEVEL

THE WOUNDED ROGUE

Approaching from the muddy street in the wrong part of town, the Wounded Rogue is certainly not the first place on anyone's list of Top 10 Bars. In fact, it would probably merit inclusion on Fantasy Trip Advisor's Places Sensible People Should Avoid at All Costs list. That suits The Wounded Rogue just fine, as it's not the smell of burnt socks permeating the tiny taproom that has hooded ne'er-do-wells coming back again and again. This relative hole-in-the-wall hides a secret only the shadiest charlatans manage to seek out.

THE FRONT

GROUND FLOOR. From the outside, this tiny dive bar has grimy windows and a crooked door that looks as if it has been knocked off its hinges more than a few times. A scraggly human barmaid named Karlga welcomes would-be guests with a toothless smile and a quiet, beady-eyed stare. The taproom (*1*) is tiny and serves two types of ale: dark and darker. Two other customers in the bar sit slumped over their table, too inebriated to react to any newcomers. The smells of burnt hair and something that may once have resembled food waft through the ajar door to the left which, on further inspection, leads to a narrow hallway where a grumpy half-orc named Unek is sweating in the kitchen (*2*).

COMPLIMENTS TO THE CHEF. The only choices on the menu are soup or ale, each for the low, low price of two copper. Both taste overpriced. If the adventurers order the soup, it is delivered quickly by Unek and immediately revealed to be the source of the bar's horrific smell. If a party member is willing to try it, have them make a DC 10 Constitution saving throw or be poisoned for the next hour.

A DC 17 Wisdom (Perception) check reveals a filthy scrap of parchment pinned to the wall behind Karlga that states "Please let the chef know if you enjoy the soup!" and also features markings in Thieves' Cant stating that a respite for all ne'er-do-wells exists below. Should the party choose to give their compliments to the chef, they are directed down the small hallway to the kitchen. Upon receiving compliments for his cooking, Unek will open an almost-seamless hidden door behind a shelf of slowly rotting vegetables, which leads to a bar beneath this one.

If the party fails to figure out the secret of the soup, a cloaked figure can enter the bar, order the soup and have a quiet word with Karlga before disappearing down the hallway. A DC 18 Wisdom (Perception) check reveals their conversation ("Compliments to the chef"/"Tell him yourself."). If the party follows, the figure is gone. The kitchen's hidden door can also be discovered with a DC 25 Wisdom (Perception) or Intelligence (Investigation) check.

THE ACTUAL WOUNDED ROGUE

> There's a refined elegance to this room that is immediately apparent upon entering. Polished wooden floors and stylish leather chairs accompany this beautiful cocktail bar. Hushed conversation permeates the room and is intertwined with the dulcet tones of a harp that makes it extremely difficult to eavesdrop.

The people reclining on the chairs in this well-appointed lounge (*3*) all have a certain hard edge to them, and it takes skilled eyes to see beyond the shadows of many hoods in the dim, lantern light. A skilled harp player (*4*) obscures most low-level conversations, and those wishing to listen in must make a Wisdom (Perception) check with disadvantage (DC 20). Lip-reading is equally difficult, as most patrons obscure their mouths with hands or mugs of ale to keep their conversations discreet.

In the corner next to the bar (*5*) and surrounded by shelves of leather-bound ledgers is a beautiful mahogany desk (*6*). Behind the desk sits the Contractor, Mariosa McGee, a middle-aged, turquoise-skinned tiefling with graying, curly hair tied in a neat bun behind her head and framed by a pair of twisting, black kudu horns. Her flat, white eyes seemingly look at everything and nothing at once as she constantly writes in the open ledger book in front of her. Two attendants, a surly orc named Grit, and Samata, a lithe-looking female half-elf with no tongue, flank Mariosa and see to her every need.

THE GUILD OFFICES. Behind Mariosa's desk is a short tunnel (*7*) that leads to a cushy office (*8*) that can be hired out for private and sensitive conversations and is warded against eavesdroppers and scrying. A separate door leads to the Assassin's Guild office (*9*), through which all Guild business flows. This office is similarly warded and also alarmed against would-be attackers.

VARIANT ENCOUNTER (OPTIONAL) KILLERS FOR HIRE

Should the party wish to inquire about possible contracts available, they can approach and offer to buy Mariosa a drink from the bar, which costs 20 gp.

Depending on the party's standing with the Assassin's Guild, roll on the tables on the next page to determine what kind of contracts are available.

WOUNDED ROGUE: GUILD CONTRACTS

TAKE A LOOK AT THIS MENU AND SEE IF ANY OF THESE DISHES SUIT YOUR APPETITE. AT GM DISCRETION, ROLL 1D10 ON THE APPROPRIATE TABLE TO ASSIGN THESE CONTRACTS AT RANDOM.

Appetizers (a good way to begin)

1	A noblewoman wants to help her husband's mistress find a new home, possibly 6 feet underground. Maybe with room for him as well. —100 gp for one, 300 gp for both
2	A local farmer is convinced his neighbor has cursed his field and wants revenge. —45 gp
3	The town cheesemonger wants his thieving brother-in-law turned into Swiss. —90 gp
4	The proprietor of the Righteous Ale House wants to rough up her business rival at the Golden Apple, whom she believes is using underhanded methods to steal customers. —50 gp
5	A mysterious benefactor is paying to have a vial of an unknown substance tipped into the drinking water barrels of the Eastern Guard Barracks. No questions asked, no traces left. —250 gp
6	Two brothers have put a hit out on one another in order to lay full claim to their father's inheritance. The current bid is 85 gp, though you may be able to play them off each other to the tune of 200 gp.
7	A large group of young pickpockets have pooled their resources to ensure the street thief they work for finds himself penniless or worse. —22 gp
8	An anonymous donor will pay a divine sum to the soul brave enough to hide three sacks of bones in a nearby temple of life. —186 gp
9	One of the region's most prominent philanthropists has been bilking his own charity for years. Do some good by bringing the truth to light, or dispense your own brand of justice. —241 gp
10	In the town square is a statue of a woman named Philomena Morgen. People think she's great, but she was actually the worst. Her granddaughter wishes for it to be defaced or destroyed. Bonus points (and pay) for style. —45 gp, triple if the job causes a major fuss. She would have hated that.

Mains (for the more experienced palate)

1	The serfs of an iron-handed liege lord have unionized and pooled their resources, wanting to claim what's owed to them in both blood and lands. Death to the bourgeoisie! —1,245 gp
2	The Crown Prince of a rival kingdom wants his fiancé, the Crown Prince of this kingdom, to have a horrific and fatal accident immediately following their wedding day next week. Must be no trace of foul play. —3,000 gp
3	A noble is looking for assistance in "removing" a village of **druids**, **pixies** and **giants** that have taken up residence in his forest. —850 gp
4	An acolyte wants an entire temple's worth of clerics and paladins put down for what she believes are heretical practices occurring among her order's leadership. —1,000 gp in rare artifacts and artwork
5	A soldier who spent 15 years in prison for desertion is ready to exercise revenge on the corrupt general who forced him out. —785 gp and access to rare and powerful military weaponry
6	Several wealthy benefactors are interested in the complete destruction of the seat of power in this city. It should seem as though this event has been perpetrated by a supernatural or extraplanar force. —3,400 gp (double if it results in a war)
7	There's a hermit in a cave nearby. Some think he's a druid. We think he's a **brass dragon**. Whatever he is, the merchants want him gone. —645 gp, plus whatever's in the cave
8	One of our special clients will pay you 100 gp for every innocent life you take from the time you agree to this contract until the following sunrise.
9	From the client: "Please kill my dad. Please make it public. Please make him squeal. P.S. My dad is a god." —6,800 gp
10	A suspected **rakshasa** is masquerading as a minister. Take him out. Not once: forever. —4,745 gp

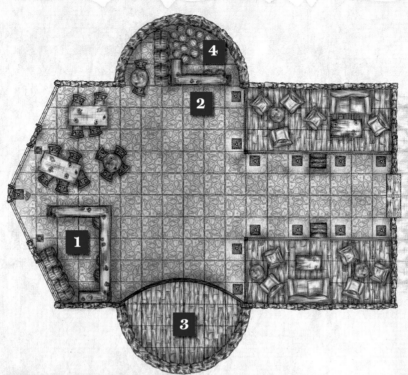

Temple Bar

> ### *"COME WORSHIP WITH US! TWO DRINK MINIMUM, NO SINGLES"* —sign outside Temple Bar

Praise a Glass

A group of enterprising hedonists bought this space when it was a run-down shrine to a mostly forgotten god, Fairguun. It now serves as a de facto dancehall dedicated to Dionysus. A space defined by its past as much as its present, Temple Bar's slab floors and open archways give it a monolithic feel—a once hallowed ground now serving as a gateway to the sometimes divine act of eating, drinking and dancing. Fairguun, a divine being long associated with fertility and a good harvest, fell out of favor many centuries ago following a decades-long drought and, as such, her temple here languished and eventually sat empty for years. Recently purchased and now refurbished, Temple Bar serves all manner of spirits, snacks and other sinful delights at its two bars *(1) (2)*. The transgressive concept of the bar is both a subject of controversy and part of its appeal. The servers and bartenders wear matching, slightly skimpy vestments and ask for tithes as opposed to tips, while a choir of bards play ribald, rhythmic tunes that equally mock gods of all pantheons from the main stage *(3)*.

Temple Bar's customers are generally cut from the same cloth—outsiders and trendsetters who have no issue thumbing their nose at the holy or sanctified. A trap door beyond the smaller bar *(4)* leads to the crypts, the sewers or another location at GM discretion.

Variant Encounter (Optional)

Roll 1d6 to reveal what sacrilege occurs at Temple Bar.

1d6	The party encounters...
1	...a **priest** of Fairguun from another part of the realm who has arrived at Temple Bar following a months-long pilgrimage and is viewing the space with a pained look in his eye.
2	...a group of 2d4 city **guards** arriving to address an indecency complaint, which the bar owners refuse to pay.
3	...a drunk patron knocking over a statue of Fairguun, which smashes into the floor, unveiling a crypt with 2d4 rising **skeletons**.
4	...three "high priestesses" of Temple Bar who challenge select members of the party to a dance contest.
5	...an **assassin** hired by one of the city's more devout nobles who will attempt to poison the drinks at Temple Bar in order to put them out of business.
6	...a lecherous dwarf who calls himself "Cleric of the New Fairguun" overtly offering to help anyone within earshot with all their fertility needs.

THE WIDE-EYED WILLOW

A pleasant place for a chat, a warming mug of tea or a cup of the proprietor's signature "cold brew," this café-style establishment is equal parts calming and innervating. And its customers keep coming back.

> As you enter the Wide-Eyed Willow, you feel as if you're in a sunlit forest in the Feywild. Colorful beads of light float around the interior, illuminating the shade from a central willow tree that's thriving indoors. The smell of moss, mocha and freshly tilled earth fills your nostrils as a short queue of customers wait patiently for their orders to be filled by a busy half-elven woman with braided hair and a wry smile. A small sign by the counter declares: "Tea 1 sp, Cold Brew 2 sp. Ask about our new customer policy."

INTERIOR

The Wide-Eyed Willow is an open space, but its various nooks and woodsy interior create an immediate sense of intimacy (*1*). Well-fashioned tables and chairs as well as cozier furniture offer a chance to catch up with old friends or make new ones. The serving counter (*2*) features a few barstools, though the line of customers around it makes sitting there a choice of last resort. A large willow tree (*3*) growing inside this space creates ambiance as well as a small abode for two **pixies**, Mink and Wink, and its trunk and branches extend from within this café out to the patio (*4*).

SERVICE COUNTER. The service counter of the Wide-Eyed Willow is piled high with pastries and other baked goods, and beyond it is a small alchemy station (*5*) where the Willow's proprietor, **Ruby Sunbeam**, mixes her brews, which she serves chilled through a combination of on-hand ice and arcane techniques.

COLD BREW. This proprietary blend of herbs, spices and a bean harvested from the outdoor garden (*6*) that's been roasted and ground gives a boost of energy along with its somewhat bitter taste. The kick keeps customers coming back for a daily dose. A new customer can enjoy their first cold brew on the house.

VARIANT ENCOUNTER (OPTIONAL)

1d6	What's happening at the Wide-Eyed Willow?
1	A surly looking half-orc has been taking up an entire table on his own for nearly three hours but has yet to place an order. He refuses to budge.
2	Mink and Wink, two **pixies** who work with Ruby, emerge from their home within the willow tree and begin teasing customers in line.
3	An elven female asks the party if they wouldn't mind watching her bag for a moment while she deals with something outside. The bag contains a **green faerie dragon** that takes the opportunity to escape.
4	Two **druids**, their faces obscured by masks, stride through the willow tree and into the café, demanding Ruby hand over her recipe for cold brew or deal with the consequences.
5	A group of four young, tragically hip humans notice the adventurers and can be overheard making fun of their attire.
6	A budding author working on his manuscript while finishing his fourth cold brew of the day excitedly solicits true stories of derring-do from the adventurers, offering 10 gp for each provable story (max 100 gp).

Cold Brew

Wondrous Item (potion), COMMON, 2 sp

For up to an hour after consuming this concoction, you feel more alert and have +2 to both initiative rolls and passive perception.

When the potion wears off, make a DC 17 Constitution save or suffer -4 to initiative rolls and passive perception, as what the locals refer to as the "cold brew crash" washes over you. This effect lasts 24 hours but can be removed via the *greater restoration* spell or by consuming another cold brew.

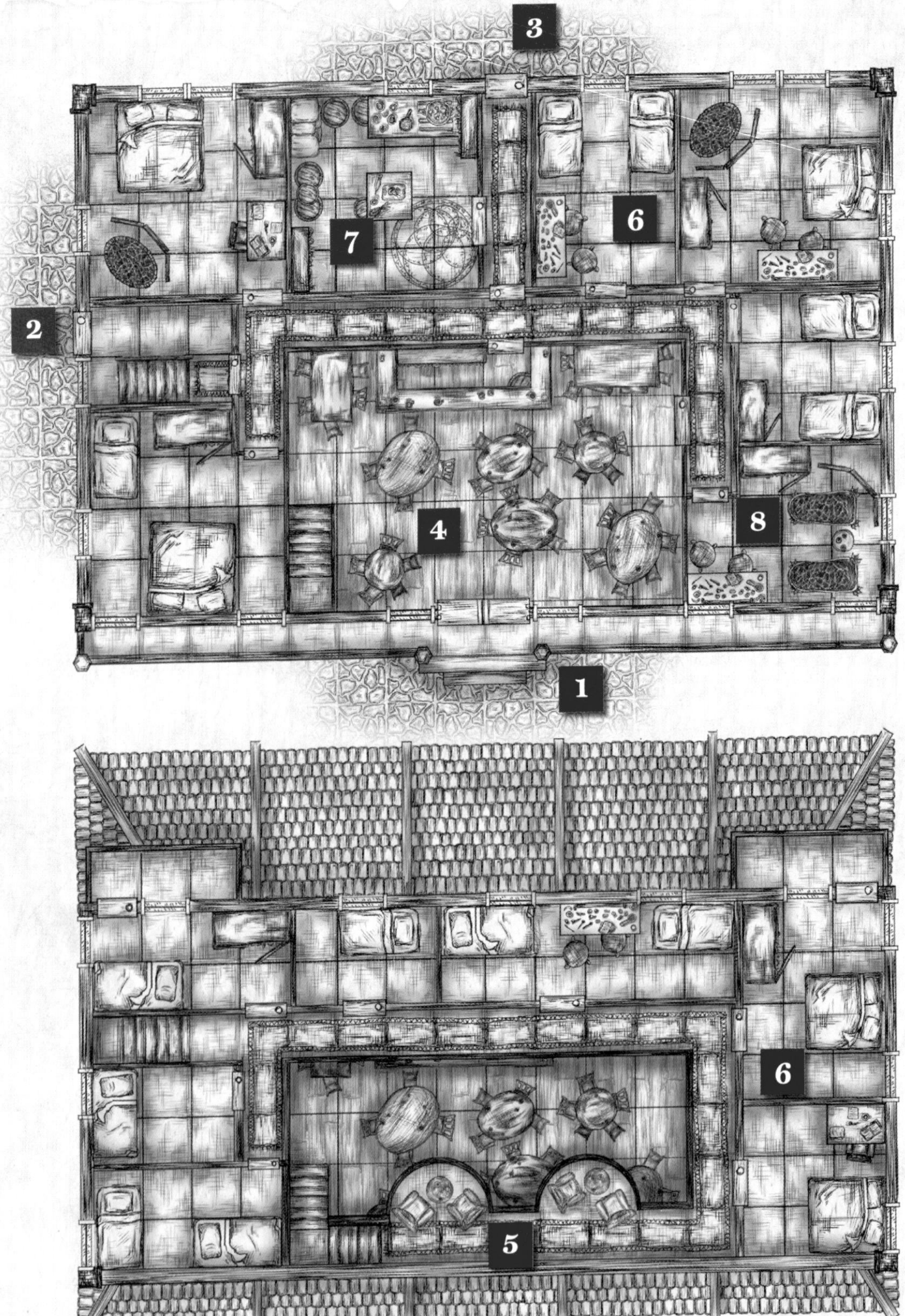
3
2
7
6
4
8
1
6
5

THE RED HERRING

For travelers seeking the softest beds and finest linens, this opulent boutique hotel offers a level of service and comfort unparalleled in most parts of the realm. The Red Herring's proprietor, a telepathic half-elven woman named **Calley O'Toole**, sees to customers' every need.

ENTRANCES AND EXITS

The Red Herring features a main entrance (**1**) that leads directly to the parlor, plus an entrance for guests who wish to avoid the parlor's typical crowds (**2**). An entrance for employees can be found along the inn's backside (**3**).

PARLOR AND PRIVATE LOUNGE

The Red Herring's parlor (**4**) is an immaculately appointed lounge space featuring dark, polished wood surfaces, gold inlays and a scuff-free marble floor. The bar's prices—more than double those of any establishment nearby—do much to keep the riffraff from spoiling the evening, but for clientele who require even more of a remove from those they deem below their station, the Red Herring does have private seating for preferred guests on the second-floor balcony (**5**). From this perch, those willing to pay for the privilege can enjoy their libations while looking down on the rest of the guests—a metaphor they knowingly embrace.

LODGINGS

Bedrooms at the Red Herring (**6**) are available on an hourly, nightly or weekly basis for those who have the coin, and in the past, arrangements have been made for guests who wished to extend their stay for a month or more.

KITCHENS

While this space features the requisite mechanisms of any quality kitchen, the cooking space within the Red Herring (**7**) is more conduit than creative arena, and it is one of the secrets to the inn's success. A teleportation circle within the kitchen ensures if the Red Herring's cooks can't prepare a particular dish, they can bring in someone who can. Guests from far-off lands can request the cuisine of their homeland and find that, remarkably, it will be available within the hour, regardless of how obscure its ingredients might be due to this feature. Much like everything else at the Red Herring, these services come with a hefty price tag.

BATHS

A long journey can sully the appearance of even the most noble of travelers, and for this reason the Red Herring offers a wide array of spa services—including washings, massages, manicures and more—in its large bathhouse (**8**).

NPC PROFILE
CALLEY O'TOOLE, HALF-ELF HOTELIER

To hear her tell it, when Calley O'Toole inherited the Red Herring from her father 14 years ago, it was in complete disrepair. Today it is considered one of the most successful inns of its size, thanks in no small part to Miss O'Toole's singular vision, attention to detail and ability to cut through the pleasantries to determine precisely what her clientele desires. She will openly discuss nearly any topic at length, but follows any formal booking with a discrete "Need anything else?" asked wordlessly within the client's mind. Though the service at the Red Herring is second to none, some attribute the inn's success to Miss O'Toole's lack of scruples when it comes to fulfilling these silent requests, no matter how strange, shocking or vile. It should also be noted that Miss O'Toole is, in reality, a **succubus** who replaced the innkeeper not long after his death and uses the Red Herring as a home base for her life's work: the slow corruption of the human soul.

VARIANT ENCOUNTER (OPTIONAL)

Roll 1d6 to determine whether riches or ruin awaits the party within the walls of the Red Herring.

1d6	The party...
1	...learns the teleportation circle in the kitchen has been commandeered by a band of 2d6 **lizardfolk** intent on looting the inn.
2	...hears screams echoing from the bathhouse as a **water weird** begins to overwhelm a wealthy patron.
3	...overhears a conversation between two merchants in the private lounge getting heated, as one challenges the other to a duel.
4	...is oblivious to a highly skilled charlatan slinking through the parlor, picking the pockets of every man she encounters (DC 17).
5	...sees an unctuous guest at the bar bragging about his last visit to the Red Herring, where his request to dine on unicorn tartare was fulfilled.
6	...meets a traveling **gladiator** who arrived with his entourage and demands to sit at the table (or stay in the room) where the party has positioned themselves.

MINI MARKET

A small shop amid the bustle of the busiest street in town, this humble space sells a little bit of everything but all of nothing and is managed by **Amadeus Thudd**, a big man who is ready to expand.

SHOP INTERIOR

The inside of the Mini Market is a mixed bag of shelves filled with a wide array of merchandise, including nonperishable foodstuffs, potions, waterskins, weaponry, hats, blankets, packs, uncured leather, alchemical supplies, tinkering wares, a wheel for a cart, a key to a chest no one's been able to find, a few pieces of farming equipment, a copper kettle, a wad of string, a bolt, a rag doll with some pins in it and a jug sealed with a large plug among other less-useful odds and ends. It is, in sum, akin to an adventurer's flea market, and there's no telling what one might find, though they'll at least find the gazing attention of Spat, a small, one-eyed rat who hangs around the shop and keeps Amadeus company.

A LITTLE BIT OF EVERYTHING

If an adventurer is seeking something specific, they can ask Amadeus, the Mini Market's sole proprietor, if he has it in stock. Amadeus will think long and hard, then suggest the adventurer look in a specific corner of the shop (at GM discretion). The character should then roll an Intelligence (Investigation) check (DC 15) to determine if they can find the item requested. Despite the fact that most of the goods sold at the Mini Market are common in nature, approximately 5 percent of the items in the shop are magical, with properties and rarities determined at GM discretion.

NPC PROFILE

AMADEUS THUDD, HALF-GIANT SHOPKEEPER

A half-giant of colossal size who makes his small shop feel even more diminutive, Amadeus Thudd ("Mad" to his friends) left the adventuring life behind after a close companion was disintegrated before his eyes by an evil sorcerer. Amadeus removed the sorcerer's arms as well as his tongue, but a hole in his heart still remained. He walked away from fighting dragons and pillaging dungeons and now spends his time outfitting others to do the same. He sells just about anything an adventurer could need, but due to the size of his shop he rarely has more than one of anything in stock—though he's hoping to get enough capital together to build a larger location. He is eager to offer advice from his years of adventuring experience, and though his greatsword is a bit rusty, his mind is sharp.

VARIANT ENCOUNTER (OPTIONAL)

Roll 1d6 to see what else might be in the Mini Market.

1d6	The party sees...
1	...a baby **orc** who wandered from its family.
2	...1d4 **bullywugs** who want to trade mud for gold.
3	...a pig that takes a liking to the party.
4	...a **yochlol** disguised as a female drow, browsing for jars.
5	...a tiny jug filled with blue liquid—and a **marid**.
6	...an angry bull that despises fine china.

VARIANT STORAGE SPACE

This large, nondescript warehouse is the perfect place to stow goods and materials for commercial or personal use, and by using the tables below, it can be modified to suit numerous purposes. Magical means are assumed if, for example, the goods being stored require refrigeration or other temperature control.

WAREHOUSE HEIGHT

1d4	The ceiling of this warehouse is...
1	20 feet high
2	40 feet high
3	60 feet high
4	80 feet high

WAREHOUSE CONTENTS

1d20	The majority of the crates, sacks and/or barrels here contain...
1	Beer and wine
2	Fine fabrics
3	Beans
4	Grain
5	Unprocessed ore
6	Luggage
7	A necromancer's clones
8	Frozen meats
9	Wax figures of nobles throughout history
10	Parchment
11	Glass containers of various sizes
12	Flour
13	Pickled vegetables
14	Medicinal herbs
15	Spices from a far-off land
16	Oil-based paint
17	Organs and pelts from creatures of all types
18	Cheese
19	Sporting goods
20	GM's choice

WAREHOUSE SECURITY

1d6	The warehouse is guarded by...
1	...2d4 **mastiffs** and doors with the *alarm* spell.
2	...2d4 **veterans** and doors with *glyphs of hold person* (DC 16).
3	...2d4 **gladiators** and 1d4 **death dogs**.
4	...2d4 **guards** and 1d4 **blink dogs**.
5	...2d4 **scouts** and an anti-magic field.
6	...2d4 conscripted **azers** and 1d4 **direwolves**.

DREAM ARCHIVE

Hidden in the darker recesses of the urban landscape, this rarely visited sanctum serves as a repository for centuries of slumbering thought. Rows of shelves create a labyrinthine interior and are lined with unmarked leather-bound tomes, each hundreds of pages thick, filled with varied script in every language one can imagine and containing detailed descriptions of thousands of dreams. Atop a pillar beyond the shelves sits a marble owl, elegantly carved, peering toward an enclosed tower. Beyond the tower's enchanted door lies a small reflecting pool offering access to the visions of kings and paupers alike—for a price.

RECEPTION

The Dream Archive is staffed by an archivist, a mute high elf named **Amaro**. He spends much of his time arranging and rearranging the books on the shelves, reorganizing based on a categorizational system known only to him. Visitors must check in with him in this space (**1**), from whence he'll escort the curious through the archive if they state a specific purpose for their inquiry, requiring success on a DC 15 Charisma (Persuasion) check.

THE STACKS

The rows of shelves (**2**) within the Dream Archive are so uniform and numerous that it's easy for one to get lost exploring them, and that's before the archive's magical effects kick in. Anyone exploring the Stacks without the guidance of Amaro must succeed on a DC 17 Wisdom (Perception) check or suffer the effects of the *confusion* spell, which lasts until they leave the Dream Archive. A single archived dream from a specific person would be difficult if not impossible to locate, if it even exists, but Amaro may be able to point the curious in the right direction at GM discretion—or if they succeed on a DC 17 Intelligence (History) check. Roll on the Vision Table on pg. 26, or reveal your own results at GM discretion.

THE OWL'S PERCH

Beyond the cramped and towering maze of shelves in the Stacks is an open atrium where six shelves of far less dusty tomes face a centralized pillar supporting a statue of a large owl carved from marble (**3**). The owl's eyes peer directly at a set of ornate doors on the opposite side of the atrium that lead into a large stone tower. Beneath the pillar, carved in elvish, is the phrase: *"Seek what thou won't find. Give what thou would take."* Upon reading this phrase aloud, the doors along the curved tower wall slowly open, and anyone within 5 ft. of the statue hears a soft voice within their mind, directing them to "peer into the pool."

THE DREAM POOL

Beyond the doors of the tower sits a magnificent pool of deep, clear water reflecting the image of whatever sky shines down from a clear glass dome that crowns the tower (**4**). A staircase winds up the stone walls, with five viewing platforms interspersed at different levels. Peering into the Dream Pool reveals visions from within the minds of the world. Once invited, a viewer can speak one name aloud—the soft voice in their heads leading them through the ritual. If the viewer's intentions are pure, they may see the most recent dream of their named subject. If the viewer's intentions are nefarious, the dream is harder to divine—in fact, a viewer may encounter a nightmare of their own. When a viewer peers into the pool, consult the Dream Table on pgs. 26–27.

Anyone looking directly into the pool before being invited to do so must make a Wisdom saving throw (DC 15). On a failed save, the target is subject to 10d6 psychic damage, or half as much on a successful save, and is paralyzed, as the haunting visions they see there corrupt their mental state.

KEEPING A RECORD. A dream must be recorded and preserved and this fact is nonnegotiable. If a viewer sees a dream, they will be approached by Amaro, his gnarled hands presenting an archive book open to a blank page, quill at the ready, his wishes clarified by the same soft voice in the viewer's mind. Any viewer wishing to exit the archive without recording their vision will find their actions impossible, as upon waking each day they will discover they are back in the Dream Archive, standing over the pool, Amaro by their side, quill in hand, awaiting their entry.

THE DREAM TABLE

When a character looks into the Dream Pool, they must name a target, then make a roll based on their alignment (Good, d10; Neutral, d8; or Evil, d6). A character led here by a deity or vision may add 1d4 to this roll.

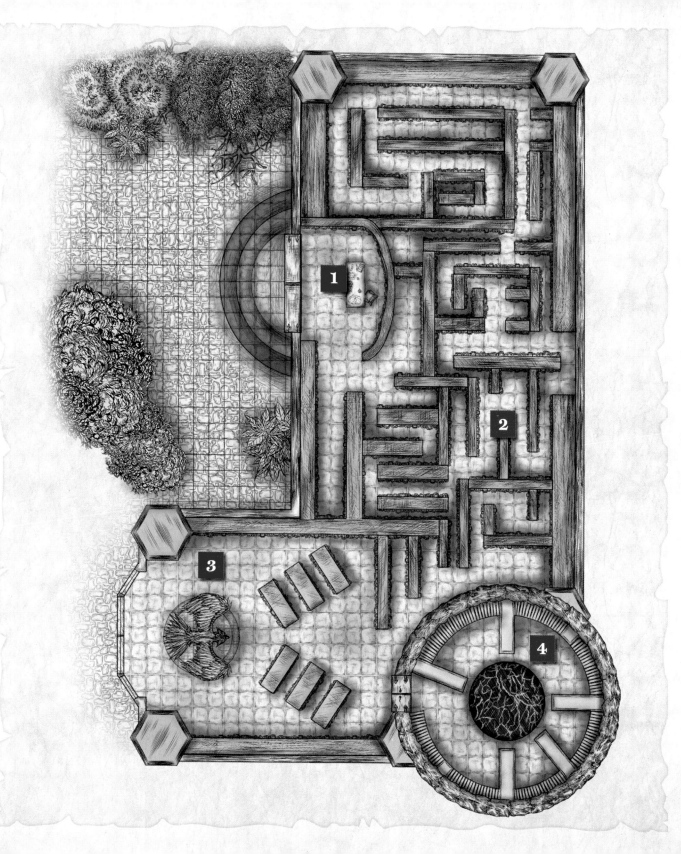

Personal nightmare

A character viewing a personal nightmare sees a vision evoking their darkest fear. They must make a Wisdom saving throw (DC 20). On a failed save, the viewer is subject to 6d6 psychic damage, or half as much on a success, and is also frightened of the Dream Pool, for fear of what they may see there. Additionally, the viewer does not gain the benefits of a long rest for 1d4 days.

2 or lower

No vision

The viewer peers into the pool but sees only their reflection. The voice in their mind suggests they "look again, without looking so hard." If they choose to roll again, they will see no vision. If they choose instead to walk away, a dream will be revealed as if they'd seen it in the pool.

3–4

A dream is revealed

The player sees a vision of the most recent dream of the person they named as part of this ritual. This vision is subject to GM discretion, or can be determined randomly by rolling on the Vision Table.

5 or higher

THE VISION TABLE

1d100	The target is...
1	...bathing in a pool of blood, surrounded by corpses—a smile on their face.
2	...running as fast as they can, pursued by an unseen force, their eyes wide with panic.
3	...leading a crowded tavern in a rousing rendition of "The Followers of Flume" and cementing themselves as one of the greatest bards of all time.
4	...enjoying a meal as the only guest at the head of a long table, which never seems to end, the food piled high and slowly beginning to rot.
5	...staring up at a burning pyre, watching the flames lick at a charred body until it falls to ash.
6	...opening a beautifully wrapped gift. Their face holds a child's innocence and wonder.
7	...floating on their back down a wide river. The distant thundering of a waterfall drawing nearer and nearer.
8	...playing with several puppies, laughing as they jump around and nibble on their fingers.
9	...scraping their bloody fingers across the walls of a prison cell, scribbling in a forgotten language.
10	...fishing by a tranquil lake. A large, **green dragon** sits with them and watches.
11	...continuously filling out stacks of neverending paperwork piled high upon their desk.
12	...riding a horse through a dark forest, whipping it faster and faster as they chase their quarry.
13	...walking through a darkened crypt until they stop in front of a casket with an open lid.
14	...kneeling atop a sheer, obsidian tower while a storm rages around them.
15	...gazing up blankly at a dead tree. Hanging from its gnarled branches are several bodies.
16	...praying in an empty temple until their god comes forth and gives them guidance on their path.
17	...sitting on a throne and staring into a dark abyss. Tears of joy run down their face.
18	...holding a plucked chicken, offering it feebly to a group of starved, knife-wielding children.
19	...small—smaller than a grain of sand—and trapped inside the eye of a celestial.
20	...aware that you are watching their dreams. The player may choose to have a conversation with the dreamer.
21	...covered in a thick goo, struggling to breathe, as their loved ones look on laughing.
22	...holding an ebony dagger, repeating the name "Ella" and stabbing the air as their voice grows hoarse.
23	...standing behind you, looking over your shoulder into the dream pool, and is not amused.
24	...attending a holy ceremony, where they are suddenly crippled by the need to vomit.
25	...calmly looking out a window as screams emanate from a nearby dwelling.
26	...carousing among the stars with ethereal creatures.
27	...staring into a portal to another realm, as a creature of immense power stares back.
28	...desperately trying to peel off their own face, a tome in Abyssal open at their feet.
29	...arguing with a goat about the deeper meaning of life as the goat stoically gazes back.
30	...enjoying a ticklish warmth between their thighs until they look down into a sea of glowing eyes.
31	...clutching the necklace they always wear, as shadows swirl in and out of view.
32	...gambling all they possess, despite the cards in their hand all being blank.
33	...casually discussing the events of the day while slowly roasting on a spit.
34	...planning the execution of their betrothed.
35	...careening down the side of a rainbow.
36	...kissing the **succubus** that dwells in their closet.
37	...emerging from a dark forest, dragging the head of a dead lycanthrope. Their own head is missing.
38	...all alone, all alone, all alone, forever alone.
39	...drenched in sweat, trembling atop the highest building around, holding a small raven's feather.
40	...on the back of a tiny horse, leading a vast army.
41	...hammering away at a forge, crafting an ornate mace.
42	...investigating the entrails of a slaughtered calf, and pulling out a beautifully cut emerald.

43	...carving a name you don't recognize into the floorboards of a house you've seen before.
44	...wrapped in furs, controlling a deadly blizzard.
45	...glowing with radiant light, enveloped by love.
46	...starving within the stomach of a giant beast.
47	...skipping across an open ocean, leaping over the waves, racing for the horizon.
48	...moaning and swaying in time to a drum beating on a distant continent.
49	...hurling fireballs into a rockstrewn canyon as they scream your name in anguish.
50	...following a spectral voice down a dark corridor, their breathing growing ever more ragged.
51	...savoring the last drop of wine from the last bottle aboard a ship at the edge of the world.
52	...wearing a crown made of teeth and sharpened bone, climbing out of a hole filled with devils.
53	...giving birth to a beautiful baby eel.
54	...being dragged through town beneath the floating body of a dragon set on destruction.
55	...picking their teeth with a giant's greatsword.
56	...opening an elegantly carved trunk, admiring the village of pixies trapped inside.
57	...convinced a **bugbear** is truly a cursed prince.
58	...invisible, and loving every minute of it.
59	...incapable of dreaming.
60	...staring into a well, aging one year each second.
61	...bargaining with an **empyrean**, and winning.
62	...suffering through their third day in a harpy's nest.
63	...commanding a legion of **kobolds**, who cackle in glee at the word "SOON."
64	...putting away their armor, their padding, their topshirt, their skin, their organs, their bones.
65	...cursed to teach a **troglodyte** to dance.
66	...haunted by visions of the night they were forced to kill someone innocent.
67	...infatuated with their reflection.
68	...the guest of honor at a vampire wedding.
69	...entertaining a **sphinx**, who asks them a favor.
70	...one of a **hydra**'s seven snarling heads.
71	...a ghost haunting their own home, terrorizing their own family for want of a warm embrace.
72	...mocking a vision of themselves from the past, teasing, "You gave the seeds away for a song."
73	...poring over scrolls that speak of an ancient treasure beneath their doorstep.
74	...being carried like a martyr through the town market by an army of **giant spiders**.
75	...chained in a damp dungeon, screaming without making a sound.
76	...gliding with their limbs completely stiff and still, across an incredibly long drawbridge toward a crumbling black castle.
77	...sitting in a leafless tree, laughing maniacally as they pick a buzzard's carcass clean.
78	...falling from the sky with no sign yet of the ground below, shouting "Fly! Fly! C'mon, fly!"
79	...keeping watch over a flock of sheep, who suddenly bare fangs and attack.
80	...peering into a pool in a library almost exactly like this one, your name on their lips.
81	...laughing uproariously while drinking ale in a tavern full of rotting corpses.
82	...trapped within a portrait of themselves, watching as admirers stare in silent reverence.
83	...escorted in a sedan chair held aloft by cats on their hind legs, as a kitten feeds them sardines.
84	...raining over the continent as a violent storm.
85	...hiding behind the curtains in a merchant's bedroom as his wife explains why she's still in bed at noon.
86	...struggling to keep their head above water as waves crash around them, a ship's lamp receding in the fog.
87	...on horseback charging toward an **orc** horde, who scatter into dust upon first contact.
88	...dead, and always has been.
89	...strolling through an open battlefield, as arrows and battleaxes fly past without consequence.
90	...begging in the street for a crust of bread, before cursing your name and swearing vengeance.
91	...buried in the scabbard of a great warrior **mage**, quietly aching to be unsheathed, hungry for the taste of an enemy's blood.
92	...soaring over the nearest mountain range, following a pulsing gold light as a voice whispers "Find me."
93	...overlooking a gathered populace from a balcony, their speech suddenly inscrutable.
94	...looking back at you, shouting "PLEASE—I'm trapped here. Please kill me!"
95	...counting their gold piece by piece, before swallowing each one.
96	... diligently gardening in a desert, each sprout and flower withering in the oppressive sunlight.
97	...hurriedly carving themselves out of stone, as their shadow begins to shift and slip away.
98	...celebrating their newfound immortality by raising a poisoned glass, as the demon they unleashed devours what's left of their family.
99	...butchering a hog into ever smaller pieces.
100	...carving the names of each member of your party inside a simple wooden bowl.

CARAVAN BAZAAR

Trade routes across the region convene in this outdoor market, with dozens of small shops of all types popping up for a tenday or two. The impermanent nature of the bazaar ensures it's rarely the same experience twice, as transient merchants sell what they can then take their carts to the next town. The market is full of people at all hours of the day and nearly as busy at night, making it a prime spot for pickpockets, charlatans and other ne'er-do-wells.

SHOPS

To determine which merchants are present at the bazaar during this visit, roll on the table below for every tent visited by a potential customer to determine what might be for sale. For each of the merchants, use the races suggested or, for even more variance, use the Random NPC Generator (pg. 125).

1d20	This tent is operated by...
1	...a human blacksmith.
2	...a human bookseller.
3	...a gnomish jeweler.
4	...an elven antiquities dealer.
5	...a halfling locksmith.
6	...a half-elf fletcher/bowmaster.
7	...a human butcher.
8	...a human baker.
9	...a gnomish candlestick maker.
10	...a halfling mapmaker.
11	...a half-orc tattoo artist.
12	...a human fruit merchant.
13	...a human sketch artist.
14	...a dwarven cheesemonger.
15	...a human healer for hire.
16	...a tiefling arcane artifact merchant.
17	...an elven woodworker.
18	...a half-elf beastmaster.
19	...a human vegetable farmer.
20	...a human furniture dealer.

CROWDS

The Caravan Bazaar is often a sea of people, and moving from one end to the other takes time, patience and the occasional shove. Because of the crush of the gathered groups here, as well as the precarious nature of the cords and ties pinning the market's tents to the ground, the entire area is considered difficult terrain.

In the event of an attack, assault or other frightening encounter, roll 1d20. A roll of 10 or lower triggers a crowd surge, with an entire market's worth of people fleeing in haste. Any creature in the crowd must move away from the inciting incident or succeed on a Strength saving throw (DC 12). On a failed save, they suffer 2d8 bludgeoning damage and are knocked prone as they are trampled by the crowd.

ENCOUNTER VARIANT (OPTIONAL)
UNSTEADY SETUP

The tents at the Caravan Bazaar are meant to be portable and somewhat disposable, and most merchants choose to bring their own. Because so many tents rise and fall throughout the week, the cords that keep them tacked to the ground are often a tangled mess, so when the wind shifts and collapses one tent, odds are several more will follow, a chain reaction that is unwelcome but not uncommon. Anytime a creature walks along a space directly touching a tent, have them make a Dexterity check (DC 10). On a failed save, the player trips over one of the tent's cords and causes a partial collapse. Roll 1d6 to determine how many other tents are affected.

THE COMMUNAL OAK

A large tree (**1**) shades much of the Caravan Bazaar, with many of its branches older than the town that rose up around it. Its lowest branches are 10 feet off the ground, but beyond that they are numerous and easy to climb among.

VARIANT ENCOUNTER (OPTIONAL)
Roll 1d6 to determine what other adventures might await the party at the Caravan Bazaar.

1d6	The party sees...
1	...a group of 2d4 hired **thugs** attacking from the trees, killing a merchant before trying to escape.
2	...a **dire wolf** break loose from its cage at a beastmaster's tent and begin growling near the Communal Oak.
3	...nothing, as an expert pickpocket (+15 to sleight of hand) takes advantage of the party at GM discretion.
4	...a starving **xorn** erupt from the earth beneath the Bazaar, menacing a gem merchant and pleading for "delicious stones."
5	...a band of 2d4 **goblin** raiders gallop in on hungry wolves looking to menace the entire market.
6	...a **djinni** released from a small box among the relics of an antiquities dealer who is displeased with its captor. Roll 1d20. On a roll of 18 or higher, the djinni has the power to grant 1 (18), 2 (19) or 3 (20) wishes.

Peerless Potions

Derisively nicknamed "Perilous Potions" by the locals, this overstocked shop is practically overflowing with vials and beakers and flasks of all sizes. The proprietor, a rather gaunt halfling mage named **Damian Cleese**, rarely leaves the shop, as much a shrine to his own alchemical artistry as a place for adventurers to stock up on all manner of potions—assuming they can be found among the myriad bottles that line every wall, shelf and free tile on the floor. A clear message greets any who would enter the shop: *"All sales final. You break it, you buy it. Potions may be poison—steal at your own risk."*

ENTRYWAY. The foyer of the shop (**1**) is a harbinger of things to come. Tall shelves precariously packed with potions are placed quite close together, forming narrow aisles with clinking glass bottles through which patrons must pass if they're inclined to shop here. Any creature wishing to walk down an aisle must do so with care, as any errant movement is likely to knock over a potion or three (see "Mind the Bottles" table).

BASEMENT. This trapdoor (**2**) is locked and requires a DC 20 to pick. It leads to a tunnel connected to the city's cavernous sewer system, and evidence suggests it might be used by Damian to sell goods to customers who don't want to be seen entering the shop, a fact revealed with a DC 20 Intelligence (Investigation) check.

GOODS. Damian's renown for potion-making is well-earned, but his lack of a meaningful organizational system is equally legendary. Pretty much any potion imaginable can be purchased at his shop, provided you possess the coin and the ability to find it. An Intelligence (Investigation) check based on the potion's rarity is required for a shopper to locate the potion they seek (see "Did You Find It?" table).

For his part, Damian is generally too consumed with his work to bother in assisting the search, though he can be utilized to procure specific goods via a DC 20 Charisma (Persuasion) check (or at GM discretion).

Pricing is also at GM discretion, and market price is fair, however, Damian can be convinced to reduce prices through meaningful haggling if adventurers are so inclined.

SHELF TOWER. Along one side of the shop, the shelves stretch higher (**3**), haphazardly stacked atop one another, filling the silo-like space and reaching heights of almost 80 feet—rising up through the entirety of what was once a former guard tower. Reaching potions located on the uppermost shelves in this area requires success on 5 consecutive Dexterity checks (DC 15). A fail constitutes a fall, which also forces a roll on the "Mind the Bottles" table as the shelves shake and sway with the sudden weight change. Additionally, should an adventurer attempt to climb the shelves after a fall, the DC increases by 1 for each fall (up to a max of 20) as the shelves become less stable with each attempt.

ENCOUNTER VARIANT (OPTIONAL) MIND THE BOTTLES

Each time an adventurer passes down an aisle, either to enter, exit or otherwise explore the shop, they must make a Dexterity (Acrobatics) check to avoid knocking bottles off the shelves or to avoid knocking over full cases of goods. Due to their less cumbersome frames, small creatures may roll with advantage.

DC	
1–5	1d4 bottles fall off the shelf and break.
6–14	One bottle slips, but the player in question can make a Dexterity save (DC 15) to prevent it from breaking.
15+	No bottles fall.

ENCOUNTER VARIANT (OPTIONAL) DID YOU FIND IT?

An adventurer may seek a specific potion by making an Intelligence (Investigation) check in a specific aisle of the shop and meeting the DCs outlined below. Each subsequent search of an aisle requires a Dexterity save as outlined in the "Mind the Bottles" table.

DC	
10	Common Potion
15	Uncommon Potion
20	Rare Potion
25	Very Rare Potion
30	Legendary Potion

NPC PROFILE
Damian Cleese, Halfling Mage

The shop's owner and sole manager, Damian is obsessed with the meticulous magic art required to brew alchemical wonders. His slim build and shabby exterior suggest a man who would rather work than eat, sleep or bathe. In fact, it's rumored he doesn't need to do much of all three, his potions keeping him alert, sated and, when necessary, smelling of fresh dew and summer pine. He gets surly when kept from his work for too long and will just as soon usher individuals out of his shop than wait for them to buy something.

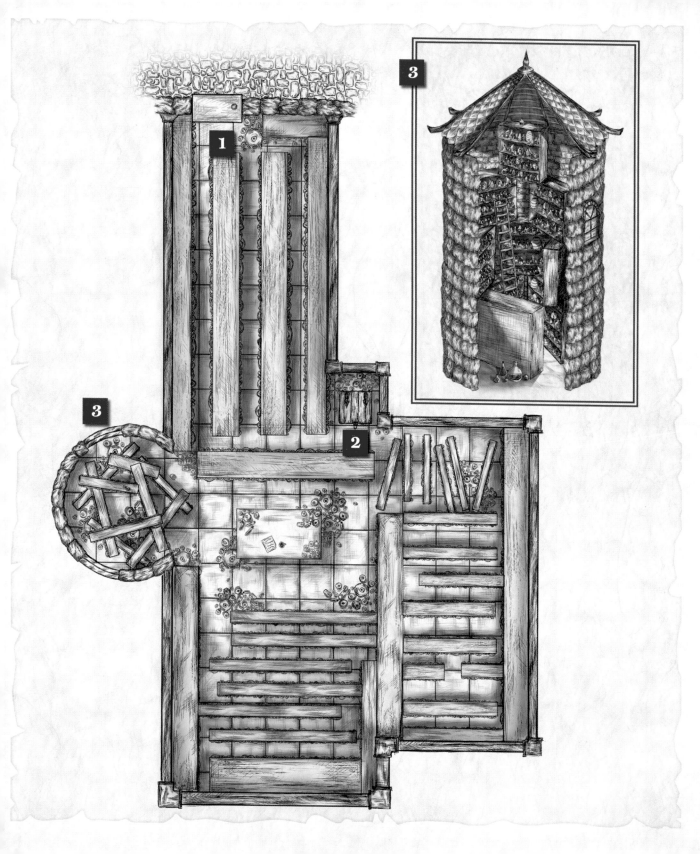

Gant's Alchemy Emporium

A well-stocked alchemist's shop, if small for a self-styled "emporium." Highly appointed with various potions and necessary sundries for any willful adventurer, it features a small side room where its owner, **Gant Guntergunt**, has a bed and a workstation, as well as a hidden door to an underground cellar.

The Storefront

The proprietor of this establishment, a spry gnome named Gant Guntergunt, spends most of his time standing on the shop counter to get a better look at his customers and retail space (*1*). A secretive sort, a DC 15 Wisdom (Insight) reveals he appears to be hiding something—namely that he's been conducting magical experiments on creatures in his basement, accessible via a secret door under the rug in his shop's side room.

GOODS. Gant refuses to haggle. Any attempt to achieve a price lower than market value could lead to a swift shutdown of his store, at GM discretion. He is susceptible to charm and flirtation, however, as well as intelligent discussions about the arcane. A DC 19 Charisma (Persuasion) or Intelligence (Arcana) check will net a discount on goods—buy three, get one free.

SIDE ROOM. Gant's side room (*2*) is private but accessible, particularly if he is distracted or in deep conversation—DC 19 Charisma (Deception, Performance, Persuasion) or Intelligence (Arcana). He sleeps in the side room from late evening to early morning. If he is not in the shop, there's a chance he's in the cellar. His desk and trunk are locked (DC 15), and he carries the key. An individual succeeding on a thorough search of the desk drawers will find a diary with notes on **water elementals**, taming **mimics**, **basilisks**, general necromancy and an incomplete recipe for **black pudding**. Within the room, a DC 15 (Perception/Investigation) check reveals a few ridges in the rug in the outline of a 4-by-4 square. Pulling the rug away reveals a hatch-style door to the cellar.

The Cellar

A balmy, almost sauna-like cellar accessible through a hidden door in Gant's side room features an old, roaring furnace, a few barrels and visibly crumbling support arches (10 hp each) that upon further inspection—DC 15 (Perception/Investigation)—could be brought down with a few strong kicks. A dark, waterlogged tunnel (3 feet of water), blocked by metal bars, appears to lead elsewhere.

THE FURNACE. This large cast-iron furnace (*3*) is continually lit, keeping the cellar nice and toasty.

THE BARRELS. These barrels (*4*) hold alchemy supplies. Two barrels are full of "in process" *potions of healing* and upon inspection (DC 15) could be used by an individual proficient with an Herbalist's Kit to create up to 4 *potions of healing* or 1 *potion of greater healing* (DC 15). Players lacking proficiency who attempt to make their own healing potions suffer 2d6 acid damage.

SUPPORT ARCHES. If two or more of these support arches (*5*) are damaged, the ceiling will collapse. Anyone under the ceiling must succeed on a DC 15 Dexterity saving throw, taking 4d10 bludgeoning damage on a failed save or half as much damage on a success. Once the ceiling collapses, the floor of the area is filled with rubble, potions and possibly the shop owner (at GM discretion) and becomes difficult terrain.

THE TUNNEL. Blocked by a steel gate (*6*), further inspection (DC 16) reveals a lock at the base of the gate, beneath the water's surface. The lock can be picked (DC 17), but must be done so at disadvantage due to its placement underwater. The tunnel either leads to another location in this book determined by rolling on the Random Location Generator (pg. 3) or a location at GM discretion.

Variant Encounter (Optional)

Roll 1d6 to reveal the wonders that might be unleashed on the party in the cellar of Gant's Alchemy Emporium.

1d6	The party finds...
1	...a glob of **black pudding** that reveals itself if the barrels are inspected.
2	...a **basilisk**, lurking in the water near the tunnel. Gant sells an oil which can cure petrified adventurers for 50 gp.
3	...a **water elemental** guarding the tunnel gate, non-hostile unless provoked.
4	...2d4 **skeletons**, which rise from the floor of the cellar if a creature interacts with the furnace.
5	...a **minotaur skeleton**, which rises from the floor if a creature interacts with the furnace.
6	...a **mimic**, which is indistinguishable from the other barrels in the basement.

GROUND LEVEL

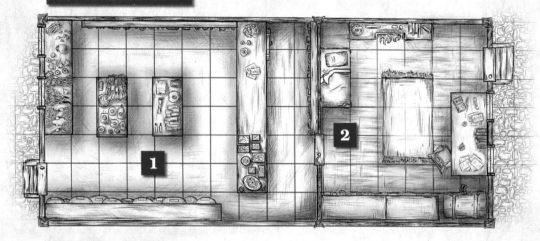

CELLAR LEVEL

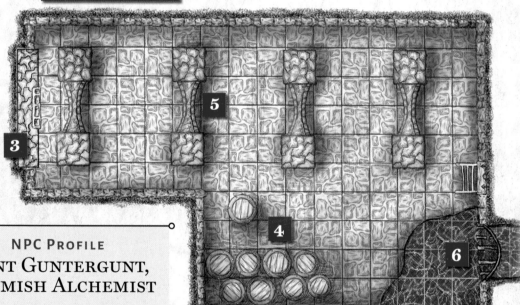

NPC PROFILE

GANT GUNTERGUNT, GNOMISH ALCHEMIST

A proud, prolific (but also somewhat persnickety) practitioner of the arcane, Gant Guntergunt is an avid researcher— one who wouldn't let small details such as morals, ethics or laws get in the way of big discoveries. He has twice been fined for conducting experiments that got out of hand, and he's been forbidden from continuing his research within the city limits. It hasn't stopped him.

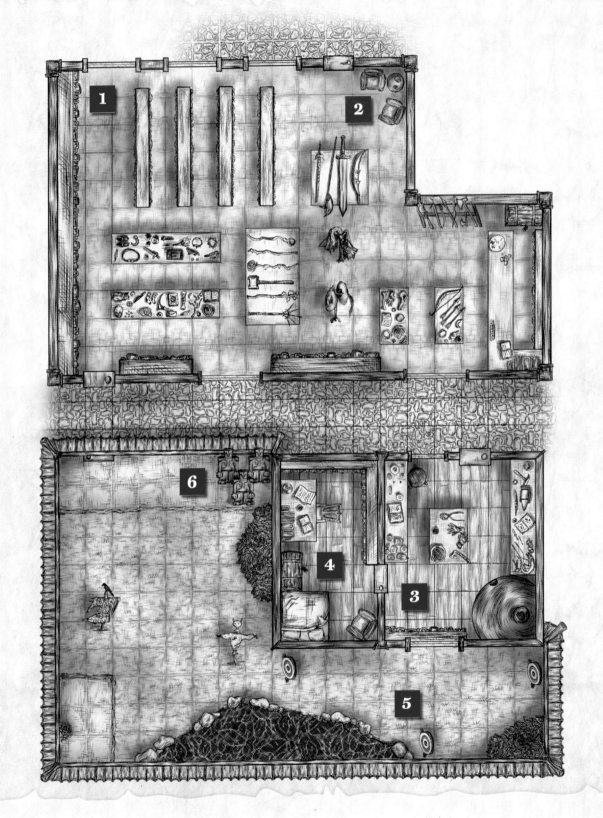

MAGE YOU LOOK

A storefront renowned for its unique magical artifacts, it's a popular location among would-be wizards, war mages and other spellcasters looking to increase their efficacy. The shop's owner and operator, a powerful artificer named **Gal Powers**, spends most of her time conceiving, creating and testing magical objects. A back door leads to a slim alleyway, beyond which is Gal's workshop and residence, as well as an outdoor area for experimenting with magical equipment. Gal takes custom orders and, if the supplies are as plentiful as your coin, can typically engineer nearly anything you can imagine—and many things you can't.

MAGIC ITEMS SHOP

INTERIOR. Mage You Look's retail space (**1**) seems unassuming compared to other high-profile locations that sell valuable merchandise. There are no guards, no golems and no locks on the doors. These appearances are, in short, deceiving. Every item in the shop is a fake—a stand-in for its match, which exists in a pocket dimension only Gal can access. The items in the shop are warded to prevent theft, and the well-disguised runes covering each object are triggered at the slightest touch. Anyone attempting the *identify* spell on these facsimiles will find the spell unnecessary, as the wards will fire off the moment they touch the item to cast the spell. When the wards are triggered, everyone within 20 feet of the item must succeed on a DC 20 Dexterity saving throw, or suffer 8d8 thunder damage (half as much on a success). When a customer is interested in purchasing an item, Gal gleefully asks for payment upfront, no exceptions. She will then generate the item from within a pocket dimension and share it with its new owner.

NPC PROFILE
GAL POWERS, THE ARTIFICER

A passionate tinkerer with an eye for small details, Gal is among the most celebrated enchanters in the realm. Her knowledge of legendary magical items is immense, as is the grin on her face when she's given the opportunity to converse about them. A middle-aged human with auburn hair and freckled skin, her life's work is the shop, but once a season she'll close down for weeks at a time to explore the world and put some of her more outrageous enchantments to the test to sate her cravings for adventure.

A FAMILIAR SPOT

A small post in the corner of the shop (**2**) is also home to Gal's familiar, Glenn. Roll on the tables below to determine Glenn's form.

1d4	Glenn is a...
1	celestial
2	fey
3	fiend
4	roll again

1d6	Glenn is a...
1	crab
2	frog
3	hawk
4	spider
5	weasel
6	bat

WORKSHOP

INTERIOR. Gal's workshop (**3**) is well-organized, with numerous solvents and materials labeled in her flowery script. An enchanter's table shows signs of well-worn use, and a magical kiln offers enough heat to forge or fire even the most difficult material components.

BEDROOM. A modest bedroom by any standard, Gal's living quarters (**4**) reveal a rather spartan private space and speak to her preference for late nights in the workshop as opposed to the bedroom.

COURTYARD

EXTERIOR. The back alleys behind Mage You Look (**5**) have been outfitted with various elements to allow Gal to test and make adjustments to some of her more outlandish inventions. A makeshift targeting range allows for the perfection of ranged weaponry, and a defensive shield of Gal's own design keeps an errant blast, rogue spell or unpredictable curse from destroying half the town.

GOLEMS. Three **stone golems** (**6**), which can be activated upon hearing the command word "ANIMATE," are chipped in places and battered in others. Flame scarring mars one golem, while another shows signs of acid damage. The statuesque figures will roam around the courtyard but cannot leave it, and they are primarily used by Gal or prospective customers to determine the power and usefulness of a magical artifact.

MAGE YOU LOOK:
ARCANE ITEMS FOR PURCHASE

ALL THE GOODS YOU CAN IMAGINE, AND MANY YOU CAN'T! ALL SALES
FINAL, ALL CURSES ARE THE RESPONSIBILITY OF THE NEW OWNER.

Traveling Hole Punch

Wondrous Item, RARE, 500 gp

Once per long rest, as an action, you can use this handheld mechanical device to create a 5-foot hole in any structure or surface. It has a 10 percent chance of opening a portal to another plane (at GM's discretion).

Hairshirt of Healing

Wondrous Item, RARE, 500 gp

Requires attunement

This article of clothing, used in some religious orders, can be used to facilitate healing through the act of self-harm. As a bonus action, make an attack against yourself. A creature that you can see within 60 feet heals three times the amount of damage you inflict on yourself.

Marble of Slipping

Wondrous Item, COMMON, 80 gp

Once per long rest, this tiny, unassuming glass ball becomes one thousand marbles for just a moment. As an action, you can toss the marble up to 30 feet and shout its activation phrase ("slippity boppity boom"). Upon impact with the ground the marble creates difficult terrain in a 15-foot radius for one turn. Any creature entering the area of effect or starting its turn there must succeed on a DC 18 Dexterity saving throw or fall prone, taking 1d8 bludgeoning damage on a failed save. After one turn, the marble returns to its bag and the effect dissipates.

Vest of Solar Power

Wondrous Item, UNCOMMON, 300 gp

Requires attunement

This tasseled buckskin vest features a large yellow beadwork sun on its back and has the ability to transfer the sun's warming rays into invigorating energy. While wearing this vest in direct sunlight you will rarely tire, and can remove the effects of up to three points of exhaustion.

Chef's Knife

Wondrous Item, UNCOMMON, 250 gp

Requires attunement

This finely balanced dagger is as sharp as it is deadly and offers +1 to attack and damage rolls. Its damage die is 1d8.

Additionally, once per short rest, when the blade hits its target you can speak its command phrase, "Order up," causing the blade to deal an additional 3d6 slashing + 1d6 fire damage as it sears the flesh of its target and creates a delicious-smelling Maillard reaction.

Immediate Anchor

Wondrous Item, RARE, 700 gp

Prerequisite: Strength 17

A small, black cast iron anchor on a heavy chain. As an action, you can throw the anchor at a target (living or not). On a successful hit the target takes 2d6 bludgeoning damage and must succeed on a DC 17 Strength saving throw as the chain wraps around them, becoming restrained on a failed save. At the end of the creature's turn it can attempt to escape by rerolling the save.

As an action, you can speak the Anchor's command phrase "Anchor's away," and it will exert 4,000 pounds of force toward the earth (or correct gravitational orientation). A creature caught under the anchor's weight and/or grappled by its chain can make a DC 25 Strength (Athletics) check to push the anchor off themselves for every 100 feet they fall. When calculating fall damage with the anchor's crushing weight multiply the number of damage dice by three.

Shades of Night

Wondrous Item, UNCOMMON, 120 gp

A pair of shades that can morph into the shape of any glasses their wearer desires. You gain darkvision up to 60 feet and +2 to Perception. Once per long rest—but only at night—use a bonus action to activate the shades to gain *truesight* up to 60 feet for one minute.

Nimble Hand Wraps

Wondrous Item, RARE, 800 gp
Requires attunement

These hand wraps resemble strong, reinforced bandages that strengthen the wrists of the bearer. Once per day (per hand wrap worn) you can manipulate the bandages causing them to whip out to a range of 20 feet to snag a creature or object and pull yourself toward it. To do so, make a ranged attack. On a successful hit, the bandage wraps around the target before beginning to wind up again, pulling you toward it at high speed. If making an attack against a creature as part of this action, add 1d4 to your unarmed attack against the creature per 5 feet traveled in this manner (max 4d4). This ability does not trigger if you are within melee range of the creature or if the object/creature is one or more size(s) smaller than you are.

Stampede in a Bottle

Wondrous Item (potion), VERY RARE, 500 gp

Within this bottle swirls a dark smoke that forms into a roiling mass of swiftly moving creatures. As an action, you can uncork this potion and release a stampede of epic proportions, the type of which can be determined by rolling 1d6 on the table below. The stampede moves out of the bottle in a 30-foot cone on the first turn and on subsequent rounds becomes a 30-foot-wide line with a movement speed of 40 feet. The stampede lasts for three rounds before disappearing. Any creature caught in the path of the stampede must make a Dexterity or Strength saving throw (target's choice, DC 17), taking full damage on a failed save or half as much on a successful one.

1d6	The stampede is...
1	...a herd of cats dealing 6d6 slashing damage.
2	...a battery of elk dealing 8d10 bludgeoning damage and on a failed save targets are knocked prone.
3	...a fleet of bats dealing 8d4 slashing damage and blinded for one turn on a failed save.
4	...30-50 feral hogs dealing 8d8 bludgeoning damage and on a failed save affected creatures are carried 15 feet in the direction of the stampede.
5	...a cavalcade of giant spiders dealing 4d6 piercing damage. A creature who fails the first saving throw must make a Constitution saving throw (DC 13). On a failed save, the creature takes an additional 2d6 poison damage and is poisoned.
6	...a tornado of sharks dealing 10d6 slashing damage. On a failed save, the affected creature takes an additional 2d6 damage as a shark latches onto a limb.

Pocketwatch Wizard

Wondrous Item, VERY RARE, 2,800 gp

As an action, you can activate this stopwatch and for 60 seconds (10 rounds) a drowsy wizard named Steve appears and can begrudgingly cast one spell during your bonus action (+5, DC 14). The wizard has an AC of 12, 22 hit points and a movement speed of 30 feet. He has the following spells prepared:

    Cantrip: *firebolt*
    Level 1 (4 slots): *magic missile, disguise self, feather fall*
    Level 2 (2 slots): *scorching ray, darkness*
    Level 3 (1 slot): *fireball*

Once this property has been used, it can't be used again until the following dawn. If your Pocketwatch Wizard is reduced to 0 hit points before their time is up, they will disappear and not return for 1d6 days.

Earth Rumble Boots

Wondrous Item, VERY RARE, 3,000 gp
Requires attunement

Leather and slate boots molded to look like boulders and clay. Once a day, as an action, you can stomp the earth (must be dirt or stone) to trigger one of the following effects:

    Sandstorm. Dust and dirt fly up and form a raging 30-foot-tall sandstorm in a 20-foot radius centered on you for one minute. The storm creates difficult terrain and limits visibility to 2 feet. Any creature starting their turn or entering the sandstorm for the first time must make a DC 13 Constitution saving throw or be blinded. They can repeat the saving throw at the start of their turn.

    Earthquake. You cause a small seismic earthquake in a 20-foot radius centered on you. Any creature caught within the blast radius must make a DC 13 Dexterity saving throw or take 4d6 bludgeoning damage, or half as much on a successful save.

    Rock Stomp. You cause a boulder in the shape of a 5-foot cube to rise from the earth, before kicking it at a target of your choice. Make a ranged Strength attack. On a hit the target takes 8d6 bludgeoning damage and must succeed on a DC 15 Strength saving throw or be knocked prone.

Cloak of Daggers

Armor (cloak), RARE, 315 gp

A shimmering cloak built entirely out of woven blades, this dangerous cape can be a lifesaver, or a potential stab in the back. This cloak gives you a bonus +2 to AC, but disadvantage to any Acrobatics or Athletics skill checks due to the danger of moving while wearing a cloak made of daggers. While wearing the cloak, you can whisper the cloak's command word, "daggerfall," as an action and cause all the daggers in the cloak to shoot outward at once. Every creature in a 30-foot radius sphere centered on you must succeed on a DC 15 Dexterity saving throw or suffer 4d4 piercing damage, or half as much damage on a success. This property can be used once per long rest.

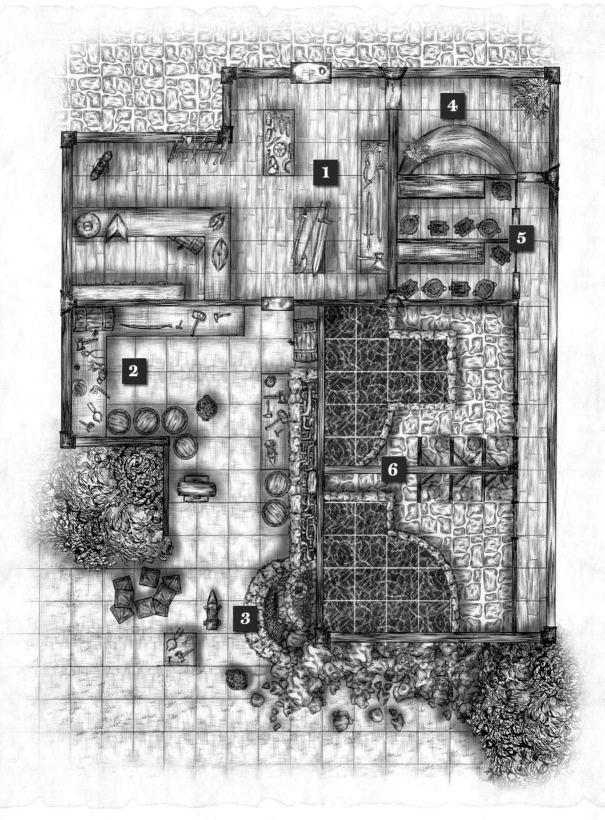

THE STEAMY SMITHY BLACKSMITH & DAY SPA

Envisioned, built and operated by husband-and-wife duo **Eager and Esme Everlong**, the Steamy Smithy is a tribute to ingenuity and economy of space. Half the shop is dedicated to Esme's blacksmith trade and the other is a stonework bathhouse run by Eager, featuring deep pools heated from pipes that circulate water through the blacksmith forge. Whether coming for a quick steam or new steel, the shop is a welcome respite for adventurers looking to sharpen their minds or their blades.

NPC PROFILES

ESME & EAGER EVERLONG, HUMAN SMALL BUSINESS OWNERS

Esme and Eager Everlong are humans in their mid-40s with shock-blond hair (and a beard, in Eager's case) and the can-do positivity with which many Northerners carry themselves. Esme's steelwork is highly regarded in the region and there's very little she can't craft out of even the most difficult of materials. Eager's commitment to customer comfort is as hospitable as it is unrelenting. Their marriage is built on a foundation of trust, mutual respect and cheerful jokes at one another's expense.

THE BLACKSMITH

THE SHOP. Esme's arms and armor are available for sale in the shop (*1*). Some of her finer works adorn the walls, but she also takes custom orders.

THE WORKSHOP. If Esme isn't asleep or at the forge, there's a solid chance she's here (*2*) working on her next piece.

THE FORGE. The Steamy Smithy's forge (*3*) runs hot both day and night and can be leased for use by other metalworkers whose equipment isn't available (or reliable). Water pipes running through the forge help maintain its temperature and also heat the large baths within the spa.

THE SPA

RECEPTION. The bathhouse area is open as long as customers are willing to pay its 1 gp entry fee—a steep price that acts as a bit of a gate along class lines. When the bathhouse is packed, it's typically with merchants or other tradespeople with coin to spare. If Eager isn't at the desk (*4*), he'll have left a sign directing potential customers to check next door at the blacksmith shop.

CHANGING ROOMS. Small lockers (*5*) are available to stow personal belongings for customers as they soak in the tubs. The locks have a DC of 18.

BATHHOUSES. There are two separate bathhouses of equal size (*6*), and the water in the large, inset soaking tubs is kept hot throughout the year. Steam released from within the piping system every hour or so keeps the bathhouses balmy.

VARIANT ENCOUNTER (OPTIONAL)

To determine what's in store for the party when they stop in to visit the Steamy Smithy, roll 1d6 on the tables below depending on which half of the shop they're visiting.

The Blacksmith

1d6	The party finds...
1	...a belligerent customer and his 1d4 friends trying to return a sword Esme didn't make.
2	...the forge flaring up as a **fire elemental** bursts forth from its coals.
3	...1d4 **flying swords** on the wall springing to life, the work of a saboteur bent on destroying Esme's business.
4	...Esme feeling generous and offering half off labor for all custom merchandise, provided the materials are paid for or supplied.
5	...a panicked guard demanding enough pikes to battle a rampaging **hill giant** lumbering toward the shop.
6	...a flock of 1d4 **cockatrices** menacing the forge looking for something to eat.

The Spa

1d6	The party finds...
1	...a crafty pickpocket has pilfered the gear locked in the changing rooms.
2	...signs of violence emanate from within one of the bathhouses, as a group of 2d4 hot-tempered **thugs** battle one another.
3	...the heat in the bathhouse rising and feel the door is barred from without—the work of a **crawling claw**.
4	...1d4+2 **bugbears**, part of an exploratory party, bursting through the stone floor of one of the bathhouses.
5	...three of the bathhouse's fine cotton towels are actually **rugs of smothering**, planted at the Steamy Smithy by a rival business owner.
6	...two hooded figures who are **jackalweres** in disguise, hoping to sneak off with a lone traveler.

THE NIGHTMARE MARKET

On moonless nights, the dead take over one of the city's forgotten catacombs. Their purpose is not to instill fear or devour flesh, but rather to buy, sell and trade in one of the most unique open bazaars in the realm. The living are welcome, but must abide by The Nightmare Market's strict laws of commerce, with gibbets awaiting those who choose to ignore the rules.

> The temperature plunges as you descend the broad stairway, your breath misting before you. You can hear the echo of softly spoken words ahead, blending together into a murmuring tide. You reach the base of the stairs and see the vaulted ceiling of the chambers ahead rise above your head. Caged will-o'-wisps hang from the ceiling illuminating the market with their steady blue light. The market's centrally suspended gibbets, which cast a darker mood as the live and dead bodies within them moan and decay, also hang in the space.
>
> The dead have dominion. Animated corpses shuffle between the market stalls, eyes lit by a dull balefire. Ghosts and specters glide among and through the other customers, filling the air with their quiet aching. The merchants are as dead as their clientele, from the translucent bookseller to the pair of ghouls standing protectively over their butcher's stall and its overtly humanoid wares.
>
> As you go to enter, a skeleton garbed in the armor of the City Watch steps forward. You note with some bemusement that, though the skeleton itself is yellowed with age, its armor and tabard are new and clean. It grins at you, for it cannot do otherwise, and hands each of you a slip of paper. At the top of the page, stamped in an ancient Gothic print, are the words: "Conditions of Entry: Living."

THE LAWS OF THE NIGHTMARE MARKET

There are many obscure bylaws and conditions for entry to The Nightmare Market, many that are easily broken and involving little serious punishment. They range from a ban on silver within the Market's premises to the requirement that all cats wear a muzzle. Some of the laws apply to the living alone. There are three inviolable laws of the market that apply to all—living or dead—and breaking them leads to being eternally bound to the gibbets at the market's center *(1)*.

1. Unlife, like life, is sacrosanct.
2. Do not steal.
3. The living cannot be touched.

A NEW TRADITION

The Nightmare Market is only a few years old. It began when the city had the upper levels of the old catacombs cleared out in order to allow workers to reinforce the city's foundations. But the newly opened space attracted a great deal of interest among those bereft of life, and within weeks a thriving market was in operation. Scholars and sages have not yet been able to determine why the undead gather for The Nightmare Market. All that is certain is that on moonless nights, the living know to cede the ground. By and large, the people of the city have come to accept the market's operation. The dead do not harm anyone who abides by the market's laws. Some even view The Nightmare Market as an attraction or novelty, though their enthusiasm is often met with equal fervor by opponents of the gathering, who view any attempt to normalize the undead as anathema to the natural order.

COMMERCE OF THE DEAD

Most undead are driven by an overwhelming compulsion that dictates their behavior, whether it be to drain life from the living, feed on mortal flesh or haunt the site of their tragic death. Whatever rules bind them, The Nightmare Market liberates all undead within the city limits until dawn. In return, however, it hands down a new set of iron dictates: the laws of The Nightmare Market.

Without the same needs and wants as the living, and with many of their number unable to even touch corporeal objects, the dead deal mostly in fragments of identity and glimmers of life. Ghosts and specters often feel incomplete—trapped ✹≫

SLIVERS OF EMOTION, JARS OF MEMORY, ALL FOR A PRICE

For the more spectral dead (and a few of those with bodies), emotion and memory define their entire existence. Through the magic of the market, the undead and the living alike may decant their memories into containers found at the market stalls. These containers range in size and can be filled merely by recalling the intended memory and exhaling into the jar. A "full" container appears to hold a dark, inert mist. The creature giving up the memory loses all recollection of the event permanently, which can only be restored through a *wish* spell or by drinking the memory itself.

Emotions can be decanted through the same process, in which case the memory is retained but loses all emotional resonance for the creature. Some use this magic as a form of therapy, creating emotional detachment from traumatic events.

within the confines of their state when they died—and the market offers them tastes of emotions they have been unable to feel since their passing. One stall might feature a revenant selling cups brimming with her love for the man who betrayed her, while beside her a wraith offers bottled memories of the companionship among the bandits he once led.

Many of the dead do have some need for physical items, of which the most popular are bodies. Ghouls are traditionally the primary purveyors and consumers, in every sense, of humanoid bodies that flow through the market, but they aren't the only ones. Ghosts in need of a body to possess, revenants in need of a replacement arm after a bloody scuffle or even living magic-users looking for components for a flesh golem can all be found bidding on whole corpses and body parts at the butcher stalls.

THE TOUCH OF LIFE

Practitioners of necromancy aren't the only ones who like to shop at The Nightmare Market, and they are welcome so long as they obey the rules. Scholars come to learn secrets only the dead still know, while jaded dilettantes come to revel in sensations only permissible here.

The problem facing the market is that the living all have something the dead want dearly: life. The energies within their mortal frames have enormous value and must be regulated. Any deal involving the trade of essence or life force must be witnessed and signed for by one of the market authorities, typically one of the more powerful undead. A cap is placed on such transactions each night and prices are fixed so as to prevent a bidding war from leading to an unholy one.

Of course, in the corners of the market exist less scrupulous traders who see no need to bother the authorities with these transactions. They are willing to risk the wrath of the market for another taste of life, but without oversight allow their greed to get the better of them. Virtually anything in the market can be purchased by offering to give up 3d4+2 maximum hit points, which can only be restored with a *greater restoration* or *wish* spell. If the deal is not witnessed by an adjudicator, however, the merchant may roll d8s instead.

Because it makes them feel alive again, the dead devour this life force voraciously, giving them Inspiration a number of times equal to the amount of health drained.

VARIANT ENCOUNTER (OPTIONAL) DEALS WITH THE DEAD

The dead have little need for coin, so deals in The Nightmare Market almost exclusively use the barter system. Each merchant has their own price and idea of what might be valuable. For an idea of what you might encounter in the market, roll on the table at right.

1d6	The party encounters...
1	...a **banshee** beneath the gibbets at the market's heart, crooning a gentle melody. She is a soothsayer among the dead and is willing to trade a vision of a character's next moment of mortal peril in return for the memory of their greatest loss. This vision will allow the character to twist out of the way and survive on 1 HP the next time an attack reduces them to 0 hp.
2	...a silent **wraith** watching them approach, remaining motionless until they reach its stall. It gestures with one arm toward the collection of bottled memories on the table before it, each carefully labeled with a title and previous owner. "*The Day I Died*, Merineous Ghorsk," "*A Knight's Shame*, Sir Dmitri Pellirian" and "*Buried Treasure*, Captain Murk" leap out. The wraith then wordlessly draws attention to a sign attached to the side of the stall. "These memories are carefully curated. One may be purchased for the price of two."
3	...a **ghoul** with a predilection for fingers who keeps a large bucket of rings beside his stall. While disappointed they aren't interested in his famous "Finger Food," he is happy to trade the entire bucket (about 100 gp worth of regular rings and one magical *ring of protection*) in exchange for just a little bite—one of their fingers should do.
4	...an enticing smell that leads to a short queue in front of a hulking, hooded figure stirring a large pot filled with a thick, red liquid. As they wait, they realize they recognize the man in front of them. He is a local noble-man, and he looks very hungry indeed.
5	...the ghost of their most recently slain humanoid foe is working behind a stall. The spirit appears to have no recollection of them, but is willing to part with memories identifying their allies still within the city so long as they take a special memory to give to their young daughter.
6	...the sound of a quarrel leading toward one of the market's entrances. A corpse lies at the feet of a solidly built **revenant** who is protesting that the dead human had "too little life to give." Nevertheless, the price was paid, and the adjudicating specter states the revenant must honor its side of the deal and give the dead man one of its eyes. The eye, containing a single use of the revenant's Vengeful Glare, will belong to the corpse if it animates via any means before the end of the night, otherwise it will revert to the revenant. The eye could be stolen if the party can make the corpse stir long enough to claim it.

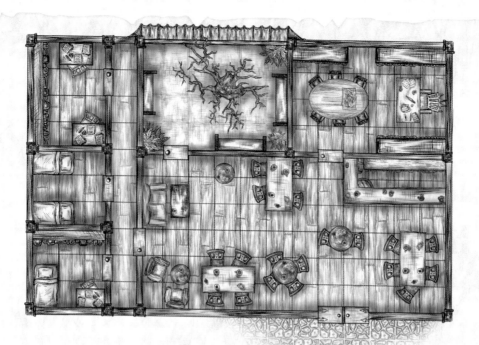

VARIANT GUILD HALL

This space can stand in as the headquarters or regional office for any guild you choose. Just roll a few dice.

GUILD

Roll 1d20 to determine the nature of this guild.

1d20	This is the hall for the Esteemed Guild of...
1	Alchemists and apothecaries
2	Armorers, locksmiths and finesmiths
3	Brewers, distillers and vintners
4	Calligraphers, scribes and scriveners
5	Carpenters, roofers and plasterers
6	Cartographers, surveyors and chart-makers
7	Cobblers and shoemakers
8	Cooks and bakers
9	Glassblowers and glaziers
10	Jewelers and gem-cutters
11	Leatherworkers, skinners and tanners
12	Masons and stonecutters
13	Painters, limners and sign-makers
14	Potters and tile-makers
15	Shipwrights and sailmakers
16	Smiths and metal-forgers
17	Tinkers, pewterers and casters
18	Wagon-makers and wheelwrights
19	Weavers and dyers
20	Woodcarvers, coopers and bowyers

UPKEEP

Roll 1d4 to reveal the state of things within the hall.

1d4	The space appears to be...
1	**Thrifty.** The guild spends very little on furnishings or decorations within its hall.
2	**Vandalized.** The hall has been set upon by someone intending to send a message.
3	**Well-appointed.** The fixtures and trappings suggest a fair amount of bartering and trade led to its upstanding appearance.
4	**Over-the-top.** An opulent atmosphere where craftsmanship meets a bottomless budget.

GUILD LEADER

Roll 1d4 to learn a bit about your host in this establishment.

1d4	The head of this guild is...
1	**Corrupt.** More interested in the coin than the craft, this leader has let power go to their head.
2	**Humble.** This individual would prefer to be left to their craft rather than bureaucracy.
3	**Charismatic.** Unafraid to boast about the benefits of the guild or the quality of its work.
4	**Drunk.** No matter the time of day, you're likely to find this leader deep into their cups, even as they handle guild business.

THE TOWN TAILOR

A tiny shop along a crowded street in the merchant district, the Town Tailor's glass storefront showcases the latest fashions and classic cuts, as well as simpler wares for the less style-obsessed. The shop's owner, **Hugh Followell**, is sharp and agile for his age and his shop is clean, if a bit musty.

NPC PROFILE

HUGH FOLLOWELL, HUMAN TAILOR

The sole proprietor of the Town Tailor since it opened its doors more than 50 years ago, Hugh Followell is a living legend in his industry, though few in town would know it. At 83 years of age, he's got twice the energy of most half his age, and his wrinkled visage spreads wide with a smile anytime a would-be customer arrives. Though he has outfitted kings and queens and nobles of all stripes, his true passion lies in helping any who walk into his shop look their best. Hugh's work is especially popular among traveling bards and acting troupes, who will often veer days off course for a chance to be sized up by his measuring tape.

INTERIOR

The shop features a display area with styles for every occasion, with tall windows facing the street (*1*). A side room packed with reams of fabric, as well as a loom and Hugh's workstation (*2*), is also the entry point for two small changing rooms (*3*).

VARIANT ENCOUNTER (OPTIONAL)

Roll 1d6 to determine what events might unfold at the Town Tailor.

1d6	The party...
1	...sees a disgruntled **noble** and his 1d4 attendants refusing to pay Hugh for a recent order.
2	...discovers 1d4 **giant badgers** have burrowed into one of the changing rooms.
3	...hears screaming as an **invisible stalker** arrives to attack Hugh at the behest of a demented **mage** for whom Hugh refused to create a robe.
4	...eventually learns Hugh inadvertently wove a long-dormant family curse (roll on the Curse Table on pg. 136) into the next garment he sells.
5	...sees 1d4 **kenku** storm the shop and begin stripping most of the display garments of their finery.
6	...sees 1d6 of the display garments springing to life (animated armor, AC 14, hp 22), forcing themselves on the party, hoping to be worn.

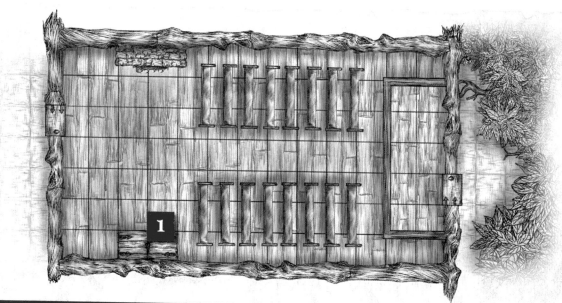

THE COMMUNITY MEETING HALL

This large, somewhat imposing wooden hall was built using massive logs when this area was first settled. It stands as the central meeting place to discuss important issues relevant to the community, including marriages, deaths, births and declarations of war, as well as less consequential gossip such as "What's the deal with Marge's cabbage patch?"

ENTRANCES AND EXITS

The hall is built out of ancient heavy timber, and its thatched roof, made of dried long grass and heather, could stand to be replaced. There are two doors at opposite ends of the hall. There are no windows, as they were deemed impractical at the time of the building's initial construction.

DRY STORES

With a successful DC 15 Intelligence (Investigation) check, the party would notice a large trapdoor (*1*) in the floor of the Community Meeting Hall that leads to a basement storage area equal in size to the center itself, with walls made of carved out clay and earth, reinforced with wooden beams. This area serves as storage for the town during the harvest so that there is ample food during less bountiful seasons. Sacks of grain and milled flour are the primary feature, though there is also enough solid food to keep the townsfolk satisfied in case of an emergency. The corn collected here is rotten and has a sulfurous smell, but is as safe to eat as brown water is safe to drink. Due to its size and composition, this door requires a DC 15 Strength (Athletics) check to open.

VARIANT ENCOUNTER (OPTIONAL)

Roll 1d10 on the table below to determine what conversations are ongoing in this meeting hall.

1d10	The gathered villagers are discussing...
1	**...how the town youths** have been using the *message* cantrip for illicit purposes and it has to stop.
2	**...Old Nellie's daughter**, who has eloped with the local lord to become his mistress.
3	**...that the Reddick family's bull** and the Urif family's cow are having a calf and neither can agree over who will own it.
4	**...the traveling tinker** in the town who has been accused of stealing 3 chickens, but he claims his inventions did it.
5	**...a local supposed witch** who is stealing the stray cats in town to use in her "dark rituals." She is, in fact, just feeding them.
6	**...one of the largest apothecary chains** in the land coming to the village, which some fear will put the local hedgewitch out of business.
7	**...Young Ygritte**, who goes missing for a couple of days each month. The town elders have determined her absences coincide with the full moon.
8	**...the soothsayer** who has predicted the village will fall to cropblight unless they pay him 100 gp to get rid of the "bad spirits" plaguing their fields.
9	**...that Perrin boy** who has developed magical powers, giving anyone he touches bad dreams.
10	**...nothing at all.** Silence reigns in the old hall as the entire village gathers in a circle to stare at a frightened young man in the center. Each of the villagers holds a heavy rock in their hand.

TEMPLES, TOMBS & CRYPTS

A SELECTION OF HALLOWED HALLS,
HAUNTED GRAVEYARDS AND
BLESSED BURIAL GROUNDS.

SUNKEN TEMPLE

A flooded sanctuary that hasn't yet lost its divine spark, this holy place stands in honor of its god by enduring despite its circumstances.

WATERY ENTRYWAY

This temple is completely immersed in water and can only be accessed by swimming through a large opening at the top of its ceiling (*1*). The holy power within this space creates an aura of water-breathing within its walls, and anyone who chooses to stay inside the temple cannot drown.

A DAMP INTERIOR

Reef-like walls and swaying seaweed are as prominent in this space as its large altar (*2*) and holy symbols. The temple's large support columns have also been co-opted by the underwater creatures that reside here, and an entire ecosystem seems to thrive inside and around each of them. Anyone curious about what it's like to sleep under the sea will find the opportunity to do so within the antechamber of the temple, which features a few sturdy ropes with which to secure a creature for rest so that they don't float or take a somnambulatory swim outside the confines of the breath-giving temple walls.

VARIANT ENCOUNTER (OPTIONAL)

Roll 1d6 to determine what underwater adventures await the party in the Sunken Temple.

1d6	The party...
1	...feels a rush of panic wash over all within the temple as 3d4 **quipper swarms** rush through the rooftop searching for a meal.
2	...watches as 2d4 **sahuagin** and 1 **sahuagin priestess** dive into the temple and attempt to destroy the altar.
3	...a tactical group of 3d4 **merrow** surround the temple, menacing anyone who attempts to leave.
4	...feels a horrible wave of fear surging through the temple as the shadow of an ancient **aboleth** blocks much of the light from above.
5	...sees a cleric within these walls accidentally summon 1d4 **water elementals** they cannot control.
6	...hears a horrible, gurgled cry erupting from one of the acolytes here, as she holds up the pieces of a broken holy artifact. It becomes very clear very quickly that the magic that allowed residents to breathe within this underwater space has been removed.

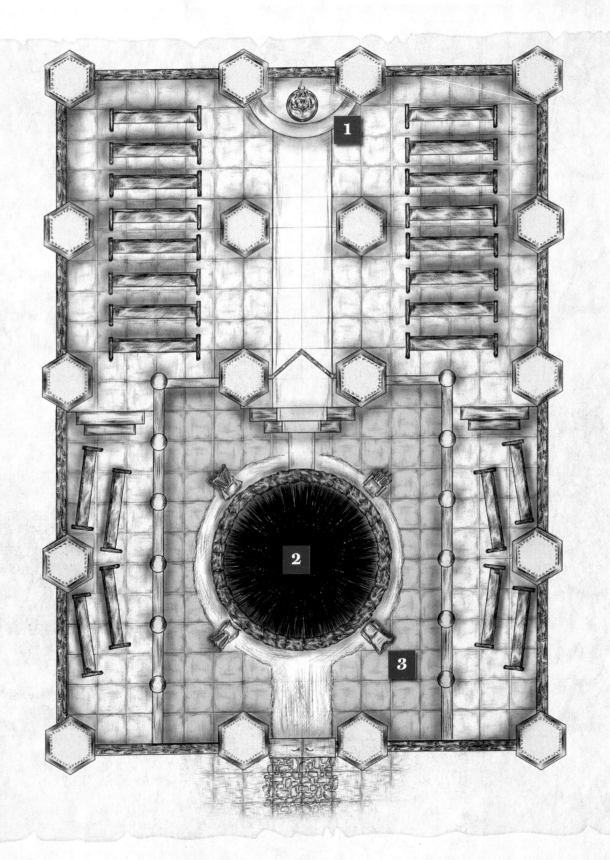

THE TEMPLE OF THE FALL

"...I SAW IT ALL AT ONCE, THIS MAGNIFICENT OPEN TEMPLE LINED WITH WOODEN PEWS, A BRIGHT FLAME FLICKERING AT THE BACK OF THE HALL OPPOSITE ME, AND BEFORE ME, THE PIT. THE ENDLESS. ITS CALL IS SILENT, BUT HAS YET TO LEAVE MY MIND. I NEED TO LOOK CLOSER. THIS WILL BE MY LAST LETTER. TELL TABITHA HER FATHER WAS A FOOL."

—The Endless Call, Volume V.ii

When one follows the path through the column-framed doorway and into the open-air courtyard of the Temple of the Fall, more often than not they'll encounter a small group of worshipers encircling the 30-foot-wide chasm that predates the building by centuries. It is, in layman's terms, a bottomless pit. But to the faithful who maintain this space, it is nothing less than a gateway into the depths of the soul. It may also be something more. They call it The Endless.

A DIVERSE HISTORY

The origins of The Endless have been lost to time, lending credence to the theory that it is as old as the earth itself. One thing that is certain is that since its discovery, curious minds have made the pilgrimage to see it for themselves. Peering over the edge of The Endless and into the breezy black void is a meaningful experience for most, but for a select few it is revelatory. The temple was built centuries ago, a lasting structure meant to endure for as long as the source of its existence. Those who worship at the Temple of the Fall are transfixed by The Endless, but few agree on why.

Expeditions to plumb the depths of The Endless have delved beyond 1,000 feet, but no one seeking the "True End" has ever returned. These expeditions evolved into annual rituals that still continue, with brave explorers volunteering to divine the full scope of The Endless. Clarity on this matter remains elusive, and is part of the Temple of the Fall's hold on those who choose to worship here.

INSIDE THE TEMPLE

Beyond the courtyard and elevated roughly 5 feet higher is a covered space with rows of pews abutted by enormous columns supporting the temple's high ceiling.

THE ALTAR. Along the back wall is a dais featuring an altar with a continual flame (*1*), which emits enough light to illuminate the space regardless of the time of day. The rows of wooden pews affixed to the stone floor face away from the altar, allowing those in attendance to keep their focus on the temple's central feature: The Endless.

THE ENDLESS. This gaping chasm (*2*) is surrounded by a well-trod tile border, as well as four wooden thrones (*3*). No one on hand can remember how long they've been part of the temple, nor does anyone recall their specific purpose—all those who worship here agree that sitting in these thrones is a bad idea, as the last person to try was dead within the week. Peering over the edge of The Endless is an almost irresistible experience and devotees choose to do so in many different ways. Some walk close to the edge and look in, while others sit on the edge and let their feet dangle over the abyss. A handful of attendants choose to prostrate themselves by the edge and crawl toward it on their bellies, their heads peering beyond the rim, eyes into the void. As the allure of leaving the known world behind calls to everyone in one way or another, anyone who looks into The Endless is subject to a DC 8 Wisdom saving throw, with a failure pulling them perilously closer to the edge. Those failing this save can make a DC 10 Dexterity save to steady themselves or else plummet over the side and into the unknown.

VARIANT ENCOUNTER (OPTIONAL)

Roll 1d6 to determine what might befall the party in the Temple of the Fall.

1d6	The party encounters...
1	...worshipers, in accordance with their traditions, preparing to cut the rope of a "True End" explorer who has decided he's gone far enough and is screaming to be pulled back up.
2	...a man desperately seeking his daughter, who was last seen wandering into the temple doors.
3	...the massive beast that lurks beneath the temple beginning to crawl out of its burrow, after centuries of slumber.
4	...a woman begging her betrothed not to attempt to leap across the chasm in an effort to impress her father.
5	...worshipers transfixed by the hole, who begin slowly walking off the edge one by one.
6	...authorities actively searching for a master **assassin** who is hiding among the temple's faithful.

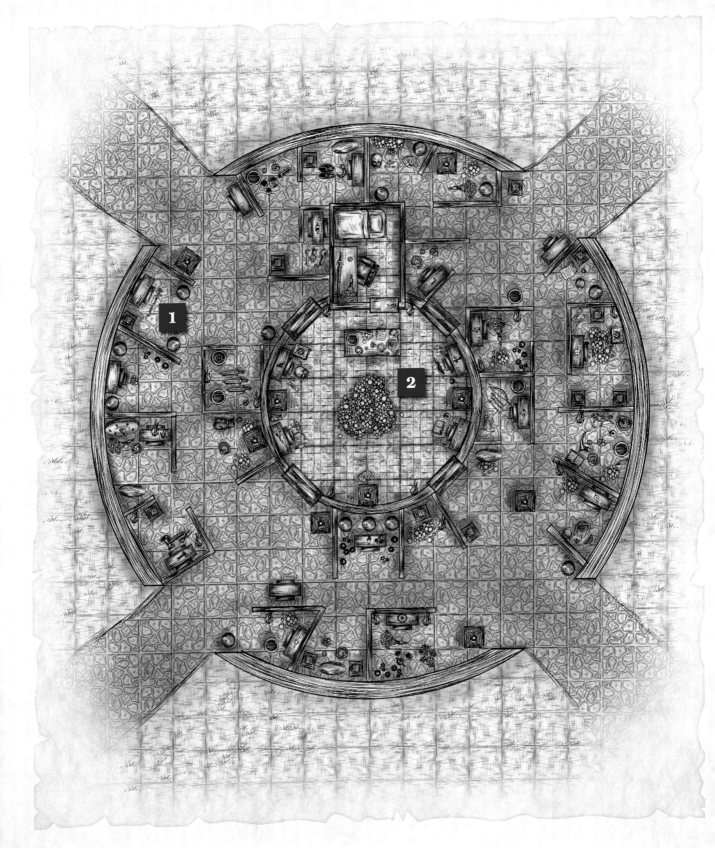

THE HALL OF MANY GODS

"LOTS OF FOLK CLAIM THEY'VE SEEN DEVILS AT THE CROSSROADS. BUT I'VE SEEN GODS THERE TOO. 'COURSE, I'D BEEN DRINKING."

—Benjen Tarrymaster, Acolyte of Ale

At a crossroads between four of the realm's larger cities is an open-air monument to the very idea of worship: a circular collection of private temples, called altarooms, where those whose steps are guided by a deity's blessing can seek further direction, pay homage or pray for forgiveness in communion with their god and other like-minded travelers. A modest shelter—the post of a single, stoic paladin—doubles as a supply store selling all the necessary elements for rituals of all stripes. The paladin, **Catherine the Godless**, also acts as a conduit for messages from the gods, making the Hall a popular destination for those seeking an audience with the divine.

NPC PROFILE
CATHERINE THE GODLESS, HUMAN PALADIN

Most days, and well into the evening, Catherine the Godless can be found sitting in silence in the shade of her post at the Hall of Many Gods. When she speaks, it is to offer assistance to those who require it—either by providing sacramental elements for rites and ceremonies or by pointing them in the direction of an available altaroom. But on occasion, Catherine opens her mouth and the voice released is not her own; deities across the pantheon utilize Catherine as a herald of sorts. As such, her mind is typically elsewhere even when she is going about the business of her charge at the crossroads, as the wills of dozens of celestials weave their way in and out of her consciousness on any given afternoon.

THE ALTAROOMS

Within the circular structure at varied intervals, these enclosed spaces (*1*) offer privacy and proper sanctuary for travelers in need of a place to practice their faith. Within each is an altar, a proper place for cleansing, shelving for small votives and enough room to lie fully prostrate if necessary. There are a handful of larger altarooms suitable for small groups, but most only fit a few worshippers at a time. Despite their architectural similarities, the major deific domains are reflected within individual altarooms. For example, those hoping to commune with a god of war can do so within an altaroom that features a grindstone wheel for sharpening steel, while those who look to guidance from a deity associated with knowledge will be pleased to find available altarooms featuring walls lined with books on numerous subjects.

PART HERMITAGE, PART RELIQUARY

The sheltered space at the center of the Hall of Many Gods (*2*) is both a lodging for Catherine the Godless, the caretaker here, as well as a makeshift storefront for holy items. Incense, holy water and other sacramental necessities are on offer for prices that would seem absurd within the borders of a major city.

PROTECTION FROM ON HIGH

Catherine the Godless is inherently nonviolent, and her vow is to protect this space and be a vessel for its purpose. Though she can readily handle herself in the event of conflict, if any of the travelers who journey through the Hall of Many Gods choose to endanger her or her mission here, they'll be met with consequences they may not be able to overcome. If she deems it necessary, Catherine can call on the aid of 3d4 **planetars**, each representing a different god from within the pantheon, to help her in defense of the Hall.

VARIANT ENCOUNTER (OPTIONAL)
Roll 1d6 to discover what circumstances the party may find themselves in at the Hall of Many Gods.

1d6	The party...
1	...hears a heated exchange between followers of disparate gods that has come to blows.
2	...is nearby when a group of 3d4 **bandits** posing as holy men are making their way into the Hall, with plans to steal all they can.
3	...sees a **deva** perched atop the shelter at the center of the crossroads in the guise of a falcon, asking the party if they require aid.
4	...sees a swirling black cloud pouring out of an altaroom, announcing the presence of a raging **glabrezu**.
5	...is caught off guard when a flaming wagon packed with barrels of pitch speeds toward the crossroads, its horses fleeing the 3d4 **worg-riding goblins** on their heels.
6	...sees a wounded cleric dragging himself along the crossroads, angrily refusing aid from all passersby.

THE BONE FIELDS

Massive piles of bleached-white skeletal remains create a desert of crumbling skulls and broken bones in this uninhabitable space. The air is thick with a haze of particulate matter, and towering dunes of bone dust create natural pathways through this unforgiving valley. Any adventurers who speak of the Bone Fields do so with humble reverence, and are all keenly aware each minute they spent there could have been their last. If you're lucky, the subtle tones of remains as they shift and crunch is all you'll hear. There are few good reasons to come to the Bone Fields, and far fewer to linger.

CREATURES GREAT AND SMALL

The Bone Fields are littered with the skeletal remains of all manner of monstrosities and beasts, as well as ancient dragons and beings that were once humanoid. Large claws extend up from beneath the rubble, cradling the skull of a gargantuan creature, its large eye sockets a black void in a sea of white.

A HANGING SENSE OF DREAD

The moment a creature enters this space they are overcome with the sense that they shouldn't stay and must succeed on a Constitution saving throw (DC 15) or be poisoned as they breathe in the foul air of this corrupt landscape. Additionally, for every 10 minutes a creature spends in this space, they must make a Constitution saving throw (DC 10), taking 4d6 necrotic damage on a failed save or half as much on a success, as a malevolent presence within the Bone Fields drains their life.

A SKELETAL COMPANION

Players approaching the Bone Fields may sense they're being followed, and a DC 15 Wisdom (Perception) check reveals their feelings to be justified. A small quadrupedal skeleton patiently follows the party from 30 feet back with the energy of a loyal sheepdog. A successful Animal Handling check (DC 15) will earn the creature's trust, and it will follow the party more closely and even come to their aid here in times of need. If any member of the party attempts to attack the creature, they will suffer 3d6 psychic damage, after which the skeletal creature crumbles into dust.

THE MIND OF A TITAN

Within the skull of the gargantuan creature that rests at the center of the Bone Fields (*1*) is a portal to the mind of a reigning king or queen (at GM discretion). Moving within the portal allows access to the mind of the monarch, and a creature can manipulate that ruler's thoughts and memories from within this portal by rolling on the Mind Portal Manipulation table.

MIND PORTAL MANIPULATION

Roll 1d20 and add the modifier of your choice (Intelligence, Wisdom or Charisma).

1–5	You see nothing within the portal, but the moment you exit you are blinded for 3d6 days.
6–10	You see the current thoughts of the monarch but are unable to influence them in any way.
11–15	You can access all of the monarch's memories but are unable to influence them in any way.
16–20	You can access all of the monarch's memories and can modify one sequence of events, as in the *modify memory* spell.
20+	You can access all of the monarch's memories and can author as many as three new ones, which will be incorporated into their thoughts as though they were their own.

VARIANT ENCOUNTER (OPTIONAL)

Roll 1d6 to determine what dangers await the party within the Bone Fields.

1d6	The party finds...
1	...1d4 **shadow demons** emerging from within the piles of bones and encircling the party.
2	...one **nalfeshnee** and 1d4 **quasits** attempting to move the gargantuan skull at the center of the field.
3	...a gust of wind carrying stacks of bone, which begin to form into 5d6 **skeletons**.
4	...a **bone devil** emerging from the rubble, seemingly hungry for flesh.
5	...2d4 **drow** and one **drow priestess of Lolth** searching the Bone Fields for an artifact of great cultural significance.
6	...a skeletal **stone giant** emerging from behind a dune, charging the party with an oversized jawbone in his hand.

THE SUN TEMPLE

Though many deities are worshiped as sun gods (Lathander, Pelor and Re-Horakhty among them), no single temple or path of faith can claim ownership over the sun's life-giving radiance. The Sun Temple was built as a central space of worship for any individual who wishes to commune with the light, regardless of their deific affiliation. The Sun Temple's most striking features are its solarium, which maximizes the amount of sunlight emitted into the space, as well as its shifting clockwork gyrolens, which rotates just enough each day to ensure a direct beam of light strikes the Solaraltar as long as the sun is in the sky.

LIGHT UNDERGROUND

After climbing several steep steps, one can find the half-buried Temple of the Sun built into the side of a hill, its surface a large, open space with worshipers milling about above, soaking in the sunlight. Descending a few steps down to the temple's open foyer (*1*) reveals the gyrolens (*2*), a series of interlocking circles and lenses housed within them that collect the sun's rays and redirect them into a single, powerful beam of light focused into the worship hall to the left. The foyer's ceiling is a massive solarium, ensuring that light can be captured and directed toward the Solaraltar (*3*) while serving the dual purpose of illuminating the space at all hours of the day. The temple's location within the hilltop ensures maximum exposure to the light with minimal shadows, and the glass top solarium's surface is aligned with the rest of the hilltop, which also helps maximize the interior's exposure to the light.

THE GYROLENS

Part arcane construct, part engineering marvel, the gyrolens rotates, shifts and swirls in time with the movement of the planet, aligning itself to collect and bounce sunlight into a solid beam that's always directed at the Solaraltar until the light diminishes once the sun sets. The mechanisms by which the gyrolens adjusts itself are magically warded, and watching it operate is akin to observing the complex systems powering a living creature. The gyrolens is so powerful—and central to the act of worship here—that some who commune with the sun in this place think of it as a demigod. The beam of light created by the gyrolens can also be focused and aimed using a lever along its base. When focused, the beam can generate a staggering amount of radiant energy—a creature hit by this beam must make a DC 15 Constitution save, suffering 12d8 radiant damage and blindness on a failed save or half as much on a success.

THE SOLARALTAR

The worship hall directly to the left of the gyrolens is home to the Solaraltar, a point of reference and reverence for those wishing to worship the light. The gyrolens ensures that a beam of light is always directed at the Solaraltar, a gilded, crystal-covered surface that can occasionally shine as blindingly as the sun itself.

THE RISING ROOM

To the right of the gyrolens is the Rising Room (*4*), an observatory space with windows and balconies built into the hillside and offering year-round views of the sunrise over the town below. Many pilgrims to this temple choose to sleep on the open floor in this space overnight in order to observe the coming of the sun once dawn arrives. With its sweeping views of a large portion of the realm, it's also a popular spot for small, dusk-lit social functions. A small library with a door (*5*) leads to a series of steps to the hilltop and is also a feature of this space.

VARIANT ENCOUNTER (OPTIONAL)

Roll 1d6 to determine what trouble may be on the rise at the Sun Temple.

1d6	The party discovers...
1	...a war of words between an acolyte of Pelor and a knight of Lathander getting out of hand, with one holding the other over the side of one of the balconies in the Rising Room until he recants his disrespectful tone.
2	...a flock of 2d4 **harpies** descending on the solarium, their collective weight threatening to crack one of its glass panels.
3	...a band of 2d4 **cultists** who support a dark demonic force storming the temple and attempting to dismantle the gyrolens.
4	...a group of 2d4 **bandits** and their **bandit captain** disguised as worshipers attempting to raid the Rising Room while the 3d4 pilgrims there are settling in for an evening's rest.
5	...the gyrolens malfunctioning, seemingly taking on a mind of its own, swirling around, firing focused sunlight at random. The gyrolens is resistant to all damage, has 150 total hp (its six lenses have 25 each, with each one damaged removing 1d8 from the sunbeam's power) and makes one attack with its sunbeam lens for 12d8 radiant damage on a failed DC 16 Constitution save. A DC 20 Intelligence check will shut it down, as will relentlessly pummeling it.
6	...a griffon rider losing control of its mount, crash-landing through the solarium. The **griffon**—understandably upset—begins to wreak havoc within the temple.

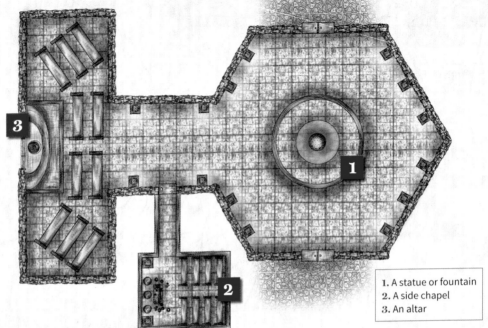

1. A statue or fountain
2. A side chapel
3. An altar

VARIANT TEMPLE

This space is suitable for the worship of any god in the pantheon—all it takes is a couple of dice rolls.

DOMINION

Roll 1d6 to determine the domain of the deity worshipped within this space, or choose one for yourself.

1	Life
2	Death
3	War
4	Nature
5	Trickery
6	Light

GENERAL ATMOSPHERE

Roll 1d4 to determine the overall feel of the space and those worshipping within it.

1d4	This space appears to be...
1	**...Reverent.** This is a hallowed and sacred temple. Quiet and serene if a bit stuffy, stepping into the temple feels like standing in the presence of something divine.
2	**...Welcoming.** A convivial atmosphere, replete with smiling faces and warm salutations, walking through this temple's halls is akin to visiting a friendly bar as opposed to a stuffy commune.
3	**...Cloistered.** Siloed off from the rest of civilization, either by choice or as a result of unique geography, those who worship here are devoted to their god and blissfully unaware of much else.
4	**...Jaded.** A bitterness hangs in the air, as doubt and frustration permeate every aspect of temple life. Though there are plenty here who worship their god, many do so out of habit or fear rather than true devotion.

UPKEEP

Roll 1d4 to reveal the overall state of things within the temple.

1d4	The temple is...
1	**...Spartan.** This temple is practically bare, its occupants wearing simple robes in an effort to focus their attention where it belongs.
2	**...Desecrated.** Crumbling and battered, the worshipers here are working to rebuild as an act of devotion.
3	**...Well-appointed.** Comfortable though not extravagant, the temple features fixtures and surfaces that wouldn't be out of place in the home of a noble.
4	**...Opulent.** A space suitable for royalty as much as divinity, from the tapestries to the statuary to the spotless floors, nearly everything in the temple looks outrageously expensive.

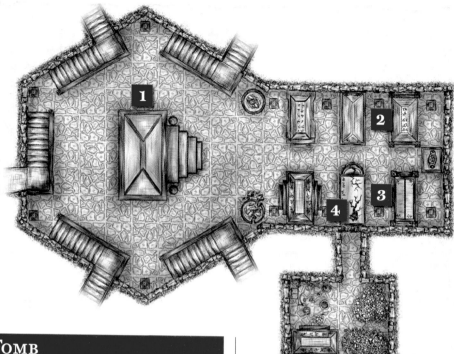

NOBLES' TOMB

Beneath the foundations of one of the city's most elaborate noble houses, this crypt is the final resting place for a great family's former scions and kin.

REVERENT REMAINS

This dusty, dimly torchlit tomb is as old as the city itself and was dug into the dirt when the foundation of the home above was laid. The bodies of generations of the family who built this crypt as well as its most revered member (*1*) are buried here, some in elaborate stone tombs (*2*), others in more modest miniature mausoleums (*3*). Statuary of the more significant members of the family can be found standing watch over various locations within the crypt, and there are a handful of plots that have been organized and cleared out in preparation for the coming inevitability of another noble death. Candles and torches illuminate different corners of the space, and the gold, jewels and other trinkets left in memory of the family members buried here glitter and scatter the flickering flames.

CURSED GOODS

On a DC 12 Intelligence (Investigation) check, the party uncovers a cache of 1,000 gp's worth of coin and jewels as well as an uncommon magic item hidden away behind a busted casket (*4*). These baubles are not meant for the living, however, and any who choose to remove these items from the crypt will fall under a baleful curse. Roll 1d4 to determine which curse takes effect.

1d4	The player(s)...
1	...lose 1d6 hit points from their total hp each day until the curse is removed.
2	...are menaced by the spirits of the fallen family, causing disadvantage on all attack rolls until the curse is removed.
3	...are under the effects of the *bane* spell until the curse is removed.
4	...fall under a curse as outlined on the Curses table on pg. 136.

VARIANT ENCOUNTER (OPTIONAL)

Roll 1d6 to see what dangers rise from the grave.

1d6	The party sees...
1	...2d6 noble **zombies** shuffling around inside the tomb. They seem hungry.
2	...1d4 **ghosts** encouraging the party to avenge their family—but can't recall what happened to them.
3	...a **bearded devil** waiting to make a deal with a noble. He is growing impatient.
4	...a group of 1d6 grave robbers currently battling a hungry **troll**.
5	...the slick walls of the tomb are actually 2d4 **gray oozes** lying in wait.
6	...a **psuedodragon** sitting quietly by the grave of its former master, and can be convinced to join the party with a DC 17 Wisdom (Animal Handling) check.

THE ICE TOMB

Among the highest peaks in the realm, this rarely visited, crystal blue cavern serves as a gallery showcasing the frozen bodies of the ancestors of those who currently dwell in this mountain range. A serene if somewhat eerie space, corpses left alongside the ice wall eventually freeze into it, kept from decay within a surface as smooth as glass.

A MOUNTAIN MAUSOLEUM

Because of the sacred nature of the Ice Tomb, its location is known only to those whose family members are buried here. The secret of its location is revealed when it comes time to entomb another member of the community in a ceremony known as the Cold Goodbye. Rumors of the Ice Tomb's existence have floated down from the mountaintops, but none who have journeyed to look for it have returned to share its location. If the party is journeying among frost-capped peaks, they might spy a nigh indiscernible pathway leading up along a craggy cliff, which can be found with a successful DC 20 Wisdom (Perception) check. The pathway then cuts into the heart of the mountain, revealing chunks of pure blue ice, as if within a glacier. These glacial walls are illusory and can be passed through by succeeding on a DC 10 Intelligence (Investigation) check. Once on the other side, the Ice Tomb is revealed as row after row of frozen corpses come into view.

CORPSE WALLS

The walls in the center of the Ice Tomb are frozen solid, and within each are generations of corpses standing shoulder to shoulder, their faces in serene repose. Some walls are thicker than others and contain more bodies—in some instances six deep. All of the corpses face the center of the chamber. The surface of the floor is slick ice and difficult terrain for anyone not wearing proper gear.

VARIANT ENCOUNTER (OPTIONAL)

Roll 1d6 to determine what chilling terrors await the party in the Ice Tomb.

1d6	The party discovers...
1	...evidence that a **young remorhaz** has been feasting on the corpses here.
2	...a sleeping **yeti**.
3	...2d6 **ice mephits** emerging from the walls.
4	...1d4 **poltergeists** that swirl around the chamber.
5	...a **wight** clawing at a body in the wall.
6	...a pack of 1d4 **winter wolves**.

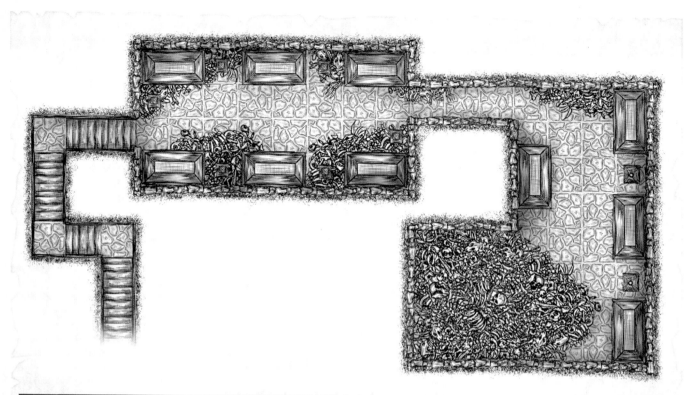

COMMONER CRYPT

> "THERE MUST BE A PLACE TO BURY THE
> BODIES OF THE COMMON PEOPLE. I TIRE OF
> SMELLING BURNT FLESH."
>
> —Ommander Levianto, Archduke of Antiamo

An underground area gifted to the town's poorest citizens as a final resting place for their dead, this once beautiful tomb is now largely a pile of bones and rotting flesh.

THE SMELL OF DEATH

The first thing one encounters in this space is its stench, the slow decomposition of dead bodies rotting on top of one another permeating the air. Any creature moving within 20 feet of the Commoner Crypt must succeed on a DC 12 Constitution saving throw or spend an action losing their lunch. To enter the crypt they must reattempt the save, with a +1 to the DC for each failure. Three successive fails of this save prevent a creature from entering the Commoner Crypt for 24 hours.

WITHIN THE CRYPT

Artfully crafted mosaics on the walls of this tomb, the final visible vestiges of its former glory as a nobleman's resting place, are smeared with dried gore and rot, as bodies stacked 12 high in some corners of the crypt buzz with a thick cloud of flies. The piles are considered difficult terrain.

VARIANT ENCOUNTER (OPTIONAL)

Roll 1d6 to determine what horrors await the party within the walls of the Commoner Crypt.

1d6	The party encounters...
1	...a stirring among the pile of bones is a mix of 1d4 **rat swarms** and 1d4 **zombies**.
2	...a group of 2d6 **skeletons**, which rise and begin menacing the party.
3	...a pair of **shadows**, which stalk the party from the darker corners of the crypt.
4	...a **mud mephit** wallowing in a pile of dirt near the bone pile, a harbinger of the arrival of 3d4 more of them.
5	...a scream from within the crypt, as a woman is being buried alive under the bones by 3d4 **bandits**.
6	...a horrible buzzing, which heralds the arrival of a **chasme**, a demon trapped within the walls of this crypt.

TOWN GRAVEYARD

Though some races are more long-lived than others, eventually all must succumb to the limits of mortality. Those who achieve fame, fortune or a measure of both might find themselves enshrined in a tomb, while the lowest of classes are lucky to have a marker designating their final resting place. For all those in between, there are graveyards like this one. A collection of centuries-old plots, freshly dug graves and well-manicured greenery, mausoleums and monuments rise alongside simple headstones in a space suitable for quiet reflection or, from time to time, battles against the undead.

GRAVEYARD GATES

The main thoroughfare (*1*) into the graveyard is marked by large wrought iron gates, which are unlocked each day at dawn then closed and locked again approximately one hour after sundown (DC 17). The iron fence surrounding the graveyard is approximately 15 feet high.

REFLECTION TEMPLE

A roofed but unwalled space for meditation or communing with the spirits of the dead (*2*), this temple disallows altars dedicated to one specific deity and is free of any of the markers typically present at a place of worship. Instead, it hosts an array of offerings to various gods—particularly those most associated with notions of life and death—a custom that throws off far-flung travelers but that locals agree is for the best given the size of their community.

STONE CASKET

This large stone casket (*3*) has a crumbling top and a false bottom, which upon further investigation (DC 17) appears to lead to an underground tomb. The large heavy lid of the casket can be removed with a successful DC 18 Strength (Athletics) check.

OPEN GRAVE

A pile of earth sits alongside a hole about 7 feet deep (*4*), the site of a recently departed citizen's soon-to-be final resting place. Anyone tumbling into this hole is subject to a DC 12 Dexterity saving throw, suffering 1d6 bludgeoning damage on a failed save. A DC 10 Strength (Athletics) check is required for anyone wishing to climb out without the aid of rope or a hand from above.

FAMILY PLOT

A larger mausoleum within the graveyard (*5*), this plot belongs to a long-forgotten family who buried their dead here for decades. Its maintenance is now handled by a single heir, who makes his home within the modest surroundings of the mausoleum (*6*). A grate within this space (*7*) leads directly to the underground tunnels that permeate the town, and while the party may find evidence that someone lives here, whether they meet the man who keeps this grave—as well as the pertinent details related to his family—is entirely up to GM discretion.

VARIANT ENCOUNTER (OPTIONAL)

Roll 1d6 to determine what adventures await the party within the graveyard.

1d6	If the sun has set...
1	...a group of 2d4 **bandits** are attempting to rob a grave.
2	...a **necromancer** and her 2d4 undead minions are systematically ripping up gravestones.
3	...1d6 **will-o'-wisps** hover among the gravestones.
4	...a pile of grave dirt is actually a **shambling mound**.
5	...2d4 **mummies** emerge from one of the mausoleums and start chasing anyone nearby.
6	...four **ghosts** float among the gravestones and mausoleums. One is hostile. One will aid the adventurers. Two will only attack if provoked.

NPC PROFILE
CALLOWAY REACHRUN, HERMIT OF THE GRAVES

Long before the noble families in this region made names for themselves, the Reachruns owned or profited from much of the land and businesses here. Their name was synonymous with success, forthrightness and honor—but that was long ago. Today their name is largely forgotten, their wealth and standing evaporating almost overnight following a series of bad deals, worse luck and—or so it was rumored—a horrible, irreversible curse. Today, the only man who knows the truth about the Reachruns is the family's sole heir, an elderly but spry hermit named Calloway. His inheritance amounts to little more than a *bag of magic beans* he keeps close to his bony chest and this family plot, where he spends most of his time maintaining the Reachrun mausoleum.

THE GREAT OUTDOORS

FOREST FORTRESSES,
BEACHFRONT BATTLEFIELDS
AND PLACID PARKS FOR WHEN YOUR
PARTY NEEDS SOME FRESH AIR.

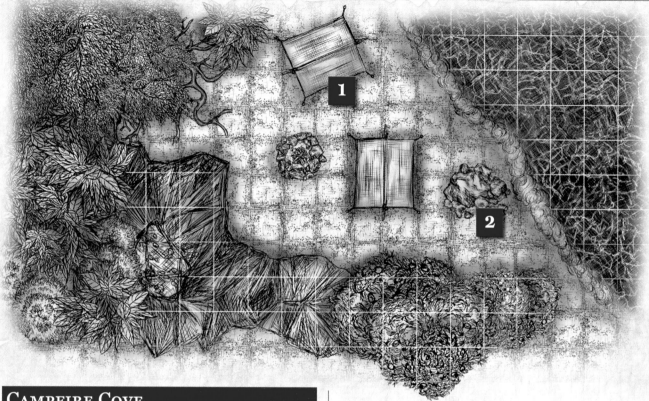

CAMPFIRE COVE

A coastal clearing that's a perfect spot to bed down for the night, this serene space is also an attractive watering hole for beasts of the nearby forest, as well as bandits looking to lie low.

FOREST COVER, OPEN SHORE

The surrounding woods give Campfire Cove enough cover so that a small campfire doesn't alert the entire realm to one's campsite. Any light source can be seen from the sea, however. In fact, rumors of the creatures who dwell beneath the waves being tempted to come to ground by the glow of a warming fire have persisted almost as long as those that tell of this site's location. In other words, it's a great spot to stay the night, though it's only as safe as any other in this land.

A SPACE TO REST, OR STASH

Members of the merchant's guild, who travel along the path that passes this space more often than any other organization, sponsored the erection and continued upkeep of semi-permanent structures (**1**) on the shoreline, which offer modest shelter from the elements, as well as cover from incoming attacks should things turn south. A large boulder at the beach's edge (**2**) is partially illusory, with a dug-out hole for treasure or dead drops hidden within the rock itself. The illusion can be discovered with a DC 16 Intelligence (Investigation) check or if someone leans against the base of the rock while facing the shore. The contents of this hidden space are at GM discretion.

VARIANT ENCOUNTER (OPTIONAL)

Roll 1d6 to determine what dangers lie in wait for adventurers who stop off at this cove.

1d6	The party sees...
1	...a small trio of **owlbear** cubs wandering to the shoreline. Their mother isn't far behind.
2	...3d4 **bandits** posing as merchants willing to trade with the party before stealing all their stuff.
3	...2d4 **ettercaps** silently investigate the creatures disturbing their carefully hidden (DC 18 Investigation) webs.
4	...an **ettin** lumbers into the cove for water. One of its heads appears to be asleep.
5	...a scouting party of 2d4 **merrow** creep onto the shore to investigate the noises emanating from camp.
6	...a massive tidal wave washes onto the cove, pulling any in the party who don't succeed on a DC 15 Strength saving throw into the sea.

POSSIBILITY PARK

> *"WHAT IF, INSTEAD OF DESTROYING THIS FOREST, WE, I DON'T KNOW, BUILT A WALL AROUND IT. FOR OUR CHILDREN'S CHILDREN. OR IS THAT A DAFT IDEA?"*
>
> —Sir Halifax Megalomo, Corporal of the Great Expansion

Featuring quiet corners for casual conversation, trees for shade and man-made structures that accentuate the natural landscape, Possibility Park is a place brimming with the opportunities implied by its name.

GREEN SPACES

Much of Possibility Park is open lawn (**1**), with well-trod paths (**2**) connecting points of interest among the rolling hills within its borders. Small benches are positioned strategically throughout the park, offering lovely views of the natural environment or of the cityscape beyond its formal confines. Small pagoda-like structures (**3**) offer shade, though not nearly as much as the dense forests (**4**) on either side of the park—left to grow wild to enhance the atmosphere of the space, as well as to protect the plant and wildlife within. Visibility within the forest areas is diminished by half, and any Wisdom (Perception) checks made in the park's packed forests are made with disadvantage. The forest also counts as difficult terrain for the purposes of determining a character's movement speed. Torch boxes illuminate most of the park and are lit after sundown.

POSSIBILITY POINT

A large stone obelisk sits on a white marble platform (**5**), casting a long shadow as the sun makes its way across the sky. Constructed as part of the park's initial design, the obelisk has become a bit of a tourist attraction, and lore suggests it has magical properties—at least anecdotally: Those who choose to touch the obelisk may find other possibilities open for them. If a character touches the obelisk, have them roll 1d20. On a 12 or higher, they are granted one extra d20 on any attack roll, skill check or saving throw. On a roll of 5 or less, they have disadvantage on a roll of your choice. This property can only be used once and fades after 24 hours.

SIGNIFICANT STATUARY

Physical likenesses of several of the area's most prominent figures dot the landscape here (**6**), equally spaced along the numerous paths within the park. Each is carved from a similar type of gray stone.

FISHING POND

A small creek feeds a modest body of water within the park (**7**), a popular spot for fishing, skipping stones and contemplating the day's dealings. A small dock juts into the pond and is a lovely spot to sit and try to reel in small fish.

HEDGE MAZE

The park offers visitors an opportunity to enter a large hedge maze (**8**) and explore its 10-foot-tall hedge walls and elegant topiary.

ENCOUNTER VARIANT (OPTIONAL) EXPLORING THE MAZE

If the party is so inclined they may enter the maze built within Possibility Park. Roll 1d4 to determine what, if anything, the party encounters within it.

1	The walls of this maze are teeming with life and are themselves alive. Any time a creature turns a corner in the maze, roll 1d6. On a 1, the creature must succeed on a DC 12 Strength (Athletics) saving throw or be grappled by vines attempting to pull them into the shrubbery.
2	At the center of this maze is a blind man who offers to read the palms of each member of the party for 1 sp. He will tell them each one truth about their future, at GM discretion.
3	The center of the maze features a portal to another realm (at GM discretion) and can be activated with a successful DC 20 Intelligence (Arcana) check.
4	Anyone who walks into this maze but does not reach its center is cursed, and will find themselves at the entrance to the maze each dawn, their body inexplicably drawn to complete it.

VARIANT ENCOUNTER (OPTIONAL)

Roll 1d6 to determine what possibilities await your adventurers in Possibility Park.

1d6	The party sees...
1	...a group of 1d4 **phase spiders** menacing the pagoda.
2	...a small boy drowning in the pond, where he's being circled by a hungry **crocodile**.
3	...a **bulette** bursting from the ground and wreaking havoc throughout the park.
4	...2d4 **insect swarms**, heralding an angry **dryad**.
5	...a park visitor tossing an apple core into the pond, offending a **water elemental**.
6	...1d4 **ghouls** emerging from within the hedge maze and terrorizing the park.

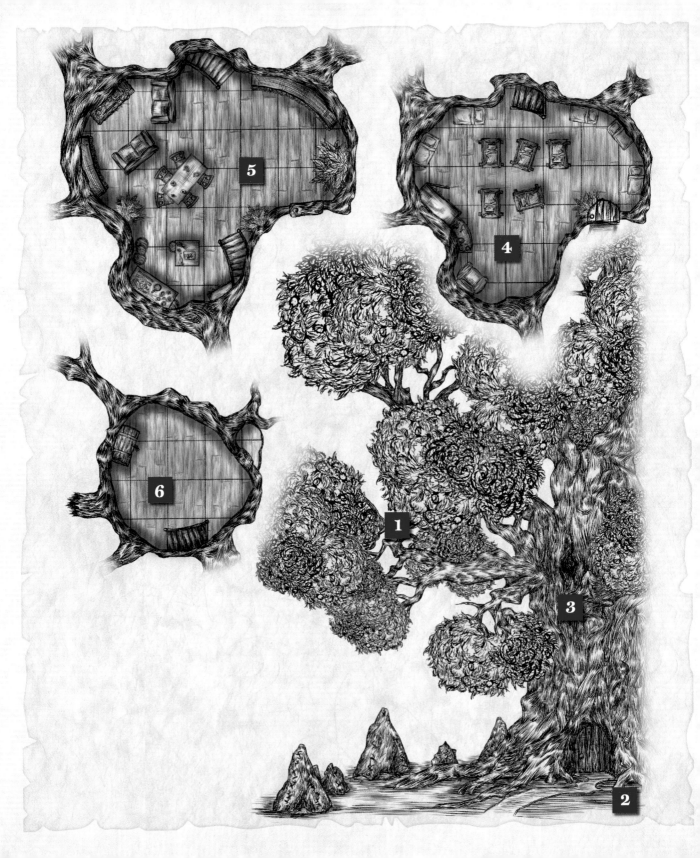

OAKVILLE HARBOR HOUSE

In a large clearing within the forest stands a massive oak, its branches thick as the average poplar. Within the tree's enormous trunk is a bustling village of pixies who have transformed the inside of the tree into a residence in order to care for abandoned or neglected babies before shepherding them to the Feywild to live a life away from the Prime Material Plane. The leader of this group of would-be do-gooders is **Nanny Flit**, a well-meaning, if misguided, minister of a specific brand of hope. If adventurers encounter Flit or her other pixie companions, they are likely to discover a somewhat unsettling plot to spirit children away into another realm, regardless of their parents' wishes on the matter. As such, the party should determine how to address this issue, if at all.

NPC PROFILE
NANNY FLIT, PIXIE CAREGIVER

This humble **pixie** just wants to make life a little better for the babies of the Prime Material Plane and, as such, took it upon herself years ago to care for abandoned infants and find homes for them within the Feywild. As the dangers of the realm became more apparent, her view of "protection" became a bit broader. Now, instead of caring for lost or neglected babes, she meticulously plots, in her words, to "shepherd" children away from potentially loving parents. She is peaceful and pleasant but will defend her cause from any interlopers who would deign to interfere.

EXTERIOR

The Oakville Harbor House appears as an enormous oak tree (*1*), with large, sprawling branches in a woodland clearing. It has weathered storms, droughts and lightning strikes, as well as a small assault from within. At its base, perceptive observers might notice what appears to be the tiny, circular entrance to a rabbit warren where the large roots begin to penetrate the earth (DC 15 Wisdom [Perception]). A DC 15 Intelligence (Investigation) check reveals a tiny wooden door (*2*) roughly 1.5 feet tall, which leads to the lowest level of the residence within the tree's trunk. A continued investigation (DC 18) reveals a knothole (*3*) approximately 15 feet off the ground, which features a door hidden inside of it and leads to the second level of the oak's interior. Both doors are locked, with a DC of 18, and are also under the effects of the *arcane lock* spell, making their total DC 28.

VARIANT ENCOUNTER (OPTIONAL) AWAKENED HOME

At GM discretion, the Oakville Harbor House can be presented as more than just a large oak—it can be a slumbering **treant** that will defend its denizens from any and all threats.

INTERIOR

The inside of Oakville Harbor House evokes a busy nursery, with fluttering, flying attendants buzzing busily about. The lowest level (*4*) features a few small cribs and a relatively airy ceiling considering it exists inside a tree trunk. The second level (*5*), accessible via the knothole door, hosts a hidden entrance to the lower level, as well as a porthole to the tiers above, and it's here that meals are prepared and served for the residents of the space. The tiers above (*6*) are home to Nanny Flit and her numerous attendants.

The babies who are being held within the tree are, as babies are wont to be, occasionally fussy—particularly if there are loud noises in or around the Oakville Harbor House. Murmurs and coos can be perceived within 15 feet of the tree with a DC 18 Wisdom (Perception) check. At GM discretion, if the infant(s) within begins to cry, the sound carries much farther (60 feet) and is easier to hear (DC 12).

VARIANT ENCOUNTER (OPTIONAL)

Including Nanny Flit, there are three other **pixies** within the Oakville Harbor House at all times. Additionally, the base level of the interior of the tree is currently home to 1d4 infant children. Roll 1d6 to determine what other excitement may be nearby.

1d6	The party encounters...
1	...1d4 **shambling mounds** beneath the ground around the tree waiting for anyone who gets too close.
2	...2d6 villagers with torches menacing the tree with claims that it "ate our babies."
3	...a **coven of three green hags** yelling at the tree, demanding the babies they are certain are hidden within.
4	...a **troll** shambling along in the woods near the tree looking for food.
5	...a single **pixie** struggling to push the back end of a particularly chunky baby through the lower door of the tree.
6	...a hunting party of 2d4 **centaurs** pursuing a **giant elk**, driving it directly toward the party.

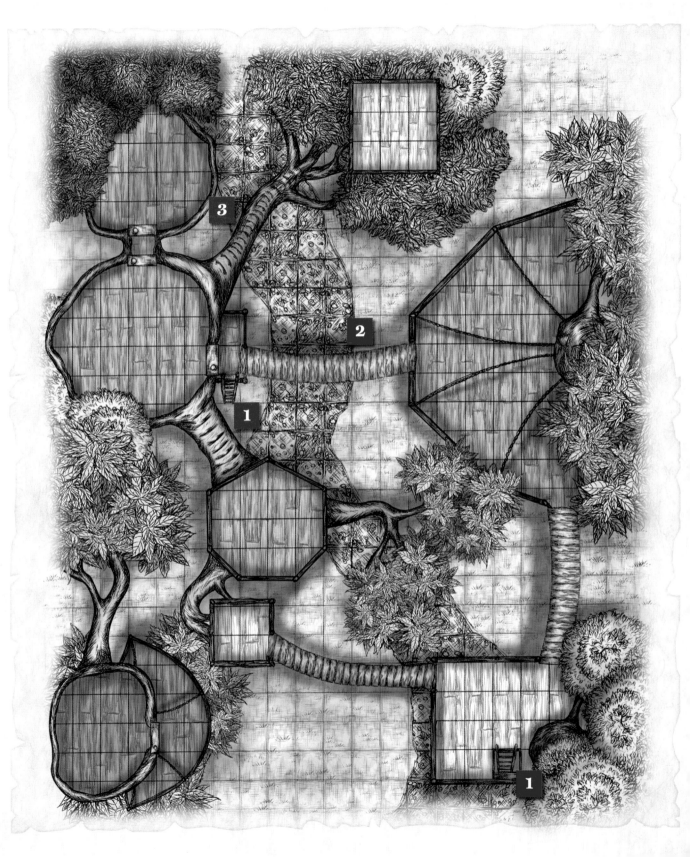

TREETOP VILLAGE

Among the trees of a dense forest and just below the canopy is a series of structures connected by rope bridges and sturdy branch walkways—a small community in an otherwise uncivilized locale.

A VERSATILE LOCATION

This place can function as a home for those seeking refuge from violence or as a home base for those who might intend harm on others. Roll on the table below to determine its residents (at GM discretion).

1d6	Who dwells in this village?
1	A group of 1d4 **druids** who have vowed to protect the creatures in the forest.
2	2d4 would-be **scouts** who use the village as an outpost during training.
3	A group of 4d4 halflings who've taken to the trees to avoid the beasts that dwell below.
4	A tribe of 3d4 **orcs** who use the elevated position to prey on any creatures that pass below.
5	A group of 3d4 human children, orphans from a far-off village that was razed by **bandits**.
6	A group of 3d4 **bandits** who impose a tax of 10 gp for anyone wishing to travel in "their woods."

VILLAGE ACCESS

For those unaware of its location, the Treetop Village is difficult to find and even harder to access. A DC 15 Wisdom (Perception) check in the surrounding forest reveals two sets of elevated ladder rungs that start 8 feet off the ground. A DC 20 Wisdom (Perception) or Intelligence (Investigation) check reveals the lowest rung is trapped (DC 15), and if used to support more than 20 pounds of weight will trigger a rockfall from a net above. If triggered, everyone within 5 feet of the ladder must make a DC 15 Dexterity saving throw, taking 3d10 bludgeoning damage on a failed save or half as much on a success. The ladders (*1*) lead to the locked access doors (DC 18) to the main platforms.

TREETOP TOWERS

Wooden platforms of varying elevation serve as the base for this village's structures (*2*). The underside of each is camouflaged with the canopy above, obscuring the entire village from the forest floor. A keen eye can detect its presence with a DC 18 Wisdom (Perception) check. The platforms are of varying heights (30, 40 and 60 feet) and are connected by a series of rope bridges and sturdy branches (*3*). Each platform is walled off to ensure protection from the elements and assailants, but there are windows on all sides of each platform that offer a comprehensive view of the area, and archery slits that allow for attacks from full cover.

BRIDGES AND BRANCHES

Passing over a rope bridge or running along a connective branch is not without its difficulties, and those who don't normally reside here aren't able to maneuver from platform to platform as easily as those who do. Moving slowly and methodically across these elevated paths is the safest way to avoid a fall. If a creature chooses to use their full movement speed to cross these pathways, they must succeed on a DC 10 Dexterity saving throw with disadvantage, falling off the bridge or branch on a failed save and tumbling over the side. A creature that falls suffers 1d6 bludgeoning damage on impact with the forest floor for every 10 feet they fall.

VILLAGE PROTECTIONS

The Treetop Village is relatively secure but not impregnable. Because the entire community is built from wood and sits just below the canopy of a dense forest, threats from fire are of particular concern. As such, fire buckets filled with sand are posted on every platform, as are glyphs that activate the *create food and water* spell if flames reach the platforms, expelling several hundred gallons of water in times of emergency. Once these glyphs are expended they must be recast.

ENCOUNTER VARIANT (OPTIONAL) FRIENDS OR FOES?

When the party discovers the Treetop Village, you can elect for its residents to be hostile, friendly or cautious. You can also choose to roll 1d6 and confront them with one of the below encounters, either while they are attempting to access the Treetop Village or once they are inside. Secondly, at GM discretion, the residents of the Treetop Village could work with the party, stand against them or attempt to stay neutral during this encounter.

VARIANT ENCOUNTER (OPTIONAL)

1d6	At Treetop Village...
1	...a group of 2d4 **gnoll riders** on **giant hyenas** charge over a hill, hungry for fresh meat.
2	...the party has been standing near 1d4 **shambling mound(s)**.
3	...1d4 **werewolves** leap into the clearing beneath the platforms.
4	...1d4 **goblins**, led by a **hobgoblin captain**, sneak through the forest on patrol.
5	...the party finds itself between a mother **owlbear** and her two cubs.
6	...a hungry **giant constrictor snake** stalks the party from among the foliage.

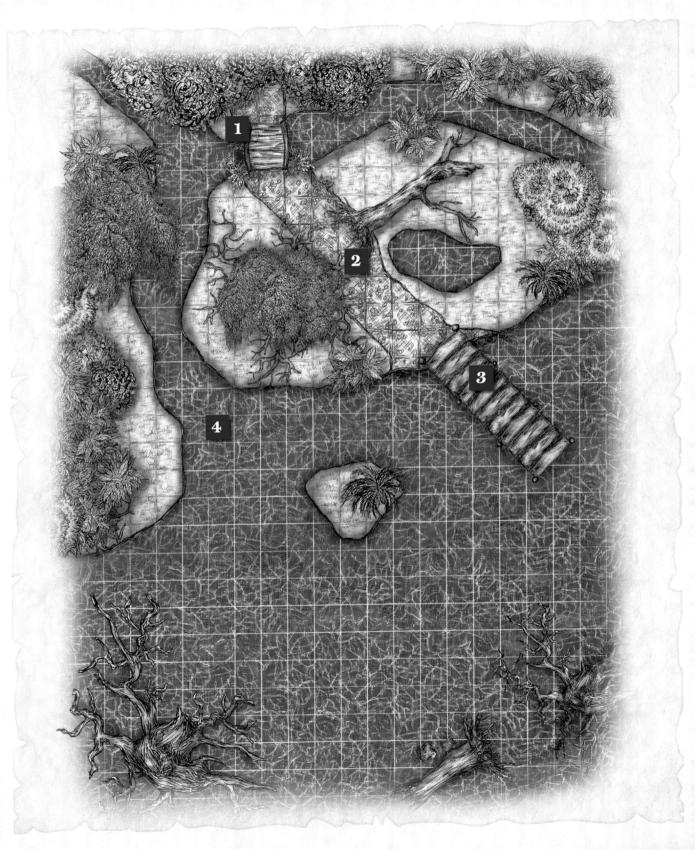

FISHING PIER

A respite from the bustle of town, this secluded spot in the forest is the perfect place to cast a line and reel in a big one (a fish, not a merrow).

FRESH AIR, FRESH WATER

The fishing pier is a known, if rarely visited, location. This is partly because of its proximity to the town (it's not close) and in part because there's not much to do here other than sit and enjoy the quiet—a pastime some are too busy to fully appreciate. Those who do choose to walk through the nearby woods and across the bridge (*1*) that leads to a pathway through the bog (*2*) will find a lovely view and an even lovelier place to sit (*3*). The larger pond (*4*) feeds a stream, which flows away from town and down toward the sea. The stream itself is freshwater, but the pond the pier juts into features a bit of a mix, as well as a few creatures who've erroneously swum upstream.

ENCOUNTER VARIANT (OPTIONAL)
APPEARANCE

Roll 1d4 to determine the current state of the pier and its surrounding forest.

1d4	The pier is...
1	**Foggy.** Visibility is hard to come by as a thick fog hangs over the water and the surrounding marsh, heavily obscuring the entire area.
2	**Flooded.** A heavy rain (which, at GM discretion, can be ongoing) has caused much of the marshland to flood. All the land in the area is difficult terrain as mud and knee-high water make each step a slog.
3	**Sunny and Still.** It's bright here, as beams of sunlight stream through the trees. It's also quiet—perhaps too quiet.
4	**Frozen.** The water in the pond as well as the creek has frozen through and is dense enough for most medium creatures to stand on. At GM discretion, roll 1d6 each time a creature is on the ice, with the creature plunging through the ice on a roll of 6, suffering 1d6 cold damage for each turn they remain in the icy water.

VARIANT ENCOUNTER (OPTIONAL)

Roll 1d6 to determine what the party might catch or prefer to throw back into the pond at the Fishing Pier.

1d6	The party finds...
1	...a man teaching his son how to fish. The boy catches something—something big (a **hunter shark**)—which promptly tugs him into the water.
2	...a small island offshore that appears to be moving slowly toward the dock. It is, in reality, a **plesiosaurus** making its way to shore to investigate the creatures now in its territory.
3	...a small jug tied to the dock with a bit of twine. Opening the jug releases a **merid**.
4	...a troop of 2d4 **lizardfolk** on patrol through the low grass by the river. They are hungry.
5	...a nest of 2d4 **harpies** observe the party from the tree by the pier, attacking if they look weak.
6	...a small boat by the dock is actually an oversized **mimic** with 102 hit points, awaiting its next victim.

DEATH BELOW

Beneath the surface of this placid pond is a nest of felled trees and broken limbs, some of them human. A creature investigating this collection of debris does so at disadvantage because of the murky nature of the water here, and will find more than just rotting logs on a DC 12 Intelligence (Investigation) check. The skeletal remains of 2d4 humanoid creatures are trapped beneath the natural clutter, and may become undead creatures who want nothing more than to drown any in their reach, at GM discretion.

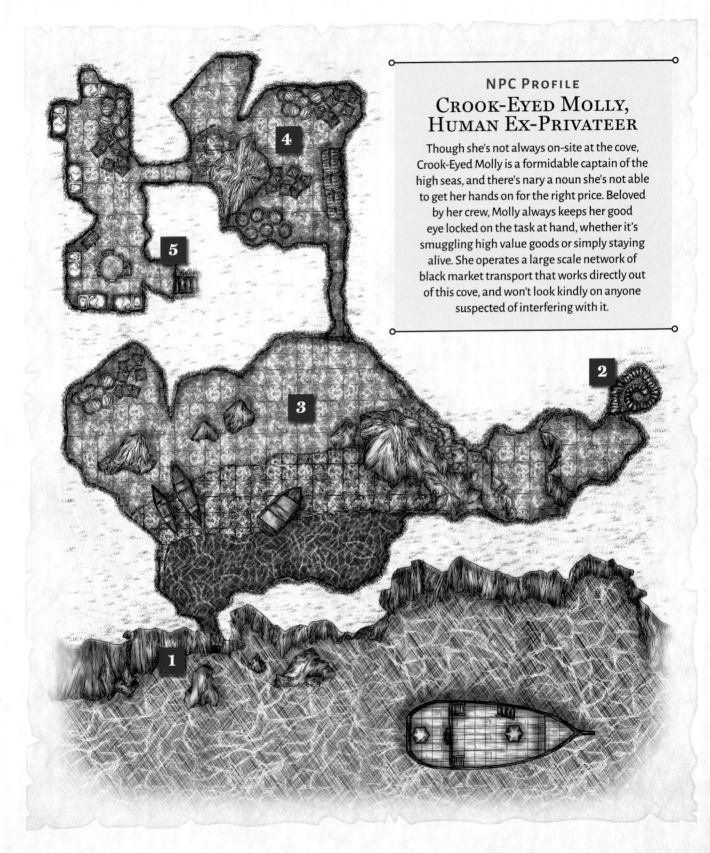

SMUGGLER'S COVE

Within a natural inlet masked by wave-battered rocks and the ocean itself lies the entrance to a cave that hosts all manner of stolen goods. Works of art sit wrapped among sacks of grain and crates of contraband within the confines of this well-protected space. Those who venture here without an invitation or a clear idea of where they're headed might never have a chance to leave.

ENTERING THE GROTTO

There are two points of entry to the natural foyer abutting the hidden corridor leading to the cove's main storage facilities. From the sea (*1*), an inlet along the sheer, 400-foot cliff wall leads to a tunnel that's only visible (and accessible) by boat during low tide. This cave leads to an open, cathedral-like grotto with a soaring, stalactite-pocked ceiling and a short span of sand-covered shore. A secondary entrance can be found atop the cliffs (*2*), where a hidden door covered in earth and visible with a successful DC 18 Wisdom (Perception) check lifts to reveal a spiral staircase that descends to a series of interior cliffs, ladders and landings.

INSIDE THE COVE

GROTTO. Jagged rock outcroppings worn by the tides are the dominating feature in this dark cave (*3*). When the tide is low, roughly half the interior space is navigable by foot, but once the water begins to creep in, the dry shoreline begins to disappear fairly quickly. Smugglers use this quirk to their advantage, loading or unloading their goods as the tide recedes, as the boats can still float but the goods can rest on solid, relatively dry ground. Signs of this activity are visible during low tide, revealed by a DC 15 Wisdom (Perception) check. Astute observers (DC 18) will notice some foot traffic leads toward an inset spot about the size of a half-orc along the cave wall. Stepping fully into this space reveals nothing, but examining the cave wall within the inlet by touch gives away its mask—an effect of the *hallucinatory terrain* spell. The illusion can also be perceived with a DC 18 Wisdom (Perception) or Intelligence (Investigation) check. Through this narrow corridor is the cove's storage facility—and the spoils of weeks' worth of illegal activity.

ENCOUNTER VARIANT (OPTIONAL)
SHIFTING TIDES

To determine whether it's high, low or mid tide, roll on the table below.

1d6	The water level is currently...
1	Low tide
2–3	Mid tide, rising
4	High tide
5–6	Mid tide, receding

STORAGE AREA. Dim torchlight from the walls offers a view of boxes, crates and sacks of goods (*4*)—so many that it might take someone quite a bit of time to separate run-of-the-mill goods from the truly spectacular, and as such, goods should be revealed at GM discretion. There is a pit trap along the walkway to the second chamber that can be discerned with a DC 15 Wisdom (Perception) check. The first creature that triggers the trap and any creature within 5 feet of them at the time the trap is triggered plummets 60 feet and is subject to 3d6 bludgeoning damage, as well as 2d6 piercing damage on the spikes below if they hit the bottom of the pit. Goods in the second chamber should be revealed at GM discretion.

HIDDEN ENTRANCE. Behind a stack of boxes, revealed as fakes with a DC 18 Intelligence (Investigation) check, is a bolthole and a long, narrow ladder (*5*) that leads nearly 400 feet down to the sea-soaked caverns below, at GM discretion.

VARIANT ENCOUNTER (OPTIONAL)

Roll 1d6 on the table below to determine what adventures await your party within the Smuggler's Cove.

1d6	The party sees...
1	...a group of 1d6 **bandits** and their captain, Crook-Eyed Molly, arriving to pick up some loot.
2	...a **banshee** behind one of the grotto's rocky cliffs about to release a terrifying scream.
3	...1d4 **basilisks** slink out from behind a collection of humanoid statues within the grotto.
4	...1d6 **sahuagin** and their **priestess** emerge from the depths, approaching the shoreline.
5	...1d4 **merrow** menacing the exit through the tidal cave.
6	...two **water elementals** swirl in the sea within the grotto.

THE HIGH DOCKS

Nestled in a private cove abutting the city wall, this well-appointed aquatic access point is exclusively for nobility or those who can pay to appear as such. With a carriage house and stables, as well as a levitating landing that ushers the upper crust to their own entrance atop the city wall, the High Docks ensure those who can afford its services need never mingle with those who cannot. A full garrison is typically on patrol to keep things orderly, leaving **Sheeva Starcaster, the High Dockmaster** to handle more pressing matters—namely who will open her next cask of wine.

FLOATING PALACES

The vessels that typically drop anchor at the High Docks rarely carry cargo (**1**). Instead, they're oceanbound residences, in many cases featuring full-time crews who cater to the whims and desires of their wealthy owners. It's not uncommon for the moneyed elite to host invite-only soirées aboard their boats in the summer months, during which most ships never leave the docks. Because space to dock here long-term is at such a premium, arrangements to do so must be made well in advance, and plenty of ships have been directed to the city's other docks—or worse, the Low Docks—due to a cap on available space (much to their owners' chagrin).

NPC PROFILE

SHEEVA STARCASTER, ELVEN HIGH DOCKMASTER

A glamorous arch-mage who found her true calling as the city's High Dockmaster, Sheeva whiles away most of her days swirling a glass of claret, twirling her fingers to cast the odd spell and hurling the rabble who might dare to make their way to the High Docks out on their respective duffs. Her attendant work at the docks has helped her cultivate connections with some of the realm's most powerful nobles, most of whom would willingly offer just about anything she asked for the promise of a permanent spot on her anchor list.

BLIND CARRIAGE HOUSE

Sometimes the city connected to the High Docks isn't a passenger's final destination on the continent and they require further transportation. Because the clientele who frequent the High Docks generally have an aversion to mingling with commoners, the carriage house (**2**) is positioned to allow for would-be passengers to be escorted into their hired carriage from within an enclosed structure while the horses and driver wait outside. Only rarely has this practice led to a passenger being taken to a far-flung city they had no intention of visiting.

THE DOCKS

Unlike their counterparts at most coastal ports of call, the High Docks are enchanted with a simple spell that displaces errant drops of water, ensuring they remain dry and easily navigable at all times. Additionally, each dock features a secondary platform (**3**) that, through magical means, can be raised to the level of the city wall (20 feet), granting access to the High Docks' private entrance (**4**).

VARIANT ENCOUNTER (OPTIONAL)

Roll 1d6 to determine what high crimes or low blows might envelop the party at the High Docks.

1d6	The party sees...
1	...a small tribe of 3d4 **troglodytes** emerging from beneath the carriage house. They make quick work of one of the horses before turning their filthy claws on the filthy rich.
2	... a **blue and a red slaad** under the control of a shadowy figure leap off the city wall and into the crowded dock below for a surprise attack.
3	...an **assassin** leap off a docked boat as screams from its 4d6 passengers carry across the water. It seems an overturned bowl of poisoned punch is also a powerful acid that's eating a hole straight through the vessel's floor.
4	...two angry **air elementals** descending on the High Docks, unsettling a lifted dock carrying 2d6 passengers on their way to the city wall.
5	...a powerful surge of dark energy erupting from the deck of one of the docked ships as a summoned **barlgura** crashes onto the dock. The 1d4 **cultists** aboard the ship gasp in glee.
6	...1d4 **helmed horrors** drop from above and immediately begin a strategic assault against Sheeva, seeking revenge on behalf of a snubbed noble.

THE LOW DOCKS

Small boats, ferries and skiffs jockey for a place to moor themselves to these docks in order to transfer all manner of cargo into the city at this crowded landing—the only space common folk are permitted to dock their vessels. Like many places where barrels, boxes and boatloads are in abundance and guards are not, the Low Docks are a target for cons, extortionists, pickpockets and other criminals.

THE DOCKMASTER'S CHARGE

A surly sea dwarf named **Aegis Mackforth** keeps a watchful eye on the arriving and departing vessels as well as their crews, and several times an hour, representatives from various ships will approach to shake his hand and attempt not to raise the ire of his large **blink dog** companion. His role is to keep the peace, ensure cargo is handled safely and to citywide standards and see that the boats and crowds keep moving.

DOCKMASTER'S SEAT. Aegis Mackforth can usually be found within or near this small office *(1)*. From this elevated spot he can observe most of the goings on at the Low Docks and intervene whenever necessary—though his presence is usually enough to keep things in line. Above his perch on the dock are markings that those who understand Thieves' Cant can easily decipher: "Pay now or pay later."

THE DOCKS. Because of their wet surface and the crowd of people commonly clamoring for goods or to board hastily moored vessels, the docks *(2)* are considered difficult terrain, but full movement can be used at player discretion: Anyone moving along the docks at full speed must succeed on a DC 15 Dexterity save or slip and fall into the drink.

ACCESS TO THE SEWERS. A water drainage grate *(3)* leads to the city's underground tunnels and sewer system, at GM discretion. Opening the grate requires a DC 17 Strength (Athletics) check. Though the water along the dock appears relatively still at the surface, beneath it flows a strong surge toward the sea. Any creature who ends up in the water moves at half speed (unless they have a swim speed). At the end of their turn they must succeed on a DC 12 Strength (Athletics) check or be swept 15 feet in the direction of the sea (at GM discretion). Creatures wearing medium or heavy armor are at disadvantage for the check.

VARIANT ENCOUNTER (OPTIONAL)

Roll 1d6 to determine what's troubling the waters around the Low Docks.

1d6	The party finds...
1	...a fight breaking out between two crews of 2d4 sailors, both trying to land their boat at the same time.
2	...a boat carrying a once-caged **chimera** slamming into the dock, its crew dead, the beast very much alive.
3	...the illusory image of an **aboleth** laired nearby sullying the water at the Low Docks, causing a panic-induced stampede of 6d6 **commoners**.
4	...a boat full of **commoners** that turns out to be a band of 2d6 **kobolds** hoping to steal some cargo on shore.
5	...a war party of 2d4 **sahuagin** and their **sahuagin baron** attacking from the depths.
6	...two mischievous peasant children arguing about who gets to open the *iron flask* they lifted off a traveling stranger. When they uncork it, a **mezzoloth** appears, willing to do their bidding for one hour.

NPC PROFILE
AEGIS MACKFORTH, DWARVEN DOCKMASTER

Aegis is often found smoking his pipe while overseeing the comings and goings of the boats at this landing alongside his faithful blink dog Max. Very little happens at the dock without Aegis's knowledge or oversight—unless he's been paid to look the other way, which in many instances he has. Most of these bribes ultimately make their way into the city coffers, as Aegis pays a premium to keep the docks and the cargo that ships in and out of them off the books. At any given time, Aegis is carrying somewhere close to 200 gp—and wearing it openly. No pickpocket in the realm would be bold enough to steal from the dockmaster lest they risk the wrath of dozens of individual guilds that rely on his willingness to keep this port open to their style of business.

PIT TRAPPED TRAIL

> *"THEY TOOK MY WAGON AND EVERYTHING ON IT. WOULD'VE TAKEN MY HORSES TOO IF THEY WEREN'T DEAD AT THE BOTTOM OF THAT PIT IN THE ROAD."*
>
> —Ernest Macall, sullen merchant

Well-traveled roads and even those that receive less traffic are often targeted by roving bandit parties, tribal warriors or groups of trained soldiers or thieves, who set deadly traps along the thoroughfares from town to town.

WELL-HIDDEN DANGERS

Those who aren't actively watching the road for signs of foul play are likely to miss evidence of the trap ahead (*1*). A DC 18 Wisdom (Perception) check reveals a false surface on the road covering a 15-foot drop, as well as a number of buried spears. Any creature falling through the trap, which triggers when a creature moves into its center, suffers 1d6 bludgeoning damage and 2d6 piercing damage. The trap is approximately 15 feet in diameter. Two smaller 5-foot traps are hidden in the woods (*2*), designed to disrupt mercenary forces that might be able to mount a counterattack during an assault.

A VIEW FROM ABOVE

An elevated platform roughly 40 feet off the ground and obscured by the trees (*3*) offers a clear vantage point from which to signal a raiding party or pick off escorts one by one. The platform is camouflaged but can be discovered with a DC 18 Wisdom (Perception) check.

VARIANT ENCOUNTER (OPTIONAL)

Roll 1d6 to determine the number, nature and motives of the assailants who built the trap.

1d6	The party must face...
1	...1d6 **lizardfolk** and 1 **lizardfolk shaman** who seem mostly interested in stealing weapons (to defend their village against an invasive species).
2	...1d6 **orcs** and 1 **orc war chief** who are seeking revenge on any elves traveling the road as part of a decades-old feud.
3	...1d6 **bandits** and 1 **bandit captain** who are just in it for the money and will flee if the tide turns against them.
4	...1d6 **hobgoblins** and 1 **hobgoblin captain** who want hostages for a parlay with a nearby town.
5	...1d6 **gnolls** and 1 **gnoll pack lord** who are interested in meat. Any meat. Your meat.
6	...1d6 **goblins** who happened upon the trap and did their best to set it but are now unsure of how to carry on.

THE BOUNDLESS RAVINE

A curving path leads to a shaded ravine among sloping foothills and features a derelict rope bridge that leads to the entrance to one of the region's complex cave systems.

CAVE ENTRANCE

A massive 20-foot gap with sheer sides *(1)* separates the cave entrance *(2)* from the trail's end, with a long-neglected rope bridge *(3)* spanning the Boundless Ravine. The bottom of this ravine is not visible, though it does end roughly 400 feet down. Those wishing to cross the bridge must do so at half speed or succeed on a DC 12 Dexterity check to stay balanced on the swaying bridge. Any creature weighing more than 300 pounds (including gear and armor) makes this check at disadvantage. On a failed check, the creature falls through the bridge and must succeed on a DC 10 Dexterity or Strength saving throw to grab onto the bridge, or fall into the chasm of the Boundless Ravine.

NOOKS & CRANNIES

The path up the mountain toward the cave's entrance is marked by a rough-rock landscape among the trees as well as a flat top mountain ledge roughly 30 feet above the path that overlooks the bridge *(4)*. These spaces are ideal spots from which to stage an ambush or to take cover in the event of one.

ENTRANCE TO THE UNDERGROUND

A massive seam *(2)* in the wall of the mountain is an entrance to the cave system that runs through this region, and stepping more than 20 feet within it is enough to require darkvision or a light source in order to see.

VARIANT ENCOUNTER (OPTIONAL)

Roll 1d6 to determine what dangers await the party as they venture along the Boundless Ravine to the cave.

1d6	The party sees...
1	...nothing, if they don't pass a DC 15 Wisdom (Perception) check. Otherwise they notice the group of 2d4 **bugbears** and one **hobgoblin** waiting to ambush them on the cave side of the cliff.
2	...a **hill giant** emerging from the cave. It asks in broken Common if they "knows the wordpass."
3	...a motley crew of 3d4 **bandits** who just want to tell the adventurers that they're big fans.
4	...the shape of a massive beast soaring closer to the bridge as a **manticore** swoops in to attack.
5	...a trio of **magmin** leaping from a crack in the mountain, before chasing them across the rope bridge.
6	...a pile of armor moving near the cave entrance, as if being dragged deeper inside, and there's the sound of a man screaming "Help...help me, please," all the illusory work of a hungry **otyugh**.

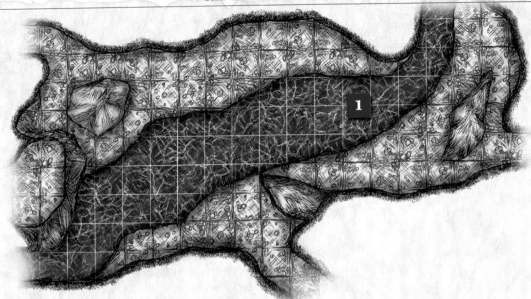

PANNING CREEK

> *"GOLD! GOLD! I GOT SOME GOLD OVER HERE!"*—Abel Nudge, murdered prospector

Gold is the most universal form of grease across the realm, and while some can create it through arcane or alchemical means, most folks work for it the old-fashioned way: through hard labor. And there's no labor that offers such an immediate intimacy with gold and other valuable minerals than prospecting. Large-scale enterprise took hold in this land long ago, and numerous mines with a host of laborers dot the landscape, but so do simple, gold-flecked creeks such as this, which beckon would-be wealthmongers hoping to hit it big one pan at a time.

A GENTLE STREAM

This portion *(1)* of the underground river that carved much of this cavernous space eons ago is flat and meandering, offering the perfect spot to pan for gold and valuable minerals cast off from within the heart of the mountain. Most of the water is less than 2 feet deep; however, there are some spots within this span of water where the flow seems to still itself.

DANGEROUS SINKHOLES

There are four spots within this creek (at GM discretion) where the water's surface is somewhat still, masking the presence of sinkholes as deep as 10 feet. The suction within these flows is powerful, and any creature engulfed by one is considered grappled with their head underwater. They, or a creature attempting to pull them out, must succeed on a DC 17 Strength (Athletics) check in order to escape.

A GLITTERING CURSE

The creek's flow of gold is long-rumored, but so is the hunger that consumes many a would-be prospector—the drive for even small flecks of the stuff consuming their every waking moment. Any time a creature attempts to search for gold in this creek, which they can do as many times as you'll allow, roll 1d10. On an odd number, nothing happens. On an even number, they've found 1 gp-worth of gold ore. On a 10, they fall victim to the Prospector's Curse and are consumed with a never-ending desire for gold: no amount will ever be enough. Their bond changes to "I will do anything for gold—anything at all," and their alignment changes to chaotic evil. This change can only be reversed by magical means, through spells such as *greater restoration, wish* or *remove curse*.

VARIANT ENCOUNTER (OPTIONAL)

Roll 1d6 to determine if the party will uncover riches or ruin in the Panning Creek.

1d6	The party finds...
1	...a dead prospector and a sack of ore worth 68 gp.
2	...the stalactites hanging above them are 2d4 **piercers** ready to ambush them.
3	...a **roper** disguised as a stalactite.
4	...2d4 **deep gnomes** who will try to scare the party into thinking the area is haunted.
5	...4d4 **goblins** who try to catch the party off guard.
6	...an **earth elemental** tired of being pickaxed.

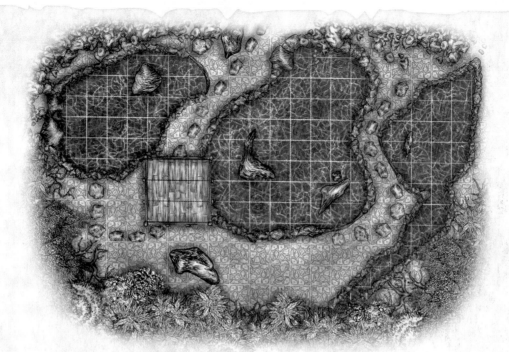

THE SISTER SPRINGS

Hidden away deep in the forests of an isolated mountain range are three ancient thermal hot spring pools. Their golden waters bubble up from deep below, bringing minerals and the acrid smell of sulfur to the surface. The name of the springs comes from an old tale of three sisters, all gold dragons, who lost their ability to breathe fire and sought the help of the springs' healing waters. When they bathed, the water stripped the gold from their scales and the heat from their bodies, but in turn gave them the ability to breathe frost. To this day, the waters of the Sister Springs bubble with the remaining heat from the three dragons and grant blessings to those who bathe there.

ENCOUNTER VARIANT (OPTIONAL)
OVERALL AMBIANCE
Roll 1d4 to determine the current state of the Sister Springs, as well as their context within the landscape.

1d4	The Sister Springs are...
1	...commercialized. There's a massive hot springs resort built around the springs. The food is nice enough but the décor is tacky. It costs 4 gp per night for a room and 3 sp to enter the hot springs.
2	...holy. The Sister Springs is the site of a temple built in tribute to the three dragon sisters (or any deity at GM discretion).
3	...untouched. The Sister Springs remain free from development and are difficult to locate.
4	...occupied. The Sister Springs is home to an **ancient gold dragon** named Mercuriel who has sought the peace and solitude of the old mountains and healing waters of the springs in her final years.

ENCOUNTER VARIANT (OPTIONAL)
BLESSINGS OF THE SPRINGS
Roll 1d8 to see what blessings the waters will give.

1d8	The waters grant...
1	...resistance to bludgeoning, piercing and slashing damage from nonmagical attacks.
2	...an increased speed of 10 feet.
3	...a hardened skin (+1 to AC).
4	...an increase to maximum hp (4d4).
5	...1d4 added to all attack rolls and saving throws.
6	...resistance to fire.
7	...the ability to reroll any skill check once per day.
8	...the ability to breathe dragon's fire in a 15-foot cone once per short rest (3d6 fire damage).

The golden waters of the Sister Springs are rumored to have healing properties. Along with a blessing, the waters of the springs grant the effect of the *greater restoration* spell. Each blessing lasts three days and each creature benefiting from the pools can only do so once every 21 days.

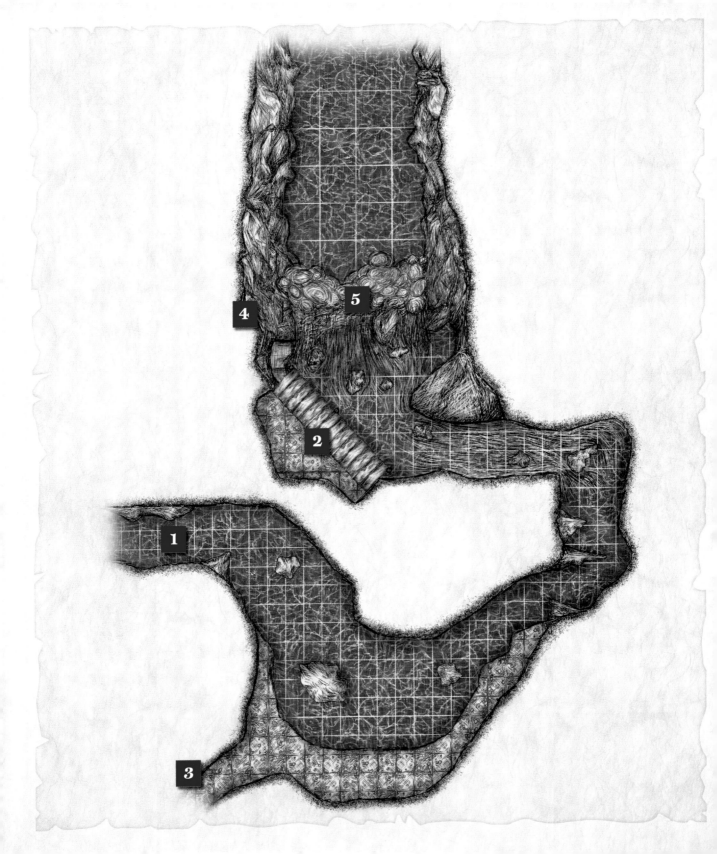

WATERRISE CAVERN

"WE HEARD THE RUSH OF THE RIVER AS WE ROUNDED THE BEND AND KNEW WE WERE IN FOR A BIT OF A DROP, SO WE BAILED AND MADE FOR THE BANKS. IMAGINE OUR SURPRISE WHEN OUR BOAT SOARED 200 FEET UP AS IF CARRIED BY THE WIND."

—Oliver Batson, journeyman explorer

This subterranean spectacle is one of the realm's most unique natural attractions: a waterfall that flows upward. The river feeding the waterfall, which locals call "the Rise," features a patch of hazardous rapids before defying gravity on its way to Waterrise Lake. The cavern is a popular destination for adventurous tourists, as well as creatures that prey on unsuspecting visitors.

THE CAVERN

The rushing river (*1*) that carved open this cavern in another age still flows, its wide curves wheeling around large rocks and splashing white over smaller ones. Stalactites hang overhead and stalagmites dot the otherwise open stretch of riverbank (*2*) that offers a full view of the Rise. A tunnel (*3*) utilized by smugglers is well hidden along one of the river's winding curves noticeable with a DC 17 Wisdom (Perception) check. A narrow pathway of inset stairs ascends 200 feet to the top of the cliff and falls (*4*). Climbing the stairs is incredibly difficult and requires both strength and patience as well as a knot (DC 10 Intelligence if not traveling with a guide) in the guide rope—with new connections required every 25 feet—a precaution against dangerous falls. Those not climbing at half speed must make a DC 12 Dexterity saving throw each time they advance, slipping on the soaked stone steps and tumbling nearly 50 feet before the guide rope snaps in to secure them on a failed save, causing them to take 2d6 bludgeoning damage as they crash into the stairs. Torches inset along the cliff wall and burning through the aid of the *continual flame* spell are the only light source in the otherwise dim cavern.

RIDING THE RIVER

Navigating this rushing current takes both strength and finesse, and anyone attempting to do so should be comfortable getting a little damp. A group of four or more must succeed on a series of checks to navigate the river, its obstacles and the shifting current. Groups featuring less than four people make these checks at disadvantage:

1 group DC 12 Strength (Athletics) check to paddle. On a failure, the boat drifts sideways and capsizes, dumping everyone over the side.

1 group DC 12 Dexterity (Acrobatics) check to maneuver the boat through a series of switchback currents, swirling backward on a failed check— which imposes disadvantage on subsequent checks.

1 group DC 12 Wisdom (Perception) check to notice a rock ahead. On a failure, the boat slams into a rock and starts taking on water.

1 group DC 12 Strength (Athletics) check to get the boat to shore before hitting the Rise. On a failed save, the boat travels up the Rise, dumping passengers overboard as it soars to the lake above.

THE RISE

This inverted waterfall (*5*) flows upward, defying gravity as well as experts in the arcane. In fact, the most powerful wizards in the realm were once consulted to determine the true origins of the Rise, and while it was revealed to be magical in nature, it also proved to be undispellable. There is an inset cave behind the watery curtain of the Rise, which can be accessed by succeeding on a DC 17 Strength (Athletics) check that must begin below the water's surface. Any attempts to access the cave without first going underwater all end the same way: a straight, almost violent flow upward to Waterrise Lake that ends with 4d8 bludgeoning damage as you are dashed against the rocks at the top of the Rise. The cave contains a chest secured with an *arcane lock* (DC 25).

VARIANT ENCOUNTER (OPTIONAL)

Roll 1d6 to determine what adventures await the party within the Waterrise Cavern.

1d6	The party shares the cavern with...
1	...a group of 2d4 tourists and their guide, a strapping **veteran**, fending off an attack by a **cloaker**.
2	...1d4 **giant centipedes** fleeing an assault by 2d4 hungry **goblins**.
3	...2d4 **darkmantles**, which descend on the party in a surprise attack.
4	...a clan of 2d4 **hook horrors** roosting along the cliff wall next to the Rise.
5	...a large puddle of water that is actually a pool of **black pudding**.
6	...1d4 **ropers** hidden among various stalagmites, surprising the party.

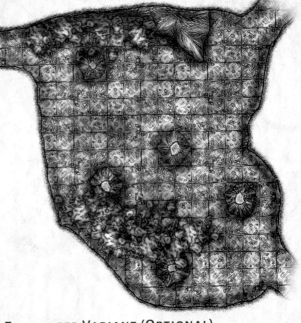

COLUMN CAVE

> "IT'S LIKE BEING IN A CATHEDRAL. EXCEPT THERE ARE CLOAKERS. AND GOBLINS. AND ALSO SOME OOZES. BUT OTHERWISE, PRETTY MUCH LIKE A CATHEDRAL."
>
> —O'thal the Unbothered, half-orc adventurer

This massive underground cavern features an airy, vaulted ceiling seemingly supported by massive natural columns carved out by the elemental forces of another age.

> An airy space filled with darkness, the Column Cave is a large subterranean cavern with a high, 50-foot ceiling and several columns that rise from the cave floor to the heights above. The columns are nearly 10 feet in diameter and cause sight line issues, making them difficult to see around if one is standing too close—assuming you can see in a cave.

VARIANT ENCOUNTER (OPTIONAL)

Roll 1d6 to determine what wonders and horrors await the adventurers in the Column Cave.

1d6	The party finds...
1	...3d4 **giant spiders** fighting over a dead halfling.
2	...1d4 **ropers** observing would-be prey.
3	...2d4 **spined devils** flying from column to column, on the hunt for signs of their master's enemies.
4	...a **barbed devil** who is desperate to find the way back to the portal that led it here.
5	...a **cloaker** swooping down from the shadows.
6	...1d4 **black pudding** slowly dripping from the columns within the cave.

ENCOUNTER VARIANT (OPTIONAL)
ENVIRONMENT

Roll 1d4 to determine the interior of this or any other cave system contained in this book.

1d4	The cave system is...
1	**...slick and humid.** The surfaces within this space are all covered with moisture and require patience to navigate without slipping. Each creature must move at half speed or succeed on a DC 10 Dexterity saving throw, falling prone on a failed save.
2	**...dry and dusty.** The air is thick with dust in this arid cavern, and torchlight fails to illuminate as much as an explorer might hope. As such, the range of vision in this space is halved and all Wisdom (Perception) checks are made with disadvantage.
3	**...dangerously luminescent.** The walls of this cave system are covered with a unique blue-green algae, its bioluminescence providing enough light to illuminate the entire area with a dim aqua glow. The algae is poisonous, however, and disrupting it causes a puff of toxin to be released in a 10-foot radius. Any creature within the cloud must succeed on a DC 10 Constitution saving throw or suffer 2d6 poison damage.
4	**...oppressively hot.** The interior of this space feels more like an oven than a cave. The walls are hot to the touch and a creature in contact with the walls for more than 6 seconds suffers 1d6 fire damage. Additionally, after spending more than 10 minutes in this cave, each creature must succeed on a DC 10 Constitution saving throw or suffer 1 point of exhaustion.

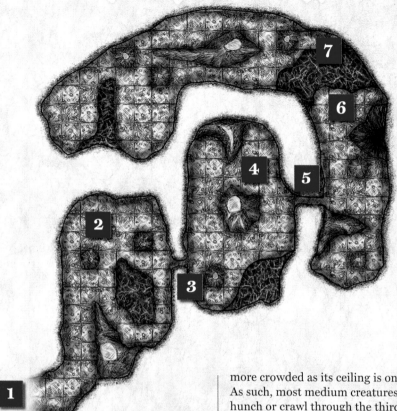

THE RAILROAD APARTMENT

An aptly named series of interconnected subterranean spaces, this trio of cave rooms is tough to navigate, making it a popular hideout for ne'er-do-wells and creatures who hate the sun but love the taste of human flesh.

ENTRANCE AND OPENINGS

The Railroad Apartment can be accessed through a single subterranean tunnel or through a cave entrance (at GM discretion) (*1*). The first room (*2*) is relatively open with a high ceiling, and most would be forgiven for assuming it's also a dead end. A DC 15 Wisdom (Perception) check reveals a small seam in the opposite cavern wall (*3*)—a seam that leads to a second, larger open space (*4*). That is, if you can fit. The narrow slit is navigable for tiny or small creatures, but medium creatures must use their full movement to pass through the crevice and must succeed on a DC 12 Dexterity (Acrobatics) check or find themselves stuck in the space for 1 turn. A similar opening (*5*) can be spotted in the secondary chamber (DC 15) and is equally difficult to navigate. The third chamber (*6*) is larger than the other two, but feels more crowded as its ceiling is only 5 feet off the ground. As such, most medium creatures may find it preferable to hunch or crawl through the third chamber. The pools of water (*7*) in each cave are connected via an underwater tunnel that can be discovered with a DC 15 Intelligence (Investigation) check.

VARIANT ENCOUNTER (OPTIONAL)

Roll 1d6 to determine what dangers and treasures may await the party within the Railroad Apartment.

1d6	The party finds...
1	...a trove of treasures in room three, (roll on the treasure table at GM discretion) guarded by a surly **troll** and 2d4 **goblins**.
2	...a group of 2d4 angry **quaggoths** in room two.
3	...a half-elf stuck in the gap between rooms two and three. He is the son of a local noble. If pulled free without the use of some form of lubricant, his body will rip in half at the torso.
4	...an angry **ogre** stomping about in room two is enough to shake the cave walls in rooms one and three.
5	...a **cambion** in room three is pursuing a group of 1d4 fleeing **bullywugs** in room one.
6	...2d4 **imps** disguised as spiders are crawling around in rooms two and three, looking for a magical item of great value to their master.

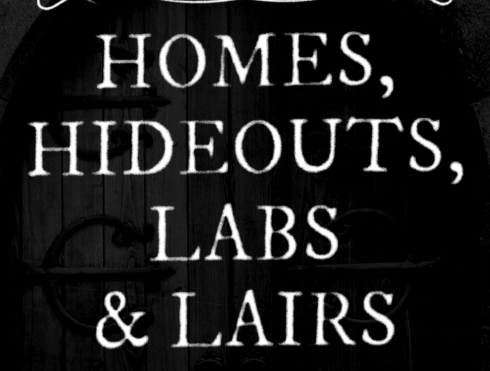

HOMES, HIDEOUTS, LABS & LAIRS

SIMPLE HOUSES AND COMPLEX COMPLEXES PERFECT FOR THOSE WHO WORK WHERE THEY LIVE OR LIVE WHERE THEY WORK.

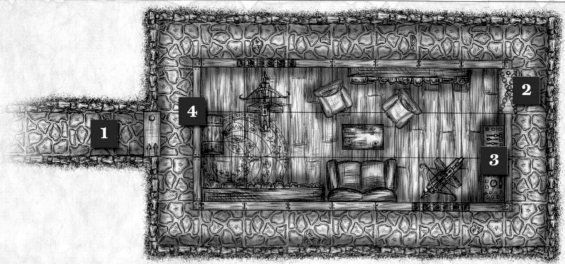

THE PANIC ROOM

Being conscious of one's own security is considered noble in many circles, but there are those who dwell in the city and amble within its seedier underbelly who take this notion to the extreme, installing within their private quarters a retreat of last resort in the unlikely event of an attempted abduction, interrogation or murder. This space, a room within a room, was conceived for just such a purpose—and woe unto those who would follow a resident within its cramped, heavily trapped hallways.

ENTRANCE HALLWAY

The exterior hallway leading into the panic room (1) has a pneumatically sealed iron door that can be locked or unlocked using a switch along the outer wall as well as from within the interior room. The hallway entrance is narrow and leads to confines that are even more cramped. The door opens directly to one of the interior room's outer walls with a heavily trapped corridor that circles around it.

INTERIOR ROOM

The interior of the panic room can be accessed through a small door (2) that features an *arcane lock* (DC 25). Within this space is an observation portal that can be used to view the goings on within the outer hallways, a teleportation circle, some comfortable furniture, two spell scrolls of *create food and water* and dry rations for four weeks. A small panel along the wall (3) features levers that trigger every trap in the hallway, as well as a remote lock for the outer door. There is also a secret, double-paneled door that can only be opened from the inside and leads directly to the exterior hallway (4). These doors swing outward, blocking off the hallway on either side, giving those who might try to pursue another obstacle in the way of their goal. These doors can be repositioned by pulling a lever within the interior room or by succeeding on a DC 25 Strength (Athletics) check. Mounted crossbows which can deal 2d10 piercing damage are also situated within the interior room and can be used to fire through a bolthole that only raises when the trigger for the crossbow is engaged.

TRAPS AND TRIGGERS

The traps within the halls are numerous and can be triggered by throwing a manual switch from within the interior room or by stepping on one of the secondary hallway's floor tiles once the traps have been activated from within the room. This gives the individual within the interior room an advantage during negotiations by both buying time and inflicting a not-insignificant amount of pain. Each trap (placed at GM discretion) has a DC of 20, and an attempt to disarm one is an attempt to disarm three—a failure springs all three traps. To determine which traps the party must deal with, roll twice on the table below to create three versions each of two trap archetypes.

TRAP TABLE

Roll 1d4 to determine which trap the party encounters. Each trap requires a DC 15 Dexterity saving throw from anyone within 5 feet of the triggering action and deals full damage on a failure or half on a success.

1	A stream of acid sprays from within the wall, dealing 3d6 acid damage.
2	A box of maces drops from the ceiling, dealing 3d6 bludgeoning damage.
3	A fire jet deals 3d6 fire damage from above.
4	A crate drops and deals 1d6 bludgeoning damage. The crate, now shattered, contained a now angry swarm of wasps.

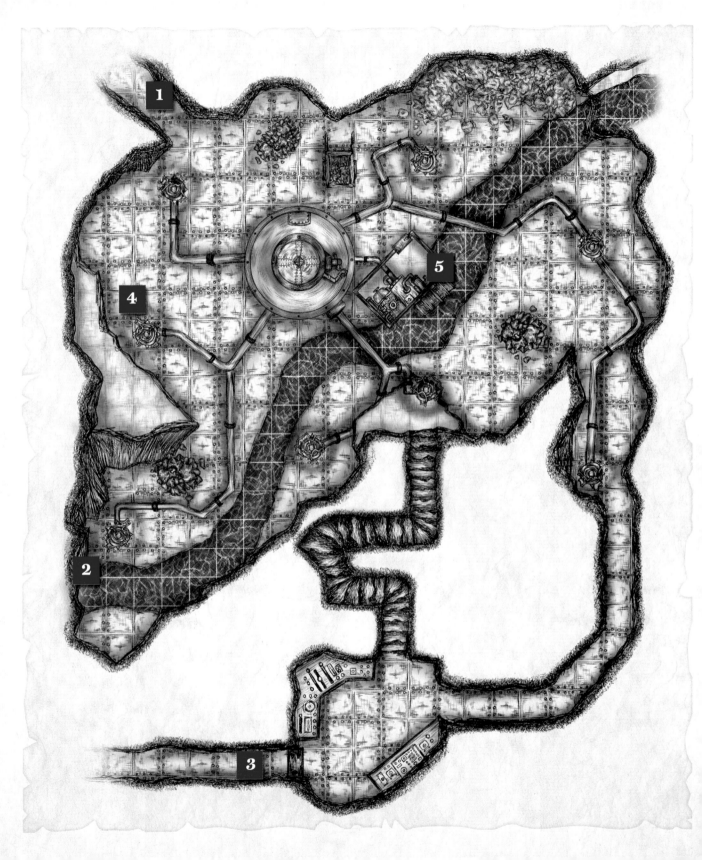

MAGNACOIL LABORATORY

The clanging of pipes and vibration of heavy machinery can be heard and felt on the streets far above this research station. Most are content to assume the effects associated with these sounds are the result of some enchantment gone awry, but the truth is far more scientific—and possibly much more sinister.

ENTERING THE LAB

A tube-like tunnel (*1*) lined with metal panels leads to a vast industrial space dedicated to discovery at any cost. Anyone wearing medium or heavy armor will find their movement reduced by half while they walk through the tube, as their armor is being pulled toward the tube's sides from all directions. A swiftly rushing river (*2*) feeds into the lab, fueling the experimental magnacoil equipment. A back entrance to the lab (*3*) that leads through its main control room is accessible through the nearby cavern system, but its heavy metal door is locked with a magnetic seal that cannot be opened while the machine is running.

INSIDE THE LAB

Tall spires wrapped with copper coils (*4*) and an imposing pump mechanism powered by a large water wheel (*5*) are the main fixtures of this mostly metal-paneled space. Piles of ore and wooden carts used to move them dot various corners of the lab, and a narrow staircase leads to the control room where **Greta Fondeaux**, a driven human inventor with an eye toward the future, runs tests on her equipment with the help of her four deep gnome assistants, Klack, Pick, Scamper and Ziggy.

CONTROLLED MOVEMENT

The towering coils positioned around the Magnacoil Laboratory can be activated individually or as a unit to affect the areas around, above or beneath them. From the control room, as an action, a creature can activate a coil to create one of the following effects. Selecting one effect cancels a previously chosen effect, as the coils are only powerful enough to enact one charge at a time.

CEILING PULL. Anything metal, including armor and weapons, is drawn upward through powerful magnetic force. Attacks with metallic weapons are made at disadvantage, and anyone in metal armor is immediately lifted off the ground toward the lab's steel ceiling. Anyone wearing medium or heavy armor takes 2d6 bludgeoning damage as they slam into the ceiling, where they remain until the ceiling pull is interrupted, or their armor is removed. Creatures pinned to the ceiling and then falling to the floor are also subject to 2d6 bludgeoning damage.

NPC PROFILE
GRETA FONDEAUX, MAGNACOIL MAVEN

Lacking the divine spark of some of her peers, Greta Fondeaux combined a tinkerer's eye with grand vision and worked tirelessly to create the magnacoil, a contraption that imbues metal with the power to attract other metallic objects. Together with her loyal assistants, she continues her research and will not stop until she's discovered not only the source of the magnacoil's power, but also how to wield it.

POWER PULL. Choose one coil. Any metal object within 20 feet is pulled directly toward the chosen coil. Anyone within the path of a weapon or other object pulled toward the coil must succeed on a DC 15 Dexterity saving throw or take damage from the weapon equal to its damage type (or 2d6 bludgeoning damage for an object or pulled creature) on a failed save, or half as much damage on a success.

FLOOR PULL. The metallic floor is activated and anything metal, including armor and weapons, is pulled downward with exceptional force. Anyone wearing metal armor finds their movement reduced by half. Attacks made with metal weapons are made at disadvantage.

VARIANT ENCOUNTER (OPTIONAL)

Roll 1d6 to determine what wonders await the party in the confines of this hazardous laboratory.

1d6	Once inside, the party...
1	...discovers Greta has been aware of the party's infiltration of her lab when she unleashes a surprise attack the moment they arrive.
2	...notices one of the magnacoils failing as it begins spewing sparks. Anything within 15 feet of the coil takes 3d6 force damage.
3	...sees the lab is under attack from a group of 2d4 **drow** and their **elite warrior** leader.
4	...finds a rival **mage** is being held and tortured by Greta and her minions while his **shield guardian** is trapped on the ceiling unable to help.
5	...ascertains that the magnacoil system has overloaded and could possibly explode in less than 10 minutes, undoubtedly causing a ceiling collapse.
6	...hears an argument between Greta and her lab technicians has turned violent—they've trapped her in the control room until they decide what to do next.

GROUND LEVEL

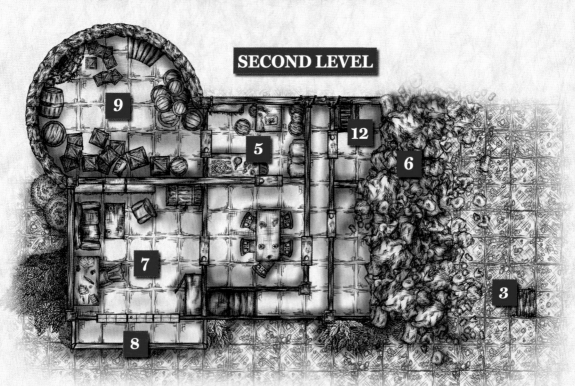

SECOND LEVEL

BAD MANOR

The former residence of a well-to-do merchant with noble ties, Bad Manor is a haven for low-level thugs and mid-tier criminals, as well as the permanent home of **Cracker LeBloom**, the self-styled Baron of Bad Manor.

EXTERIOR

Bad Manor appears as a two-story building with crumbling walls, darkened windows and a visible lack of care for its landscaping. The front door of the home (*1*) has been barricaded and barred from within but could be shoved open with a successful DC 20 Strength (Athletics) check. A DC 17 Intelligence (Investigation) check reveals the side door (*2*) leading to the barracks is locked and trapped, but each can be bypassed with Thieves' Tools (DC 20). If the door is opened without the trap being disengaged, a series of rigged crossbows deal 3d6 piercing damage to the first creature through the door.

A hidden entrance (*3*) behind a bramble bush among the rubble along the side of Bad Manor, revealed with a DC 17 Wisdom (Perception) check, is the preferred method of entrance for its residents, and its lock has a DC of 15. This entrance leads to what's left of the manor's basement, as well as a tunnel that leads to the ground level of the interior.

GROUND LEVEL

Bad Manor's barracks hold all manner of weaponry, much of it cobbled together from available supplies. A series of holding cells (*4*) that double as bedrooms when the space is packed with residents is just off the main corridor. The locks on the cell doors have a DC of 17. Bolthole blinds are placed strategically on this level to protect Bad Manor from unwelcome guests.

SECOND LEVEL

Up the stairs is the Bad Manor's kitchen (*5*), as well as a surprisingly well-to-do dining area, perhaps the only holdover from the home's former glory. Beyond the kitchen on one side of the home is a caved-in roof (*6*), and the scent of water damage and mildew often mingles with that of the day's fare.

Through the kitchen's other door is the makeshift office and sleeping quarters of Cracker LeBloom, the Baron of Bad Manor (*7*). His desk is locked (DC 15) and contains a disguise kit and several documents supporting numerous identities. A DC 15 Intelligence (Investigation) check reveals LeBloom has at least three aliases—a merchant, a barkeep and a city guard—as well as the clothing necessary to pass himself off as each. Two shuttered windows lead to the home's balcony (*8*). Beyond LeBloom's office is the storage area, where a DC 17 Wisdom (Perception) check reveals a hidden passage (*9*) that leads to an opening in the ceiling of the floor below.

BASEMENT LEVEL

This musty basement (*10*) is full of boxes, crates and a few sacks of grain, most of it pilfered from local shops and traveling merchants. A well-traveled tunnel through some of the rubble below leads directly up to the first level (*11*) and a ladder to the second (*12*).

VARIANT ENCOUNTER (OPTIONAL)

Roll 1d6 to determine what adventures await within Bad Manor.

1d6	The party will find...
1	...2d6 **bandits**, half on each floor, guarding Cracker LeBloom as he meets with an **assassin**.
2	...1d6 **bandits** battling 1d6 **bandits** from a rival force as a deal turns sour before the party's eyes.
3	...1d6 **bandits** enjoying a meal on the second floor while Cracker LeBloom snoozes in bed.
4	...1d6 **bandits** patrolling both floors of Bad Manor, with a soot-covered **bugbear** in one of the cells.
5	...the bodies of 2d6 **bandits** laid out all over Bad Manor, victims of a deal gone wrong. Written in blood, the phrase "The debt's still open" drips off the walls. Cracker LeBloom is hiding in the storage area on the second floor.
6	...the entire manor is deserted—but Cracker LeBloom and 1d6 **bandits** arrive five minutes after the party.

NPC PROFILE
CRACKER LEBLOOM, THE BARON OF BAD MANOR

A smooth-talking swindler with a dangerous mean streak, Cracker LeBloom was nothing more than a street urchin when he took up residence in Bad Manor four years ago. Since then, he's systematically, and at times ruthlessly, built a sizable band of loyal thugs and bandits who come and go, paying him a premium for a place to lie low. A consummate con artist, LeBloom is arrogant, agile and always angling for a better deal, offing (or paying off) any who might do him harm.

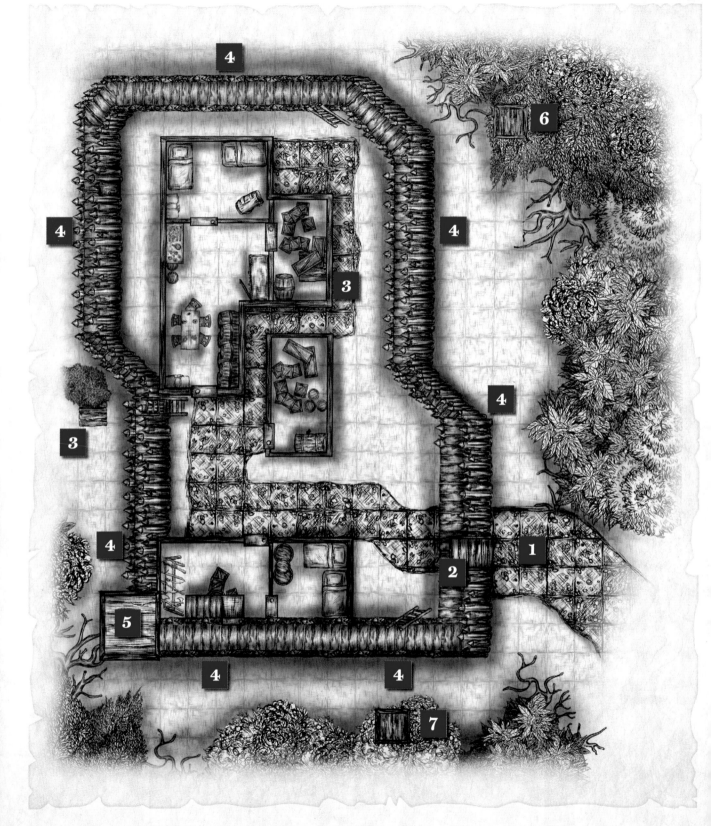

WOODPIKE OUTPOST

Surrounded by dark forest, this heavily fortified structure is a prime spot from which to launch an attack on nearby settlements or to retreat to if that attack didn't go as planned. It is typically manned by **Gurdak-Dur**, King of the Wood.

POINTS OF ENTRY

The entranceway (*1*) built into the 15-foot-high wooden wall is the only inviting element of this otherwise imposing space, but looks, in this case, are deceiving. A pit trap on the path just beyond the entrance (*2*) serves as an unwelcome mat and requires a DC 17 Wisdom (Perception) check to notice. Anyone falling into the pit trap suffers 2d6 piercing damage and is grappled by the bear traps at the bottom (DC 15). There is a hidden tunnel used by those who inhabit the outpost (*3*), and the footworn path through the brush that conceals its trapdoor can be perceived by the particularly observant (DC 20).

TRAPS ABOUND

In addition to the pit trap at the main gate, there are several traps along the walls (*4*), each with a DC 17 to uncover and DC 20 to safely disarm. Anyone triggering these trip-wire traps and those within 10 feet of them must succeed on a DC 18 Dexterity saving throw, taking 3d6 piercing damage on a failed save or half as much on a success, as numerous crossbow bolts fire in their direction.

PRIME SCOUTING

In addition to the 40-foot watchtower within the outpost (*5*), there are two elevated platforms (30 feet) obscured by the trees (*6, 7*), which both offer full cover and prime vantage points for a clear view of incoming threats, as well as tactical positioning for ranged assault. Ranged attacks from these platforms and the watchtower are made with advantage. Additionally, boltholes are placed strategically along the walls of the outpost, offering full cover to sharpshooters stationed on the ground.

VARIANT ENCOUNTER (OPTIONAL)

Roll 1d6 to determine what awaits any adventurers who might plan a siege on this outpost.

1d6	The party encounters...
1	...2d4 **hobgoblins**, one **hobgoblin warlord** and two **bugbears** hiding among the bushes are ready to settle in after a week's worth of raiding.
2	...an **owlbear** chained near the outpost's entrance being baited and abused by 5d4 **orcs**.
3	...2d4 **thugs**, one **berserker** and one **veteran** divvying up their spoils after an attack on a nearby town as 1d4 **mastiffs** roam the grounds nearby.
4	...a group of 1d4 lycanthropes (**werebear**, **wereboar**, **weretiger** and/or **werewolf**), currently in human form, bickering about the plans for their next hunt.
5	...5d4 **gnolls**, who have begun a ritual sacrifice on a peasant girl.
6	...4d4 **goblins**, who are being sternly upbraided by one **hobgoblin**.

NPC PROFILE
GURDAK-DUR, KING OF THE WOOD

A rampaging half-orc with a soft spot for the trappings of royalty, Gurdak-Dur is a hulking mass of muscle with the blood-soaked blade of a warrior and the will to impose tyranny on any who stand in his way. He is, in sum, a pretty bad guy—but his weakness is vanity, as well as a clumsiness that befalls anyone who wears a cape as long as his. Trailing behind him by a length of 10 feet., Gurdak-Dur's cape, sewn from the tanned flesh of his foes, could easily trip him up on a crowded battlefield.

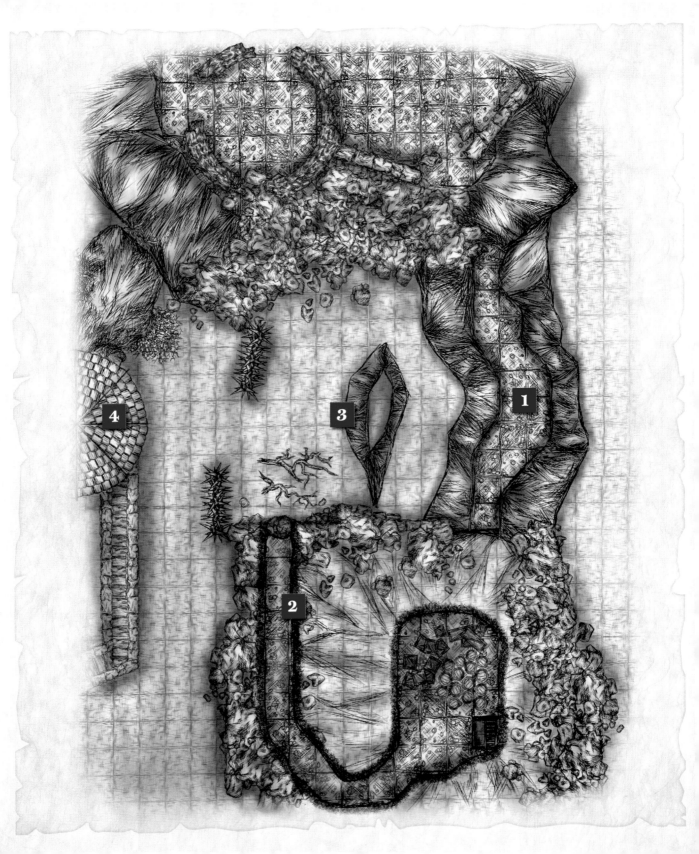

THE LAST REDOUBT

A point of retreat in a battle lost before it began, this fortified ruin is occupied by a ragtag group of soldiers who likely won't last the night.

> Crude embankments lie between two hills, a wall of packed earth and wooden stakes stand just behind a series of ditches. Men and women, some of them visibly wounded, wield shovels or sharpened stakes to expand the defenses, but many seem resigned to their coming fate. Sweat-soaked brows lift just long enough to shoot you a look of hopelessness. The battle is lost, and these are the losers.

A RALLY POINT WITH NONE TO RALLY

After a rout in battle, these soldiers fled here, a fallback position fortified ahead of time. But no one anticipated the situation would be this insurmountable. The enemy is coming, maybe in the next few hours, and this collection of demoralized and wounded soldiers can't hope to hold them off. There is little cover here, and not enough soldiers to properly fortify more than one position. **Captain Jane Sally**, a human **veteran**, does her best to organize what's left of her outfit, but many are too weak to obey commands, and those well enough to stand have begun whispering plans to desert and save their hides. A successful DC 12 Intelligence (Investigation) or Wisdom (Insight) check reveals a growing sentiment among the living that they'd be better off killing Captain Sally and making a run for it than holding this position against their battle-ready foes.

MAKESHIFT PROTECTIONS

A hastily dug trench (**1**) protects much of the Redoubt's northern front, while natural hills offer a solid defensible position from all sides. The higher of the two hills can be accessed via an underground tunnel (**2**) with an entrance on the northeast side of the trench. Ditches (**3**) and spiked barricades along the landscape make a mounted assault problematic but not impossible. The 50-foot bell tower (**4**), all that remains of the ruined castle once built here, offers prime position for scouts and snipers.

GROWING UNREST

Despite all her efforts, the soldiers know well that their commander is ordering them to stand and wait for their deaths. Some of them accept this with a calm stoicism, but others are not so willing to give up their lives. 2d4 conspirators meet in the shadows or talk quietly as they toil in the ditches, plotting ways to escape their fates.

NPC PROFILE

CAPTAIN JANE SALLY, HUMAN VETERAN

A stout, middle-aged woman with cropped black hair, sun-baked skin and the battered, bloody armor of a frontline brawler, Captain Sally tries to put on a brave face but knows her position here is hopeless. Run down by a superior force just a few miles away, she and her unit have retreated to a position she must defend—even if there's no one left to stand by her side. Valiant and headstrong, her gallows humor is starting to wear thin on all under her command.

ENCOUNTER VARIANT: NAMING THE ENEMY

Who are these soldiers fighting? Roll 1d6 or choose a foe that best aligns with your current adventure.

1d6	These soldiers are fighting...
1	...hobgoblins.
2	...orcs.
3	...rebels.
4	...soldiers of the crown.
5	...a necromancer and his undead army.
6	...gnolls.

VARIANT ENCOUNTER (OPTIONAL)

Roll 1d6 to determine the fate of the soldiers at the Last Redoubt and to see what the party comes across.

1d6	The party finds...
1	...a group of conspirators planning to kill Captain Sally at dusk before making their escape.
2	...a company of 3d8 enemy combatants preparing to attack the Redoubt from the rear with aid from the conspirators.
3	...Captain Sally, who asks them to escort the wounded to town for 3d10 x 10 gp. En route, the party is ambushed by 2d4 enemy combatants.
4	...3d8 enemy combatants attacking in force from all sides. Captain Sally begs the party to flee with a package that she says "must be kept safe."
5	...2d8 enemy combatants using a large catapult with a range of 200/400 dealing 3d6 bludgeoning damage in a 10-foot radius on a failed DC 15 Dexterity saving throw, or half as much on a success.
6	...2d4 **trolls** attacking what remains of the stronghold, with the conspirators using the distraction to try to slip away.

ENCOUNTER VARIANT (OPTIONAL) CONTROL ROOM

A successful DC 20 Intelligence (Investigation) check reveals the kitchen *(2)* is light on the necessary implements for making food, and upon further inspection appears to be an elaborately disguised control panel for a magical locomotive device: the house itself. When activated, the house's stilt-like avian legs raise and shift. The house has a movement speed of 80 feet, and when used as a vehicle has 88 hp.

THE HORRIBLE HUT

Judging by its exterior, folks would be forgiven for assuming something truly evil lurks within the walls of this small, elevated hut. They might be right.

ENCOUNTER VARIANT
WHO DWELLS WITHIN THIS HOUSE?

Roll 1d6 to determine the nature and motives of this home's owner. The home's interior reflects the personality of the one who dwells within. Roll 1d8 to determine whether they are good (odds) or evil (evens).

1d6	Inside the house dwells...
1	...**Abigail Firth**, a human witch who enjoys sculpting tiny cherubic children out of clay and then bringing them to life during major holidays.
2	...**Marjorie Baker**, a half-elven sorcerer who sleeps during the day but carouses at night, as she is convinced she's part vampire.
3	...**a coven of three hags**—Bertha, Burka and Bartab—working to subvert the government of a nearby town.
4	...**Gwyneth Torso**, a human mage hard at work on her 12th book of lore and, under a nom de plume, her 28th book of lycanthropic erotica.
5	...**Reese Anteroth**, an elven wizard who designed the house's exterior in an effort to be left alone to focus on creating her own jigsaw puzzles.
6	...**Hira Lowenlight**, a dragonborn high priestess who uses this house as a means to proselytize around the countryside in service to her god.

THE SEASONAL GARDEN

Surrounding the Horrible Hut are four distinct gardens (*1*) that grow seasonal produce at all times of year. In addition to summer squash and tasty turnips, the hut's garden features a small mushroom patch. If players choose to eat any of these mushrooms, roll on the Mushroom Table to determine the effects.

MUSHROOM TABLE

1d6	The mushrooms...
1	...**deal 2d6 psychic damage** on a failed DC 15 Wisdom saving throw. On a successful save, the creature can see into the ethereal plane.
2	...**deal 2d6 piercing damage** on a failed DC 15 Constitution saving throw. On a successful save, the creature is resistant to fire damage until their next long rest.
3	...**deal 2d6 poison damage** on a failed DC 15 Constitution saving throw. On a successful save, the creature can fly until their next long rest.
4	...**deal 2d6 acid damage** on a failed DC 15 Constitution saving throw. On a successful save, the creature gains advantage on all attack rolls until their next long rest.
5	...**deal 2d6 psychic damage** on a failed DC 15 Wisdom saving throw. On a successful save, the creature gains the ability to speak and understand all languages until their next long rest.
6	...**deal 2d6 psychic damage** on a failed DC 15 Wisdom saving throw. On a successful save, the creature knows and can cast one 6th-level spell (at GM discretion) once before the memory of how to cast it fades away.

VARIANT ENCOUNTER (OPTIONAL)

Roll 1d6 to determine what the witching hour might reveal to any adventurers passing by this abode.

1d6	The party encounters...
1	...a group of 3d6 pitchfork- and torch-wielding citizens ready to burn the house to the ground.
2	...dark clouds which portend the coming of a violent storm—caused by the owner's ex, a rather tempestuous storm sorcerer.
3	...a seemingly endless line of children parading their way out of the home, the result of a conjuration spell gone awry.
4	...war drums sounding as a battalion of 4d6 **orcs** stampede toward the Horrible Hut.
5	...an unruly **hill giant** stomping her way toward the Horrible Hut, before knocking politely to ask how things are going, how's the family, etc.
6	...a trio of **will-o'-wisps** whipping around the house's exterior as a gang of 2d4 **scarecrows** dance in the eerie extraplanar light.

WRETCHTOWN

A home for those with nothing, rising from the cast-off refuse of the city. Most others steer well clear of Wretchtown's rotten stench, but those in need of urchin-supplied information or the services of its most reclusive denizen, the Hag of Wretchtown, will find cause to slip through one of the warren's many doors.

> You can't help but feel dubious about the safety of such a tall, rickety structure, clearly sagging against the city wall at its back. A putrid stench cloaks the hovel from the outside, but it slowly gives way when you pass beneath the hanging cloth covering the entrance and make your way inside. The hovel is cleaner within than expected, though its low-hanging ceiling causes problems for the tallest among you. You are obliged to pick your way past the slumped forms of the locals as you wind your way deeper, feeling their eyes on your back until the twisted maze carries you from sight.

THE WARREN

Built from the cast-offs of the city, a collection of scrap and rubbish piled two stories high, there are no wide spaces in Wretchtown. Every wall bears a load and the seemingly random planks of timber lying across the corridors are often all that keeps those walls from collapsing. The floors are unstable, liable to send those on higher levels crashing through the ceilings of those below if they put too much weight in one spot. In some places these holes have been patched and reinforced with whatever material was on hand, in others makeshift ladders have been propped up to allow passage between floors. The entire building is a fire hazard, built mostly from flammable material and with corridors too tight to negotiate quickly. When players are navigating Wretchtown, have them roll 1d20 for every 30 feet of movement. On a roll of 3 or lower, the wall they are leaning on or floor below them collapses, at GM discretion.

Additionally, if any such character moves more than half their speed in a round, they move too quickly to plant their feet with the care required, and must make a Dexterity saving throw with a DC of 14 to leap clear as the floor gives way beneath them.

Similarly, Area of Effect damage of any kind risks causing the walls and supports to give way. Characters will need to make Dexterity saving throws (DC 12) to avoid falling debris. Any kind of fire damage being used, meanwhile, runs the risk of starting a larger conflagration within the structure as it consumes the walls here at twice its normal rate.

THE WRETCHES

An assortment of halflings, gnomes, elves, humans and a handful of others, Wretchtown's denizens all share one thing in common: They are scarred by a rotting, disfiguring sickness that deadens the nerves and steals away their flesh. The disease doesn't appear to be infectious, but the results are grotesque enough that the city would rather victims stay holed up in one place. They are a close-knit community by necessity, only safe from local criminals by virtue of owning nothing worth stealing, and have embraced the derogatory "Wretchtown" name for their home with pride. The more ambulant members of the community can be found begging in other parts of the city, but many are largely confined to Wretchtown, lacking the means to travel farther than the ability to crawl will carry them.

The denizens of Wretchtown rally to defend their homes. They will demonstrate a remarkable bravery in attacking anyone who seeks to hurt a member of their enclave or the structure itself. Use the statistics of **commoners** for the Wretches, with the suggestion that 4d6 Wretches are home at any given time. They have AC 8 and are unarmed, but make three attacks per round.

SUCH A SWEET OLD DEAR

At the heart of the second floor of Wretchtown (**1**) sits a cluster of rooms, home to the most beloved inhabitant of Wretchtown—a hag named **Sweet Lil' Annie**. She can be found hunched over a large, black pot, billowing smoke shunted out of the room by a length of brass piping sticking out through the roof of the hovel at a jaunty angle. She is every bit as deformed and scarred as the others in Wretchtown, but she moves with an energy and liveliness 🦇 ≫

NPC PROFILE
SWEET LIL' ANNIE, THE HAG OF WRETCHTOWN

Rescued from the clutches of an evil hag as an infant by a band of adventurers, none realized the babe had already been affected by the ritual through which new hags are born. When the change took her, Annie was deposited in Wretchtown, where the suffering of the inhabitants kept her busy and allowed her to pass without too much notice. She brews salves and potions to alleviate the suffering of those around her, and to reward those who go the extra mile to please her. She is protective of the other inhabitants of Wretchtown, viewing them as her pets and possessions, and they in turn will rally to her defense should she ever be attacked.

at odds with her appearance. The broth brewing in her pot lends a similar energy to those who drink it, and Annie is as generous as she can be with its contents. She also accepts visitors from outside Wretchtown, trading favors and charms for secrets and ingredients.

ENCOUNTER VARIANT
THE WITCH'S BREWS

Sweet Lil' Annie is already surrounded by so much abject mortal misery that she sees little need to delve too far into twisted, evil magics. Annie may use any of the following if attacked, or she may grant them as rewards or offer them in trade.

1d6	The Black Pot's Contents
1	**Essence of Health.** This steaming, milky broth grants the drinker immunity to disease and poison for the next eight hours and allows the drinker to ignore any penalties from disease or poison that they currently suffer, though the user inevitably finds strands of wiry, black hair caught in their teeth after drinking.
2	**Rot Flower Extract.** This spotted, stained vial holds a bubbling yellow liquid. If thrown or opened, the liquid boils out into a miasma that blankets the area. Treat this as a *stinking cloud* spell centered on the vial's location.
3	**Little Poppet.** A withered doll inside a jar of sickly green fluid. A creature may use its reaction after being hit by an attack to reduce all damage to 0. The Poppet is destroyed by the attack instead.
4	**Delicious Porridge.** The grains may be blackened or still shedding their husks, and the milk may have clearly curdled days ago, but when it hits the tongue this porridge tastes creamy and filling. The porridge also places a *geas* on the eater, compelling them to follow the next command Annie gives them.
5	**Eyeblind Powder.** A creature with this container may take an action to blow Powder into the face of another creature within 5 feet. That creature must make a Constitution saving throw with a DC 16 or be blinded for one minute. The user of the Powder must make a Constitution saving throw with a DC of 12 or be poisoned for one minute. Both creatures may repeat their saves at the end of each round.
6	**"A Friend."** Sweet Lil' Annie hands you a circular silver container. She tells you that "he" will be happy to be out in the world. Within the container is the subject of a *magic jar* spell, and the soul inside is unable to project itself or possess anyone until it leaves Wretchtown. The identity of the soul contained is at GM discretion.

VARIANT ENCOUNTERS (OPTIONAL)

Roll 1d6 on the table below to determine what riff raff and rabble the party might run up against among the muck in Wretchtown.

1d6	What encounters fester beneath Wretchtown's skin?
1	A nest of 1d4 **rat swarms** gnaws on the dull limbs of this level's 1d6 Wretches, who lack the strength to fight them off.
2	A charitable priest from the local temple would like to bring his god's light and healing to the poor sufferers of Wretchtown, but they angrily refuse to allow him entry. He asks for the party's aid.
3	A sickly but savvy pickpocket swipes at the purse of the most oblivious-seeming party member, with a +7 on the attempt, claiming half its contents on a success.
4	The local noble's 1d4 guard(s) have been ordered by their master to covertly clear out this eyesore, and they attempt to start a fire just inside its main entrance.
5	A badly misshapen elf approaches the party before they can fully enter the Warren's confines: "Sweet Lil' Annie knows about the Bad Thing." The messenger explains that all can be forgiven, for a price (at GM discretion).
6	A grizzled mercenary is on the hunt for a notorious thief rumored to reside here. He offers 100 gp to anyone who can aid in her capture.

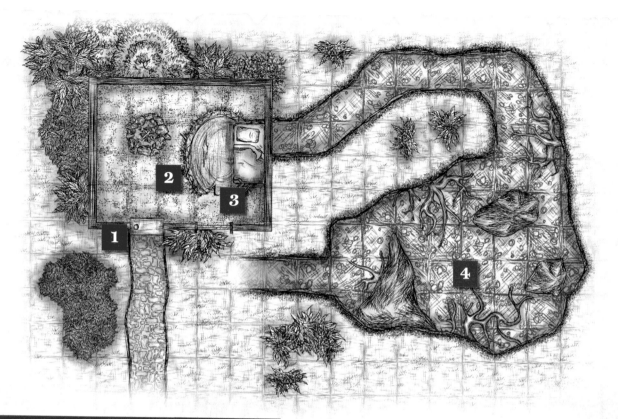

THE SHACK

A seemingly abandoned, single-room structure on a hillside hides an entrance to a system of underground passages.

THE BUILDING

The front door (**1**) to this rundown shelter is its primary point of entry. This shack has no windows to speak of, though there are cracks between the boards that keep it upright and are wide enough to let in a little sunlight or rainfall, depending on the day. Its overall aesthetic is "empty"—though there is a bed and a small area rug (**2**) that's tattered and a little threadbare. Beneath the rug, which at GM discretion can be presented as a **rug of smothering**, are a few arcane runes that are revealed to be part of a teleportation circle with a DC 15 Intelligence (Arcana) check. The bedroll (**3**), which covers the floor, is the only part of the room not covered in a layer of thin gray dust, and a DC 15 Intelligence (Investigation) check reveals an entrance to a subterranean tunnel beneath the bedroll.

THE CAVERNS

A narrow, steep-sloping tunnel about 5 feet in all directions leads down to an open cavern (**4**), itself connected to a deeper series of tunnels and cave systems, at GM discretion. The cave is cool, damp and devoid of light.

VARIANT ENCOUNTER (OPTIONAL)

Roll 1d6 to determine what the party might uncover if they go poking around in this seemingly abandoned outpost.

1d6	The party finds...
1	...a **galeb duhr**, left to guard this entrance to the caves by a paranoid **mage**.
2	...a cluster of 2d4 **shriekers** and 2d4 **gas spores** have taken root in this damp, subterranean cavern—the shriekers scream a warning that echoes down the halls of the cave.
3	...1d4 **ghasts**, whose stench is a good indicator of their presence, wandering in the cavern.
4	...a **gibbering mouther**, having wandered here from the darker corners of this cave system, is now whispering to itself in the darkness of the cavern.
5	...a small waif, clinging to life on the bedroll, claims his father was dragged under the shack by a nest of 3d4 **giant spiders**.
6	...a **bandit spore servant** wanders inside the shack, bumping into the walls repeatedly as it tries to heed the call of the **myconid sovereign** and 2d4 **myconid adults** in the cavern beneath the shack.

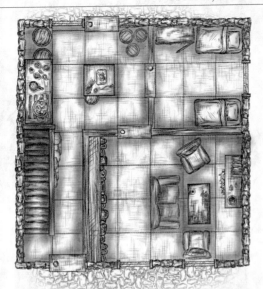
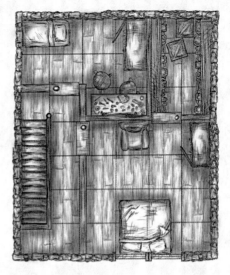

VARIANT HOME 1

Who lives in this home? A few dice rolls hold the answer.

RESIDENTS

If you're unsure of who lives in this home (meaning you aren't using it as the residence of an established NPC), roll on the Random NPC Generator (pg. 125) to create a homeowner. Then roll on the tables below to determine the status of the house itself.

INTERIOR

A kitchen, a large living space and three bedrooms represent the bulk of the interior space of this domicile. A back door leads to an alleyway/open landscape behind the house.

APPEARANCE

Roll 1d4 to determine the overall appearance of the house.

1	**Quaint.** This home is tidy if a bit cramped, and feels as though it's been lived in for years if not generations.
2	**Minimalist.** This home is free of the trappings most accrue over a lifetime and is instead adorned only with necessary elements—a modest wardrobe, a table, a few chairs, some beds and little else.
3	**Cluttered.** A hoarder dwells here and each room is stuffed with the items they've collected over the course of their entire life. Each room is difficult terrain, as creatures must negotiate the piles of accrued items to get anywhere.
4	**Abandoned.** This home is empty, and the location of its owner is unknown (except to the GM).

VARIANT ENCOUNTER (OPTIONAL)

Roll 1d6 to reveal what dangers dwell within this otherwise pedestrian abode.

1d6	The party encounters...
1	...2d4 **goblins** doing their best to impersonate the halfling family they buried in the yard.
2	...a cow on the second floor that can't seem to make its way down the stairs.
3	...a man and wife who live in fear of their child, a young telepath with psionic abilities.
4	...a pair of **ghosts** who keep pestering the family within to go solve their murders.
5	...an **arcanaloth** in the guise of a friendly old woman who loves to garden, but also really, really wants some spell scrolls.
6	...a family of **doppelgangers**, doing their best to ingratiate themselves to the local nobility.

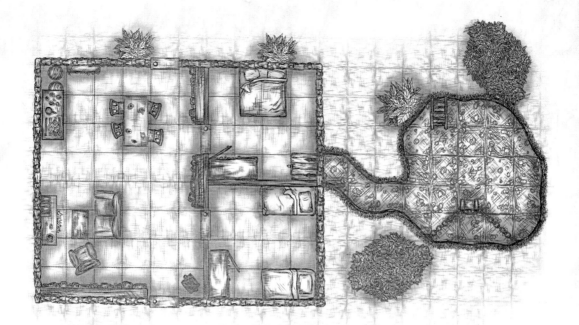

Variant Home 2

Who lives in this home? A few dice rolls hold the answer.

Residents

If you're unsure of who lives in this home (meaning you aren't using it as the residence of an established NPC), roll on the Random NPC Generator (pg. 125) to create a homeowner. Then roll on the tables that follow to determine the status of the house itself.

Interior

This home is small but efficiently appointed, with two bedrooms, an all-purpose living/dining room, kitchen area and entryway. One of the bedrooms also features a well-disguised trapdoor beneath the floorboards, revealed with a DC 18 Intelligence (Investigation) check, that leads to an underground room.

Underground

What's being hidden within this covert space? Roll 1d6 to find out.

1	**Smuggling operation.** The individual(s) residing here use(s) this space as a stopover location while shuttling illicit goods into or out of foreign territories.
2	**Shrine to a forbidden deity.** The individual(s) residing here use(s) this space to worship and commune with their god/patron, an act prohibited by law.
3	**Interrogation room.** The individual(s) residing here use(s) this space to question and/or torture political or personal enemies, and the tools and instruments positioned throughout (as well as the blood-stained walls) suggest they know exactly what they're doing.
4	**Panic room.** A place to hunker down in the event of a robbery or overwhelming attack of existential proportions.
5	**Entrance to a dark cave system.** The space leads to a secondary staircase, which in turn leads to a ladder that leads to a vast series of caves and tunnels.
6	**Portal to another dimension.** The perfect way to travel between planes, this room features a portal to a plane of your choosing beyond the prime material.

Variant Encounter (Optional)

Roll 1d6 to reveal what the party will face down in this otherwise drab domicile.

1d6	The party finds...
1	...the ringleader of a secret plot to kill a local lord.
2	...four dead bodies and 1d4 **shadows**.
3	...a nonviolent **orc** just trying to make it work.
4	...a **chasme** buzzing within the empty house.
5	...a family of recently destitute nobles.
6	...a room full of 3d4 **zombies**.

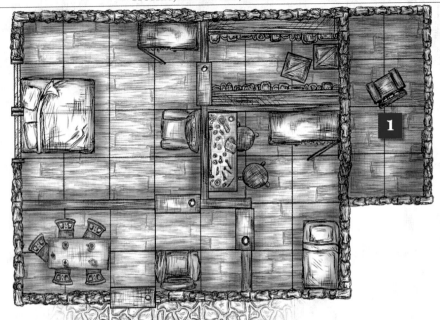

THE SECRET ROOM

Some houses have hidden corridors and cleverly covert cubbyholes for storage or study or simply for secrets. This home is an example of the form, and the secret room (*1*) contained within it—or any other location within this book—can be located with a DC 22 Intelligence (Investigation) check while your party is exploring the space.

VARIANT ENCOUNTER (OPTIONAL)

Roll 1d20 to determine what's locked away in the secret room.

1d20	In the secret room the party finds...
1	...**grasping hands** frozen in place, each reaching, clawing and crawling their way toward the door.
2	...**bodies.** They rock gently in the draft from the window as they hang suspended from giant meat hooks.
3	...**shelves and shelves of dolls**.
4	...**a big dog with red eyes** chained to the center of the room amidst a circle of dried blood.
5	...**stinking piles of trash and junk.** It stinks.
6	...**a small, thin child** who lets you know you'd best be off before "mother" returns.
7	...**20 years' worth of stolen correspondence**, all still unopened.
8	...**a rare mushroom garden,** the contents of which is worth 3,500 gp.
9	...**a taxidermy workshop** with the creations on display. All of the creatures are missing their eyes.
10	...**shelves of ancient, dusty leather-bound books**. All of the pages are blank.
11	...**an ancient woman** sitting in a rocking chair and singing the same lullaby over and over.
12	...**a collection of stunning oil paintings** of various famous battles from one of the last great artists from the previous generation.
13	...**three pedestals arranged in a triangle.** Atop each is a chalice. One is full, one is empty and the last in a state of both half-full and half-empty.
14	...**stolen socks.** Thousands of them.
15	...**teeth.** They line the shelves, are in jars and bowls and are scattered across every surface.
16	...**a flying, talking sword** named Zanith.
17	...**a perfectly carved marble statue** of the party, looks of terror twisting their faces.
18	...**a very comfortable, albeit small-looking bed.** This bed grants the benefits of a long rest after just one hour of sleep within it.
19	...**a cursed breastplate.** Anyone who touches it, or the wearer, for the first time takes 4d8 necrotic damage. Anyone who attunes to the armor is cursed to make death saving throws at disadvantage.
20	...**a vast array of hoarded gold coins** worth 13,000gp piled high in the small space.

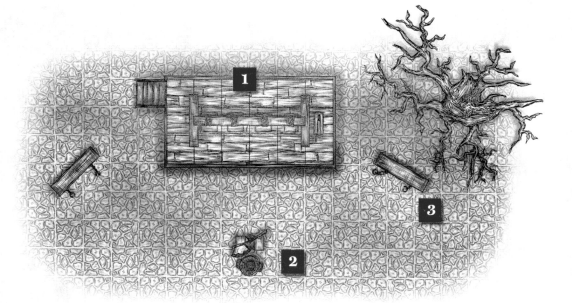

STOCKS & GALLOWS

Whether or not the punishment fits the crime, sometimes citizens of the realm are sentenced to suffer the sword or the noose or the humiliation of their peers. Though it's not quite home, this will be the last place many lay their head.

GALLOWS

The nooses on this block (*1*) are thick, corded rope (AC 12, 2 hp) and can withstand a weight of up to 650 pounds. The platform is about 10 feet off the ground and features a trapdoor system under each noose, triggered by a lever guarded by the executioner. When the lever is pulled, all the trapdoors drop simultaneously, regardless of whether each noose is occupied. A projectile aimed at the noose from a distance farther than 30 feet adds +1 to the rope's AC per 10 ft. If a noose is bearing a body that starts to sway, this attack is made at a disadvantage.

BEHEADING BLOCK

It's hard to overestimate the feeling of dread that befalls someone whose neck is placed on this indented and gore-flecked surface (*2*)—or how that feeling will influence their will to survive. A creature about to be executed must make a Constitution saving throw, the ramifications of which are detailed below.

1–5	The creature is paralyzed.
6–10	The creature is frightened.
11–15	The creature is resigned to their fate, but not otherwise hindered.
16–20	The creature is emboldened, as if under the effect of a barbarian's rage.
20+	The creature is emboldened, as if under the effect of a barbarian's rage, and has advantage on attacks.

STOCKS

Not every crime deserves an execution, but some who are set in the stocks (*3*) wish for death, particularly when their peers start lobbing rotten produce or animal feces at them as they serve their time. The locks used on the stocks have a DC of 15.

VARIANT ENCOUNTER (OPTIONAL)

Roll 1d6 to determine what fate holds in store for the party at the stocks and gallows.

1d6	The party sees...
1	...a (guilty) **thief** pleading his innocence. The gathered crowd believes he is not guilty.
2	...a coordinated group of 3d4 **bandits** working to free their **bandit captain** and his two lieutenants.
3	...a fire breaks out at the gallows as a concerned citizen tries to stop a public execution.
4	...a 9-year-old boy in the stocks for sending a love letter to the realm's princess.
5	...a man about to be beheaded is *polymorphed* into a weasel by his spell scroll-wielding wife.
6	...an old man stands at the gallows begging to be hanged for a murder he committed 63 years earlier.

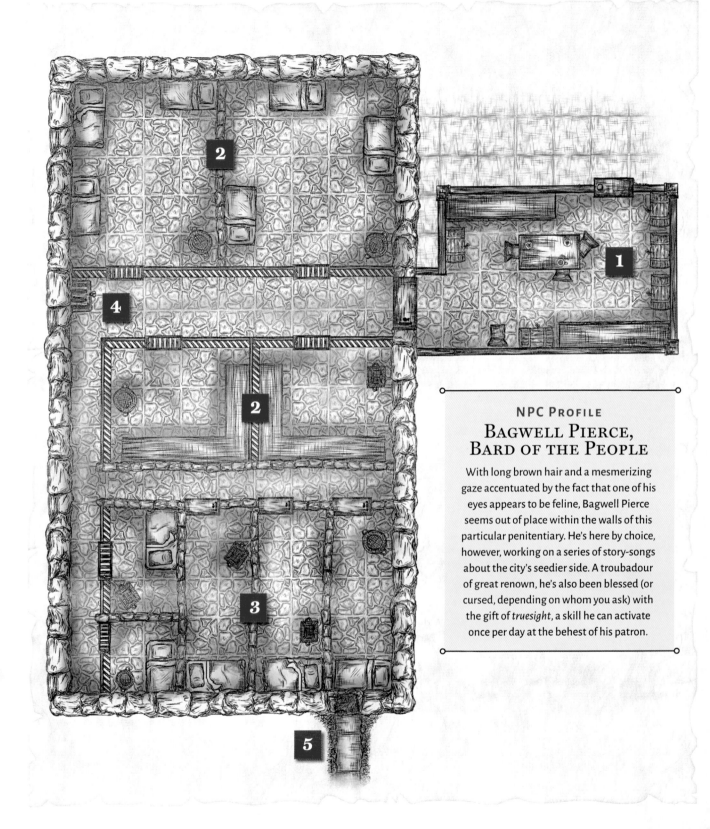

NPC Profile
BAGWELL PIERCE,
BARD OF THE PEOPLE

With long brown hair and a mesmerizing gaze accentuated by the fact that one of his eyes appears to be feline, Bagwell Pierce seems out of place within the walls of this particular penitentiary. He's here by choice, however, working on a series of story-songs about the city's seedier side. A troubadour of great renown, he's also been blessed (or cursed, depending on whom you ask) with the gift of *truesight*, a skill he can activate once per day at the behest of his patron.

TOWN JAIL

Though many may insist laws were made to be broken (or at least bent a little), those who choose to disobey area ordinances can easily find themselves contemplating their behavior from the wrong side of wrought iron bars. This facility is fairly standard, but is far from completely secure. With a little time, ingenuity, cunning or a combination of all three, most adventurers should be able to find a way to escape should they choose not to serve their full sentence. In addition to the guards and accused, a troubadour named **Bagwell Pierce** strolls the halls, seeking inspiration for his next big hit.

ENTRANCE

A large oak door leads to a small receiving room (**1**) where 2d4 guards somewhat casually man their posts.

SHARED CELLS

To the left and the right of the door leading out of the receiving room are two cells for group holding (**2**). Drunkards, louts and other nonviolent offenders are typically cordoned off together in these spaces until they dry up or cool off. Locks on these doors have a DC of 16. Roll on the Random Rabble table to determine who may already be locked up in these cells.

INDIVIDUAL CELLS

For those who can't be trusted in a group environment, a row of private cells (**3**) create separation and confinement. Locks on these doors have a DC of 18, and the cells themselves are typically under the watchful eye of a patrolling guard. Roll on the Random Rabble table to determine who may already be locked up in these cells.

MEANS OF ESCAPE

Outside of picking the locks to the cells and sneaking past, subduing or otherwise defeating the guards that attend the jail's main entrance, there are a handful of other ways to escape this space unscathed:

GRATE. A grate along the back wall (**4**) can be observed with a DC 10 Wisdom (Perception) check. A DC 16 Strength (Athletics) check will remove the grate from its fixed position, allowing for access to the tunnels below.

HIDDEN TUNNEL. A small hole in the wall of one of the holding cells (**5**) smells of mold and water rot, and a few rats scurry in and out of this slit between stones. Though rarely asked, the rats would reveal that the wall isn't particularly sound and could be knocked over with a few solid blows (AC

10, hp 18). A DC 18 Intelligence (Investigation) check would reveal the same intel. If the wall is destroyed, a gap between buildings leading to a narrow alley behind the jail is revealed.

ENCOUNTER VARIANT (OPTIONAL) RANDOM RABBLE TABLE

Roll 2d4 to determine how many individuals are being held in the jail, then roll 1d20 on the table below for each individual to determine their identity and offense. A repeated roll indicates accomplices.

1d20	Within this cell is...
1	...**a goblin** caught masquerading as a halfling.
2	...**a half-elven petty thief** ties to organized crime.
3	...**an orc woman** whose pies gave a noble indigestion
4	...**a one-armed dwarf** covered in black soot accused of blowing up a local mine.
5	...**a human painter** who claims he's been framed.
6	...**a human farmer** whose horse kicked a man to death.
7	...**the daughter of a wealthy merchant**, caught donating his money to her boyfriend.
8	...**a burly half-orc** arrested for public intoxication.
9	...**a tiefling** who mouthed off to the city watch.
10	...**the mastermind** behind a series of sheep-related thefts, a muttering gnome named Reg.
11	...**a life-size wax figurine** styled in the visage of notorious criminal Cracker LeBloom, still at large.
12	...**a human female** who refuses to stop screaming, "I'm from the future and you're all tasty soup!"
13	...**three halflings** who refuse to speak.
14	...**a half-elf** who pummeled his elven father.
15	...**a male drow** who stands accused of flouting his dark-elven heritage in public.
16	...**a would-be bard** who stole a relic on a dare.
17	...**a quick-witted woman** whose only crime appears to be her penchant for peeing in the town square.
18	...**a sweaty half-orc** covered in gore and missing his teeth, unaware of what he did in a rage.
19	...**the biggest man in town**, held without bail for trying to stomp on one of the smallest.
20	...**a buxom bartender** with a lockpick and a pair of daggers laced into her corset.

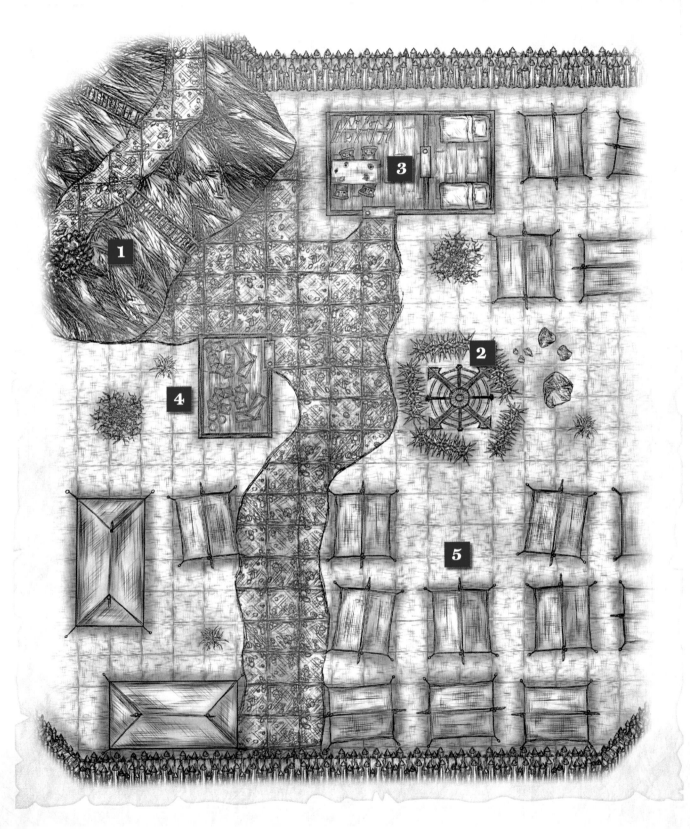

THE LABOR CAMP

Because most prisons are in some way subsidized by the rulers of the realm, it's not uncommon for those who are held within one to be asked (read: told) to pay back their debt to society through sweat and hard work. Some—including many prisoners forced to engage in it—oppose this practice, decrying it as a form of slavery. Others disagree. And others are typically the ones in charge.

ALL WORK, NO ESCAPE

The main function of those stationed at this camp is to empty the nearby mountain (*1*) of all its valuables. To determine what's being mined here, roll on the Random Mine Table. The fencing around the mine is reinforced with barbs that do 1d6 piercing damage as well as 1d10 force damage to any creature that comes into contact with them. The entire labor camp is also affected by a large anti-magic field, which emanates from a tower positioned within the center of the camp (*2*).

RANDOM MINE TABLE

The mine within this mountain is full of a valuable substance. Roll 1d8 to determine what it is.

1d8	The mine is full of...
1	Gold
2	Silver
3	Emeralds
4	Rubies
5	Diamonds
6	Red clay
7	Coal
8	Adamantine

NPC PROFILE

ALISTAR FLOGSWEAT, HUMAN FOREMAN

A grim demeanor and lack of patience are the most memorable elements of this labor camp leader's persona, and he carries himself with the air of a sadist who's lucked into being in control of a large group of people. He rules this camp with a firm hand and a pair of whips, both of which are barbed with bits of glass and metal.

GUARD OFFICE

The labor camp is overseen by a foreman, a headstrong, thick-necked brute named **Alistar Flogsweat**. He handles most of the necessary organization of work within this guard office (*3*), and when his men aren't on duty they can be found carousing within this space.

SUPPLY SHED

All the necessary implements for mining ore can be found within this shed (*4*), including pickaxes, shovels, lanterns, tinder boxes, torches and a bit of black powder. It is typically guarded by two to three **veterans** working in shifts.

MINIMUM SHELTER

The tents within the camp (*5*) lack the comforts of home, and the ones that aren't pocked with holes and tears still barely block the sun or rain most of the time. They can be useful in shielding activity within them from the guard posts, however, and provide three-quarter cover for any trying to protect themselves within.

VARIANT ENCOUNTER (OPTIONAL)

Roll 1d6 to determine what awaits the party within this prison camp.

1d6	The party...
1	...sees a group of 2d4 half-orcs repeatedly slamming themselves against the fencing trying in earnest to bust it down and escape.
2	...hears a rumble beneath the earth in the center of the camp heralding the arrival of two **goblins** inside an **apparatus of the crab**, digging their way up into the labor camp to bust out their 2d4 goblin pals.
3	...notices a flaming wagon loaded with 6d6 barrels of acid rumbling over a hill and toward the front gate of the labor camp, the start of an all out gnomish assault on the security system at the behest of a single gnome stuck inside.
4	...hears word that a collapse within the entrance to the mine has trapped 2d4 workers inside, and the foreman would like them rescued. The collapse was initiated by a group of 3d4 angry **duergar**.
5	...overhears that 2d4 **gnolls** are planning to assault the foreman and hold him hostage in exchange for their freedom.
6	...watches as a man dressed as a guard begins killing other guards as a group of 1d4 **bandits** cheer him on from the hills nearby.

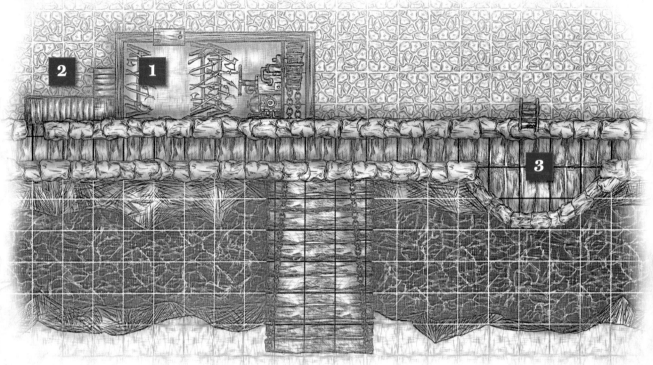

RANDOM CASTLE TABLE

When the party is exploring a large castle or sprawling estate, roll 1d6. On an odd number, roll 1d8 on Table 1. On an even number, roll 1d8 on Table 2. The end result for either roll is the room they'll have found themselves walking into (at GM discretion).

TABLE 1

1d8

1	Estate Defenses	pg. 111
2	The Grand Entrance	pg. 113
3	Council Chamber/War Room/ Map Room	pg. 115
4	Kitchen	pg. 115
5	Main Bedroom	pg. 117
6	Secondary Bedroom	pg. 117
7	Guard Barracks	pg. 117
8	Bathhouse and Privy	pg. 117

TABLE 2

1d8

1	Private Prison	pg. 119
2	Library	pg. 121
3	Dining Hall	pg. 121
4	A Guest Bedroom and Study	pg. 123
5	A Supply Room	pg. 123
6	Tower Armory	pg. 123
7	Roll on Extra Rooms Table	pg. 123
8	Roll again	

W hether surrounded by impenetrable walls, remarkable moats or the sweeping vistas of a large estate, at the end of the day a castle is still a home, and the rooms within are as primary to its function as the people who dwell there. The navigable spaces within a castle could fill an entire book, to say nothing of a single section within this one. Because of this fact, the next few pages outline spaces one would reasonably expect to find within the walls of a seat of noble power, whether a castle, keep or summer home. The rooms are presented without a planned connection to one another, leaving you free to determine where one exit might lead to another room's entrance at GM discretion. Each room described is exemplative of the visuals and themes associated with a space for nobility and royalty, though you can certainly skin them however you like as is appropriate for your game.

ESTATE DEFENSES (A)

Ensuring the safety of those who dwell within, many large homes and castles are equipped with a perimeter wall, or are fortresses unto themselves.

GATEHOUSE AND ARMORY

Walls are well and good but on occasion it's necessary to step beyond them, or welcome guests within. The gatehouse (*1*) is designed for just such a purpose, giving a set of guards a space from which to view the front door to this property and determine whether or not to open it. A massive mechanism within the gatehouse raises or lowers the drawbridge and is a two-person operation: One to rotate a gear to engage the device and another to pull a lever unlocking it and allowing it to fall. Raising or lowering the drawbridge requires a DC 15 Strength (Athletics) check. And because a wall without anyone to defend it can fall fairly quickly, it's important for those manning their post to feel prepared for any contingency. The armory is lined with longbows, pikes, crossbows and glaives to allow for those defending this wall to do so from range and with reach. A nearby set of stairs (*2*) leads directly to the top of the wall, making this room easily accessible in times of need.

THE WALL

The wall that surrounds this space (*3*) can be as imposing or welcoming as your story demands. Some walls are meant to slow an attack, or divert opposing forces toward a specific area that may be easier to defend, while others are aesthetically if not strategically pleasing. Determine a height as well as length for your wall and consider whether or not it was shoddily made or built by the finest craftsmen in the realm, a fact that could bolster or hinder its efficacy. The drawbridge door has an AC of 10 and 100 hp.

ENCOUNTER VARIANT (OPTIONAL)
OTHER DEFENSES

Bows and broadswords aren't the only way to defend an advantageous position atop a well-fortified wall. Roll 1d6 on the table below to determine the nature of the secondary defenses available for this fortress.

1d6	The wall has...
1	**...buckets filled with large stones every 10 feet.** An attack with falling rocks deals 6d6 bludgeoning damage to each creature in a 10-foot radius on a failed DC 15 Dexterity saving throw.
2	**...buckets filled with hot tar every 10 feet.** A creature splashed with hot tar must succeed on a DC 15 Dexterity save or take 4d6 fire damage on a failed save and half as much damage on the target's next turn as the tar sticks to their flesh. A target covered in hot tar is at disadvantage on all attacks, saves and skill checks, moves at half speed and is vulnerable to fire damage.
3	**...2d4 mounted ballistas.** They have a range of 200/600 feet and deal 4d10 piercing damage. They have +8 to hit and require two actions to fire: one to aim and one to trigger.
4	**...a series of hidden spikes halfway up the wall.** They can be activated as a reaction if a creature is in their area of effect, which sits halfway up the wall. If a creature is near the wall when these spikes are triggered they must succeed on a DC 15 Dexterity saving throw or suffer 3d6 piercing damage and fall back to the ground, suffering an additional 3d6 bludgeoning damage.
5	**...buckets of slop.** These pails of rotten meat and human filth are spaced every 10 feet, covered in flies and unpleasant to stand near. Any creature that starts or ends its turn within 5 feet of a bucket (thrown or stationary) must succeed on a DC 15 Constitution saving throw or spend their action and reaction retching at the stench.
6	**...glass jars full of acid every 10 feet.** An attack with a jar of acid deals 3d6 acid damage to any creature in a 15-foot radius that fails a DC 15 Dexterity saving throw.

THE GRAND ENTRANCE (B)

Most castles and opulent estates feature a greeting hall or great room, either for receiving guests, hosting galas or holding court. This space is designed to stand in as such a hall should the need arise.

GREAT HALL/THRONE ROOM

This open area (*1*) with a sprawling, arched roof features the throne of its top resident, and serves as a space from which they can listen to the populace deliver decrees to gathered yes-men or hold an upscale soiree with various members of court. If this space is not the seat of power for the realm and is instead a massive great hall in a noble's mansion, the throne should be omitted from your description of its trappings.

ENTRANCE HALL

A relatively bare space save for portraits of nobility or statues of particular cultural significance, this area of the castle (*2*) is effectively a foyer, an area in which to prepare yourself for an audience with the queen, a dance with the prince, an upbraiding from the scion of a major family or a summary execution in view of the rest of the court for crimes against the realm. You know, like the foyer of your own home.

WAITING ROOM

This area (*3*) is effectively a holding room for those who seek an audience with the head of the house, and would usually feature a few attendant guards as well as council members or footmen flitting in and out to check in on arriving guests to see if they need anything before their moment with the seated ruler here, or keep an eye on them to ensure they aren't looking to cause trouble.

OFFICES FOR CLERKS/COUNCIL CHAMBERS

Behind every great family is an individual who sets their meeting schedule, and this space (*4*) houses the individual(s) responsible for those duties. After all, a quality secretary can be as meaningful a deterrent to access as the highest castle wall.

MAIN COURTYARD/CARRIAGE ENTRANCE

The formal gateway to the Entrance Hall is through the courtyard abutting this massive residence (*5*). Some castles and noble homes feature a covered space to ensure those arriving by carriage need not fret about the weather—an option you can add here at your own discretion.

ENCOUNTER VARIANT (OPTIONAL)
PARTY TIME

There is no shortage of reasons for the upper crust of any civilization to hold a soirée, ball or other social function to which a large number of guests can be invited—and the Great Hall is where those events would take place most often. Roll 1d6 on the table below to reveal the sort of celebration taking place within this space.

1d6	The guests are...
1	...celebrating the death of a rival lord with a masquerade ball.
2	...enjoying the intoxicating glow of a wedding reception.
3	...preparing for an evening of convivial conversation and various types of dancing to honor a fertility god.
4	...at a naming ceremony for a new leader.
5	...all female, as this fancy gala is for women only.
6	...here under false pretenses.

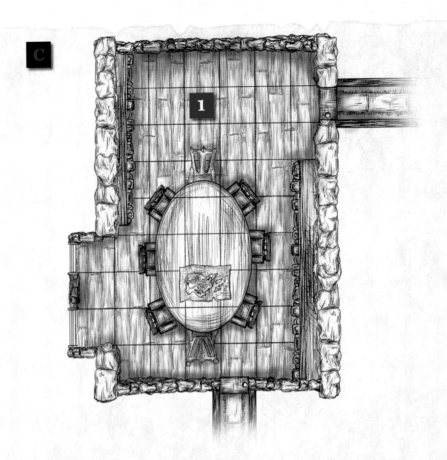

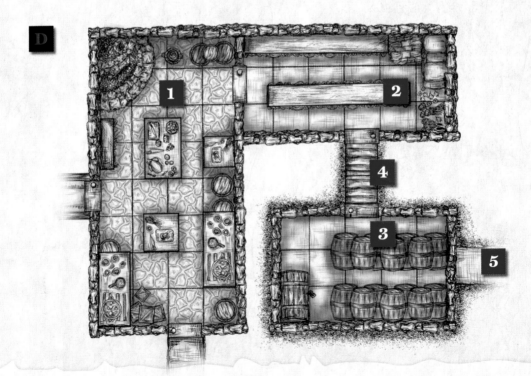

Vital Interiors

Every highborn home is unique, though they have numerous rooms in common. These spaces might feature as part of a castle exploration, or can serve as the site of specific scenes within your ongoing adventures.

Council Chamber/War Room/ Map Room (C)

Whether king or queen, lord or duke or simply a rich person with a desire to use their wealth in a way that can directly impact the world, this room (*1*) is a space to get a broader view of the realm and plan strategically in times of war or peace. Its walls are adorned with maps of the surrounding regions and there are several rolls of maps from far off lands stacked among the shelves on either side of the room's council table. The room is also perfect for gatherings featuring a king's trusted council or advisors, each of whom may be here to advance their own aims.

Kitchen (D)

A lodging with this many rooms requires a kitchen capable of preparing enough food to fill the mouths of those that dwell within them. This kitchen (*1*) features a large stone oven, a cast iron stove as well as several prep stations for breaking down sides of beef, chopping produce and plating dishes.

Pantry

A large area for short-term food storage (*2*), the pantry features stacks of sacks of staples (such as flour, rice, beans, lentils, potatoes and more), as well as any fruits or vegetables from nearby farms or far flung locations that have been collected as part of a forthcoming food menu.

Barrel Cellar

A staple of any large estate, this space (*3*), accessible through a passageway from the pantry (*4*), features rows of stored wine, mead, ale or distilled spirits ready to be cracked open for a special occasion or simple request.

Secret Tunnel

Covert passageways are not uncommon in manors such as this, and can lead below ground, up to a rooftop or simply to a different wing of the estate. This entrance to one such passageway (*5*) can be discovered with a DC 17 Intelligence (Investigation) check.

Encounter Variant (Optional) Ales Well

Every host is different, and the stores in any highborn home reflect the taste of the master of the house. Roll 1d6 to determine the drink of choice within this estate.

1d6	These barrels contain...
1	**...a rare spirit from another realm.** Upon tasting this spirit for the first time, a creature must succeed on a DC 12 Constitution saving throw to avoid temporary blindness, which lasts an hour.
2	**...a wine of the estate's own make.** This wine isn't the best, but the host is proud of it. A creature tasting this wine must succeed on a DC 10 Constitution saving throw to drink without making a sour face. A Charisma (Deception) check could also be utilized to avoid insulting the host.
3	**...a mead made from local honey.** Though it's not been made public, 1 in 6 individuals are allergic to this honey and break out in hives upon consuming it. For every creature who partakes of this mead, roll 1d6. On a 1, they break out in hives and are visibly sweaty, and their throat closes up slightly making it difficult to speak. This effect dissipates after a long rest or at GM discretion.
4	**...a dark spirit reminiscent of rum.** The drink is somewhat addictive, and any creature who partakes must succeed on a DC 12 Constitution saving throw or will immediately ask for another glass—forcing another saving throw. After three failed saves a creature becomes extremely inebriated, is incapable of lying and makes all skill checks and attack rolls at disadvantage.
5	**...a warming dark ale.** With hints of clove and allspice, this rich ale is similar to porter but with an added bonus: Any creature who consumes this ale is resistant to cold damage for one hour.
6	**...a highly flammable spirit.** With a smell like kerosene, a DC 10 Intelligence (Investigation) check would reveal this distilled spirit would immediately ignite if exposed to a spark or extreme heat.

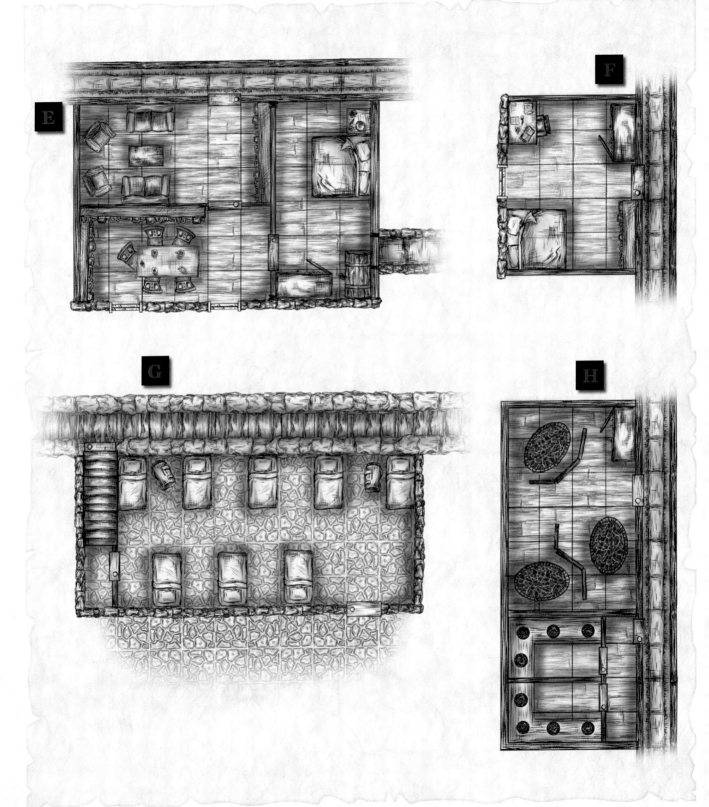

BEDS, BATHS AND BEYOND

It is true that the very, very rich are just like the rest of us in that they usually put their pants on one leg at a time and also, eventually, will need a place to lay their heads after a long day (unless they are sleepless warlocks, but that's another matter). Though most adventures may not lead directly to the bedroom of a king or archduchess, those spaces still exist, which is why they are included here. The rooms outlined below are typical of what one might find within the confines of a particularly opulent home.

MAIN BEDROOM (E)

This space features a large bed, a fully appointed reading room as well as a table and chairs for those days when its resident is hungry but would prefer not to put on pants. A wardrobe and storage chest round out the furniture in the room.

SECONDARY BEDROOM (F)

Smaller than the master bedroom but no less opulent, this room features a large bed, wardrobe, a shelf for books as well as a desk suitable for late night letter writing or for reviewing plans for the day as the sun comes up.

GUARD BARRACKS (G)

The collective home of a castle or estate's attendant guard, what these barracks lack in privacy they make up for in soft linens and stellar pay. These beds can also be shared with visiting guests of a certain class, if the host determines they are nice enough for free shelter but perhaps a bit too unruly to trust within the home's inner sanctum.

BATHHOUSE AND PRIVY (H)

A good soak can cure the ails of even the most well-to-do resident of this abode, and such a remedy can be found in this steamy escape. Personal tubs of piping hot water are separated by dividers within the room, and a large closet features some of the softest towels and robes in the realm. Beyond the bathhouse door is a spot to expel one's waste into a chamber pot without having to view it after the fact.

VARIANT ENCOUNTER (OPTIONAL)

Roll 1d6 to determine what dangers might wait within the walls of these bedrooms.

1d6	The party learns...
1	...a **night hag** is implanting dark visions inside the mind of the host as they sleep.
2	...1d4 suit(s) of **animated armor** refuse to let anyone into or out of the master suite.
3	...the host's paramour is hiding inside one of the room's wardrobes, explaining they cannot be found by the host's spouse and pleads for the party's aid.
4	...or at least suspects, that these beds are all cursed as the following morning no one who slept in one benefits from a long rest.
5	...a trap door beneath the bed in the master suite leads directly to a tavern within this book (at GM discretion), a fact currently being exploited by 6 local **thugs**.
6	...1d4 **ghosts** frequent these rooms and refuse to leave, sharing lengthy diatribes about how much they hate the current decor.

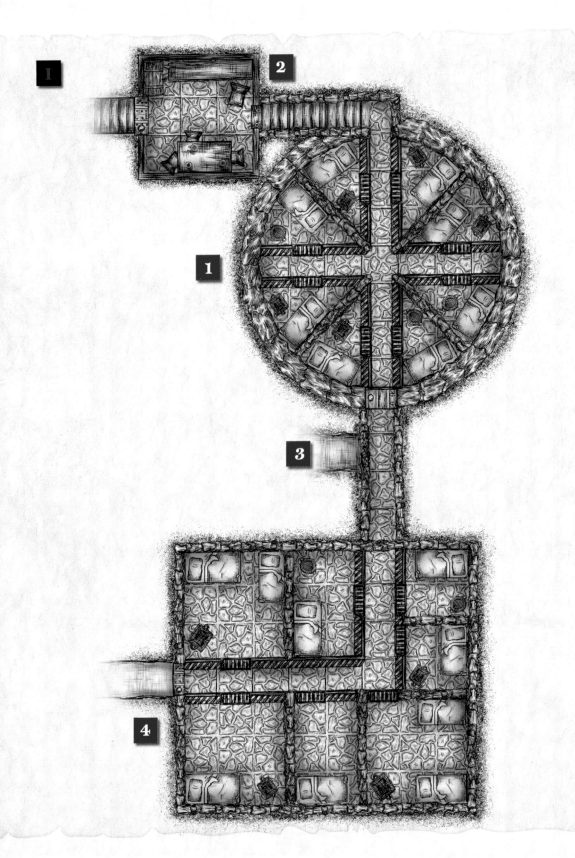

PRIVATE PRISON (I)

Many large estates and castles feature cells utilized to punish those who might wish to do harm to the head of the house, and are set up in a way that prevents troublemakers from wreaking havoc despite not having a large force in place to stand guard.

MAIN JAIL CELLS

The pie-slice construction of this block of cells built into one of the castle's spires (*1*) allows for a single guard or two to keep a watchful eye on the entire roomful of cells. The cells here each feature DC 18 locks, and each cell is equipped with a single bedroll and a chamberpot. The 2d4 **guards** who work in this space usually carry a set of keys on them, but there's a 1 in 6 chance they've left them with their superior, who is elsewhere.

GUARDROOM

When not on duty, the 2d4 guard(s) who keep this space under lock and key can be found commiserating or taking a load off in this small room (*2*) that acts as both a check point for incoming rabble and a check-in area for those interested in the status of prisoners who continue to defy those in charge. The door off this room leads to the floors above, by rolling on the Random Castle table on pg. 110 or at GM discretion.

SECRET TUNNEL

Though criminals and ne'er-do-wells occasionally find themselves locked up here, they still receive visitors from time to time—occasionally from palace insiders who would prefer not to have their movements tracked. This tunnel entrance (*3*) can be perceived with a DC 20 Wisdom (Perception) or Intelligence (Investigation) if one knows what they're looking for: tiny slits along the brickwork allow for it to swing forward just enough to allow a medium or smaller creature to slip through. These tunnels lead underground to the crypts or to other rooms within the estate at GM Discretion.

SECONDARY JAIL CELLS

A room utilized for overflow in the event of an uprising or disease outbreak, this secondary prison (*4*) is slightly less secure than the main cells, with its doors each featuring a DC 16 lock.

ENCOUNTER VARIANT (OPTIONAL)
PALACE INTRIGUE

Roll 1d6 on the table below to determine what plots may be afoot on these grounds, then have your party choose how to respond.

1d6	It appears...
1	...the host has been brainwashed by a powerful demon disguised as a court jester.
2	...the host's books are being kept by a particularly skilled and sticky-fingered accountant.
3	...the host's daughter has fallen in love with a member of the kitchen staff—a forbidden, and therefore secret, affair.
4	...a member of the council here is secretly allied with a rival house or kingdom, and is urging his master to war—and slaughter.
5	...an **assassin** from a far off kingdom has been sent to take out the host—as well as the rest of the family.
6	...a series of cries are emanating from various rooms within the estate. A DC 15 Intelligence (Investigation) check near one of the walls in this space reveals 14 hidden children, scummy and malnourished—all of them claiming they've been kept here by a member of the host's staff.

GM NOTE

For more variety, use the Variant Encounter table on pg. 107 to populate these cells with random rabble.

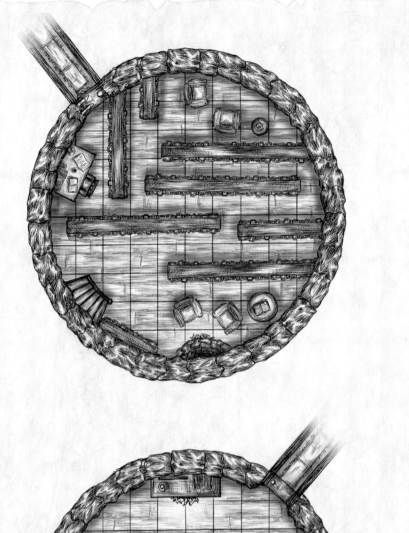

J

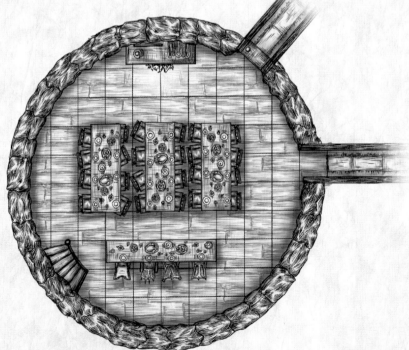

K

TOWER OPTIONS

The spire of a large castle or mansion can be utilized for any number of meaningful purposes—a potions laboratory or makeshift library, for instance. These two maps represent the possibilities for a space such as this, but can be modified as necessary at GM discretion.

LIBRARY (J)

Shelves stacked nearly 20 ft. high and stretching to the ceiling are stocked with books on nearly any subject, and this room features cozy spots in which to research and record one's findings. The doors within this space lead deeper into the castle and the stairs in the corner can lead up or down, at GM discretion.

DINING HALL (K)

Though meals can be arranged in the Great Hall or for a smaller group within the kitchen, this room is utilized for day-to-day meals and features enough seating for several members of court or castle staff, as well as a dais from which the master of the house can look out upon their guests while dining. The doors within this space lead deeper into the castle and the stairs in the corner can lead up or down, at GM discretion.

ENCOUNTER VARIANT (OPTIONAL) CASTLE FURNISHINGS

Though many noble estates shine with wealth from every corner, circumstances can change for any highborn family. Roll on the table below to determine the visual aesthetics associated with this castle once the party arrives.

1d6	The castle is...
1	**...falling apart.** The slow decay of time paired with a lack of upkeep on the part of the residents here has left a once imposing and impressive castle full of rubble with collapsing walls, damaged tapestries and rotting floors. At GM discretion, roll 1d6 each time a member of the party enters a new room in this castle. On a 1, have them make a DC 15 Dexterity saving throw or fall through the floorboards to a room below as the beams supporting them snap under stress.
2	**...haunted.** Every room in this castle has a chance of being inhabited by a **ghost or ghoul**. Each time the party enters a new room, roll 1d6. On a 1, 1d4 ghosts or ghouls appear in this space, and are friendly or nefarious at GM discretion.
3	**...frozen.** Whether through some curse or overexposure to the elements in a particularly chilly climate, every room in this castle is covered in ice. The floor is difficult terrain, and anyone attempting to dash must succeed on a DC 15 Dexterity check to avoid falling prone as they slip and fall. Heat (from a flame or other magical effect) can melt the ice here but after 2d6 minutes it begins to refreeze.
4	**...opulent.** This castle might be the fanciest any in the party have ever had the pleasure of walking within. Even the servants' quarters are gilded and feature subtle, artistic flourishes. Tapestries and mosaics and other fine artwork hang on every wall. The guard and other staff in this castle are similarly appointed.
5	**...dark.** There seems to be a purposeful effort to keep out the light in this entire castle, perhaps because its leader does not want to be seen, is frustrated by the sun or simply feels more at home when shrouded in darkness. Those without darkvision will need a torch to navigate this castle, as entering it is similar to walking within the tunnels of a pitch black cave.
6	**...under construction.** Whether there's been a recent change in ownership, a strong desire for a remodel or a significant amount of damage that must be repaired, the signs of a concerted effort to update or rebuild the rooms, hallways or even foundations of this castle are apparent throughout—and 10d4 members of a guild responsible for this sort of work are an ever present sight.

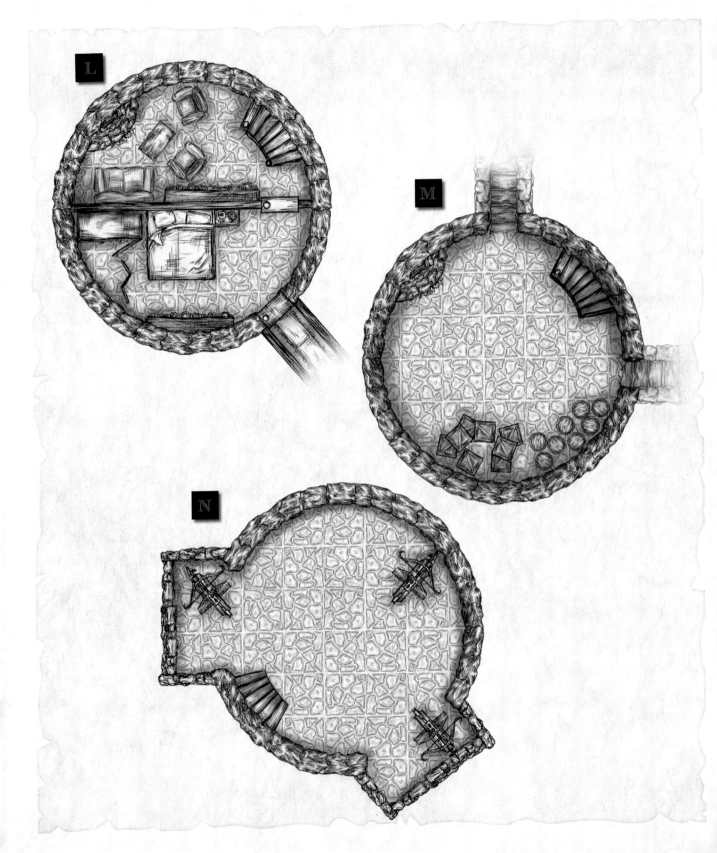

SPACE TO EXPLORE

Most homes of this size have rooms that are rarely seen, to say nothing of whether or not they get any use. When visitors arrive, however, there is often an urge to show them around the grounds and show off the comforts and luxuries that wealth or status allows.

A GUEST BEDROOM AND STUDY (L)

A space intended to host visitors for longer stays, this room features a small sitting room as well as a large bedroom with access to other halls and rooms in the castle, plus one of the lumpier beds anyone has ever had the displeasure to sleep on. The stairs in the sitting room can lead up or down at GM discretion.

A SUPPLY ROOM (M)

With so many comings and goings on the property it's natural to accrue more than you need and to prepare for those times when less is available. This storage space features ample room for amassing supplies to ride out a long winter, a hate-fueled uprising, a celebration or other event requiring large portions of necessary staples. The boxes and barrels within this space feature items relevant to the ongoing adventure, at GM discretion.

TOWER ARMORY (N)

While security of the keep is in many ways the responsibility of those keeping watch along the walls, this armory offers a strong strategic position from within one of the spires, with long range ballistas that can deal a significant amount of damage should an army begin a march on the walls or a dragon swoop in to bring death and ruin from above. The ballistas have a range of 200/600 ft. and deal 4d10 piercing damage. They have +8 to hit, and require two actions to fire: one to aim and one to trigger.

ENCOUNTER VARIANT (OPTIONAL)
EXTRA ROOMS

Roll 1d20 on the table below to determine the nature of another room in this space as your party begins to explore it. If a room is repeated, roll again on the table or let it stand—many homes of this size feature multiple kitchens, bedrooms, studies and more. Because who wants to walk?

1d20	This room is...
1	...a gymnasium with a fencing circle.
2	...a greenhouse with a massive tree inside.
3	...an observatory with a large telescope.
4	...an indoor lap pool.
5	...an archery range.
6	...an alchemist's laboratory.
7	...a doctor's quarters for observing ill patients.
8	...a launch pad for a small dirigible airship.
9	...a torture chamber.
10	...a ballroom with a stage for an orchestra.
11	...a hall with statuary lining both sides.
12	...a small chapel.
13	...a smith's forge.
14	...filled with portals, each leading to another realm at DM discretion.
15	...a teleportation circle.
16	...a bedroom with a very strong necrotic scent coming from beneath one of the floorboards.
17	...a walk-in closet, but the size of a great room.
18	...an aviary, featuring messenger birds and several hooded falcons.
19	...a distillery for making spirits.
20	...a nursery, complete with 2d4 babbling babies.

RANDOMIZED TABLES

FEATURING MORE VARIANTS THAN A MIN/MAX BLOG...

RANDOM NPC GENERATOR

FOR WHEN YOUR PARTY NEEDS A PERSON, PRONTO.

These roll tables are meant to serve as a guide for creating intriguing and memorable characters on the fly. You can use them to flesh out an NPC you've already developed, or to breathe life and some stakes into a standardized shopkeeper or tavern owner. These characters should use commoner stats at GM discretion. Once you've combined the elements from each table you'll have a name, a basic description as well as motivations and possible secrets or pitfalls they might bring to the table as they interact with your players. Most of the entries are somewhat vague, but have a specificity that will start to clarify itself once paired up with other table entries. As an example, the description below was created using some of the tables provided.

A male half-elf with flowing blond hair, a tall and thin build, a wide smile and a fashionable mole who hasn't slept in eight days and is in too deep with a local crime boss.

This character (let's call him Mandalf) is likely losing sleep because he is having trouble with the local crime boss. But that doesn't mean you couldn't be inspired by other details in the context of the description. Perhaps that large mole on Mandalf's face is keeping him up at night, whispering dark words and corrupting his thoughts. It's possible the reason Mandalf is growing out his hair is to sell it to the local crime boss. Or maybe Mandalf is super slim because he isn't getting any sleep—maybe he's just really stressed? Is he stressed about the crime boss? Or his mole? These aren't questions these tables will answer. But hopefully they are worth exploring at your table as you bring each new creation to life.

If you roll a different character and find through the magic of dice rolls that they are eerily similar to another NPC your party has encountered, try rolling one or two details again to break things up. Things would change quite a bit for Mandalf if instead of having a tall and thin build and crime boss troubles he was instead described as follows:

A male half-elf with flowing blond hair, a tall and ripped build, a wide smile and fashionable mole, who hasn't slept in eight days and is also a lycanthrope.

In this scenario it's likely the reason Mandalf hasn't been sleeping is because he's been howling at the moon. Though it could still be the evil mole. The choice is yours.

Finally, there are trillions of possible permutations using the following tables in tandem with one another, so if any of the characters generated using these tables resemble real-life individuals take it as a testament to the fact that there are billions of people in the real world (as opposed to a signal that I have been following you around taking notes on your family and friends).

RACE

Depending on your campaign setting you may determine that non-human or non-dwarven or non-dragonborn races are incredibly rare. If something like the above situation is true for your world, feel free to augment the roll generated by the table below to bring it in line with your adventure setting.

1d10	This character is...
1	...a dwarf.
2	...a halfling.
3	...a dragonborn.
4	...a human.
5	...a half-elf.
6	...a tiefling.
7	...a half-orc.
8	...an elf.
9	...a monstrous race.
10	Roll again

PREFERRED PRONOUNS (OPTIONAL)

Most people in your world are likely to ascribe to a common gender binary, but that shouldn't stop you from mixing it up and bringing diversity to your lands by rolling on the table below. After all, gender is a social construct. It can inform and be a vital part of a person's identity or be non-consequential relative to how they conduct themselves. This statement is also applicable to a character's sexuality, for which there is no roll table (maybe it comes up, maybe it doesn't). The Preferred Pronouns table is meant to guide you in creating realistic and unique NPCs. As always, your world is as diverse as you wish to make it.

1d6	This character uses...
1	she/her/hers
2	he/him/his
3	they/them/theirs
4	she/her/hers (transgender)
5	he/him/his (transgender)
6	no pronouns, only a name

AGE AND INTELLIGENCE (OPTIONAL)

In general, most of the characters your party is likely to encounter will be middle-aged and of average intelligence. But that shouldn't stop you from rolling 2d6s to fill the realm with whip-smart 9-year-old barkeeps.

1d6	Age
1	A child
2	A teen
3	A young adult
4	An adult
5	Elderly
6	Extremely old

1d6	Intelligence
1	Dumb as dirt
2	Average, which ain't great
3	Street smart, not book smart
4	Book smart, not street smart
5	Book and street smart
6	Smarter than everyone

HAIR AND BUILD

Roll a couple dice to determine this NPC's hairstyle and build, relative to the character's overall appearance. NOTE: If the race you've randomly rolled would lack hair, feel free to skip this table or push ahead and consider it a compelling part of their backstory by asking questions such as "Why is this dragonborn a towhead?"

1d12	Hair
1	Short dark/black hair
2	Short blond(e)/white hair
3	Short red hair
4	Shoulder-length dark/black hair
5	Shoulder-length blond(e) hair
6	Shoulder-length red hair
7	Flowing blond(e)/white hair
8	Flowing dark/black hair
9	Flowing red hair
10	Colorful hair (green/purple/blue/etc), with length at GM discretion
11	Bald
12	Wigged (roll again for description)

1d10	Build
1	Tall and lean
2	Tall and ripped
3	Tall and rotund
4	Medium height and build
5	Medium height and slim
6	Medium height and out of shape
7	Short and thin
8	Short and sturdy
9	Short and stout
10	Sickly (roll again for build)

WHO IS THIS PERSON, REALLY?

At the end of the day, as complex as all of us are, most of the things that define who we are to other people are pretty straightforward: "He's my boss and he needs me to raise money for his charity."; "She's my ex-landlord and she's invited me to come to her open mic."; "He's my sister's best friend and I'm pretty sure he wants to harvest my organs." NPCs in your fantasy world are no different. The next few pages of tables are meant to help you establish a few defining characteristics for random NPCs your party might encounter. For those times when you're in a pinch and need a name and description in a flash, you can go the fast route and roll 1d100 to establish one line of information across all the columns on this table. Alternatively, for a more unpredictable experience, roll 6d100 for a completely randomized character, using the appropriate line per column based on your rolls. As always, feel free to augment elements of the result so they feel more organic to the world you've created, or lean into the chaos and see where it leads your party. After all, that's why you roll the dice...

NAMES, DESCRIPTIONS AND DEEPER DESIRES

Roll 1d100 or 6d100 at GM discretion to define a character's first and last name, a brief description, their wants and needs, a secret they carry or obstacle in the way of their success as well as the items on their person.

1d100	First Name	Last Name	Brief Description	Wants and Needs	Secret or Obstacle	Also Carrying
1	Aer	Merigu	...with shaggy hair and a slight overbite...	...who could really use a hug...	...and has sticky fingers.	2 gp, 5 sp, 14 cp. Beltknife, scythe, bundle of wheat.
2	Ali	Mishala	...with deep-set eyes and an upturned nose...	...who could use a bath...	...and is an utter coward.	Empty money pouch. A silver brooch in the shape of a rabbit.
3	Archer	Mogumir	...with a wide smile and a fashionable mole...	...who literally and figuratively has no sense of direction...	...and doesn't speak Common.	1 sp, 8 cp. Small bag of butterfly wings. Pouch of herbs and a pipe.
4	Azar	Neriyra	...with a steady gaze and pursed lips...	...who is begging for help to find their **gnoll**-nabbed dad...	...and is tracking the party's movements for the spy's guild.	1 gp, 15 cp. A novel titled *Through the Weave*. One packet of beans.
5	Brook	Nialinva	...with a deep facial scar and a gruff exterior...	...who is compelled to smell everyone they meet...	...and cannot walk on their own.	Nothing, and proud of it.
6	Briar	Neeves	...with a pug nose and lots of freckles...	...who just needs a ride into/out of town...	...and is plagued by a Curse (on pg. 136).	2 sp, 17 cp. A wooden cup they carved themselves.
7	Balin	Noosecatcher	...with a round face and rosy cheeks...	...who thinks they're possessed by a vengeful warrior...	...and has lost the will to live.	73 cp painted to look like 73 pp. A small jar of platinum paint.
8	Berieve	Oakfury	...with a few hairs springing out of a wart on their face...	...who needs a cure for their incessant hiccups...	...and can't control the volume of their voice.	32 cp, 13 sp. A hoop and stick.
9	Carmen	Ootati	...with a heavy limp and a can-do attitude...	...who has developed a taste for human flesh...	...and is in deep with a local crime boss.	15 sp. A necklace that contains a ball of yak hair.
10	Chidi	Oldfur	...with a kind face and a slow drawl...	...who is just trying to get through the day, man...	...and is never wrong. Just ask them.	21 cp, 2 sp, 3 gp. An incredibly smooth rock they enjoy thumbing.
11	Chardane	Orgulas	...with shifting eyes and a hushed voice...	...who knows of a nearby cave filled with treasure...	...and is always in a hurry.	3 sp, 8 gp. A jar full of beef tallow. A crude map of the region.
12	Cyrille	Polaan	...with a few missing teeth and a hungry gaze...	...who hasn't slept in eight days...	...and gets distracted easily.	5 cp, 9 sp, 1 gp. A vial of wyvern poison.
13	Dane	Plackard	...with a massive nose and a tight mouth...	...who hasn't been sober in two weeks...	...and is addicted to a local drug.	4 cp, 16 sp. An oversized lollipop. A deck of cards.
14	Desta	Puddleswish	...with hooded eyes and a casual tone...	...who will do pretty much anything for a silver piece...	...and doesn't believe in violence.	6 cp, 8 sp, 12 gp. Loaded dice. A directory of local gambling halls.

1d100	First Name	Last Name	Brief Description	Wants and Needs	Secret or Obstacle	Also Carrying
15	Devon	Poutine	...with wild hair and a sweating brow...	...who repeats the full names of everyone they meet...	...and distrusts at least one party member.	9 cp, 2 sp. Knitting needles and half-finished scarf.
16	Dian	Questar	...with oily skin and whistling nostrils...	...who can't stop talking about the end of the world...	...and is also a **lycanthrope**.	7 cp. A large leather hat. A set of thieves' tools.
17	Eidar	Q'Tharas	...with large ears and an oval face...	...who is constantly on the lookout for grooming tips...	...and is allergic to something nearby.	6 sp, 1 gp. A cup and ball game. A trout in butcher paper.
18	Eli	Quid	...with a strong jaw and a hearty laugh...	...who compulsively says what they are thinking...	...and is comically hot-tempered.	4 cp, 3 sp, 1 gp. A book about blacksmithing.
19	Erin	Reebsa	...with a slack jaw and a tendency to mouth breathe...	...who wants to do right by their god, no matter the cost...	...and is plagued with a small bladder.	85 cp. A note that says, "Be careful, I love you. -Mum"
20	Evrim	Reyhana	...with a gap-toothed grin and gray eyes...	...who is attracted to a member of the party...	...and has terrible judgment.	64 sp. 12 gp in loose gems. A rockhammer.
21	Fabian	Rivershale	...with a pot belly and an infectious giggle...	...whose brother was wrongfully accused...	...and is a **satyr** in disguise.	14 cp, 17 sp, 4 gp. A magnifying glass.
22	Farah	Rosenmer	...with a blank expression and wild ear hair...	...who thinks they have a rat infestation...	...and seeks the perfect whiskey recipe.	10 sp. Brewer's kit and waterskin of whiskey.
23	Flynn	Sarberos	...with a face full of piercings...	...who keeps hearing voices in their head...	...and is afraid of the dark.	32 cp. A collection of dolls that look like the party.
24	Fatima	Shatterblade	...with more tattoos than uninked skin...	...who can't find their horse...	...and is a stranded planar traveler.	A whistle only a badger named Jenny can hear.
25	Gabi	Sindasalt	...with buns of steel and armor to match...	...who needs a set of blacksmith's tools...	...and is self-obsessed.	5 cp, 30 sp, 9 gp. A very small hat.
26	Grey	Srob	...with scabby knuckles they won't stop cracking...	...who lost their mother's wedding band...	...and struggles with their dad's expectations.	19 cp, 2 sp. A spyglass that can suck out an eyeball on command.
27	"Gums"	Thanar	...with a sick pompadour haircut...	...who needs to be the center of attention...	...and doesn't have teeth.	14 cp, 92 sp. An error-filled map of the realm.
28	Goose	Thermobolt	...wearing the corset of a slimmer person...	...who needs help with a dance-off...	...and insults those in charge.	A cursed pen knife (roll on the Curse table on pg. 136).
29	Hadley	Therundlin	...with a slack face on one side impeding their speech...	...who had a dream where they saw the party die...	...and a mind that's beginning to unravel.	32 cp. 7 sp. 3 gp. A pair of shoes in need of resoling.

30	Helle	Tighfield	...with a tongue seemingly too big for their mouth...	...who needs a rare coin to complete their collection...	...and is hopeless at negotiation.	8 cp. An IOU that reads "Owe you three sacks of wool. Hamm."
31	Hisoka	Underbough	...with a posh attitude and clothes to match...	...who loves to talk about food...	...and is afraid of bats.	94 cp, 1 gp. A mask that hides their face and a hit list of local thugs.
32	Hunter	Ugdough	...with a dour expression...	...who owns the town paper...	...and is a part-time cult leader.	7 cp, 8 sp, 2 gp. A dark artifact.
33	Imani	Us	...with the biggest head of all time...	...who wants to be left alone...	...and gets nervous near new people.	34 cp, 10 sp. A broken lute. A crumpled love letter.
34	Indiana	Valarnith	...with broad shoulders and a low-cut tunic...	...who is worried they might have unleashed a curse...	...and needs locks of hair from everyone.	3 cp, 5 sp, 7 gp. A sack of dates. A pound of dried apricots. A fishing pole.
35	Irati	Venderform	...with a hunched back and sores...	...who needs human contact...	...and despises being touched.	4 cp, 6 sp. A set of wooden teeth.
36	Ike	Volto	...with friendly eyes and the grace of a dancer...	...who says their family has been possessed...	...and runs a multi-level-marketing scam.	7 cp, 92 sp. A bottle of baby tears they want to sell.
37	Jaden	Vainweather	...devoid of eyebrows and a sense of humor...	...who just wants to own their own pastry shop...	...is definitely a fiend, but is making it work.	9 cp, 53 sp, 900 gp. A dark leather tome titled *How to Act Human*.
38	Jamal	Wapronk	...with a soot-covered face...	...who needs a place to hide...	...and can't read.	5 cp, 5 sp, 5 gp. Five rings worth 55 gp.
39	Joprani	Wolfsbane	...with a dent in their skull that's healed over...	...who is looking for the witch of the woods...	...and is bad luck to everyone within 30 feet.	3 cp, 81 sp. Joiner's tools. A blood-soaked rag.
40	Jack	Woolyboon	...in a purple tunic, ascot and patent leather boots...	...who is trapped in the friend zone...	...and is possessed by a low level devil.	32 cp, 5 sp, 1 pp. A crust of moldy bread. Some salt pork.
41	Kaari	Wheelmaiden	...covered in black tar and white feathers...	...who is saving to start a restaurant...	...and has a gambling problem.	45 cp, 2 sp. An undead hand that is very important to them.
42	Kyra	Xas	...with a broken arrow stuck in the side of their head...	...who wants this up-tight town to legalize dancing...	...and has a problem with somnambulism.	61 cp, 3 sp. A forger's kit. A list of noble's names.
43	Kagiso	Xeran	...with black eyes that lack irises...	...who suspects their house is haunted...	...and can't re-member their name.	92 cp, 3 gp. Cufflinks that conceal two doses of *Drow poison*.
44	Kalin	Xencord	...face buried in a book about geese...	...who wants to clean up a pond....	...and is a goose that was *true polymorphed*.	52 sp. A sack of fingernails, each more precious than the next.
45	Lin	Yesvyre	...holding a tiny dog and fighting back tears...	...who says their sister has been turned into a dog...	...and lies for fun.	89 cp, 3 sp. A belt buckle with a hidden lock-pick.

1d100	First Name	Last Name	Brief Description	Wants and Needs	Secret or Obstacle	Also Carrying
46	Lucian	Yahsquin	...humming to themselves and scratching flaky skin...	...who wants to know if you've seen a man named Reb...	...and is a member of the Assassins' Guild.	62 cp, 32 sp. A diamond that appears to be worth 500 gp. It's not.
47	Lumi	Yeoman	...with a narrow face and fine, almost too perfect features...	...who has a standup performance tonight...	...and hasn't paid their tab in six months.	25 cp, 6 sp, 24 gp. A spork, the first of its kind.
48	Lloyal	Yearender	...with a bruised eye and a busted lip...	...who needs some help dealing with local bullies...	...and has never made a true friend.	6 cp, 2 gp. A sandwich made of nut butter and smashed jam.
49	Maayan	Zeagan	...with a lumpy nose that looks a bit infected...	...who wants the party to protect them...	...and is on the run for tax evasion.	21 cp, 5 sp. An exquisite dagger carved from the bones of a dragonborn.
50	Makota	Zimet	...with a beehive hairdo that makes them seem taller...	...who needs an invitation to tonight's ball...	...and is a long lost member of the royal family.	4 cp, 74 sp. A wineskin filled with a *potion of haste*.
51	Miska	Zytal	...has a neck twice as wide as their face...	...who is looking to cure a contagious disease...	...and is struggling to get over the flu.	8 cp, 53 sp. A fake beard. A tome filled with gift ideas for hundreds of children.
52	Moriah	Aberrich	...has a face that appears stitched together...	...who is searching for the power of a *wish* spell...	...and is a runaway **zombie**.	91 sp. A recipe for pot pie. A small sack of peas. Spices.
53	Nesim	Aefrim	...looks like they're about to vomit...	...who has been challenged to a rap battle...	...and owns a treasure map to a secret island.	3 cp, 14 sp. A jar of honey. A box containing a large queen bee.
54	Nico	Altas	...is dripping in sweat...	...who just inherited an orphanage...	...and hates children.	7 cp, 13 sp. A *gate* spell scroll.
55	Nyx	Avilseer	...is expertly juggling a trio of daggers...	...who is raising money for wizard school...	...and is the very definition of chaotic evil.	A pocket-sized copy of the realm's founding documents.
56	Noose	Baelmai	...has a drippy nose and red cheeks...	...who can't find their glasses...	...and is afraid of spellcasters.	A frog. Roll 1d6. On a 1, it was once a prince.
57	Ori	Bingletrite	...is wearing clothes that are three sizes too big...	...who is on the hunt for a **red dragon** egg in the area...	...and is working against the party's interests.	31 cp. A rudimentary coloring book. Some colored wax pieces.
58	Olley	Blackreed	...looks twice their age...	...needs to catch six fish...	...and lacks common sense.	4 cp, 3 sp, 2 gp. A set of woodworker's tools.
59	Ophilia	Bronzestein	...with a pretty face and big ideas...	...who needs everyone to wise up...	...and is being blackmailed.	8 sp. A minor gem worth 1 gp.
60	Oban	Carter	...wearing goggles and chomping a smoldering cigar...	...who needs to acquire a rare **ochre jelly**...	...and feels like an extra in someone else's story.	5 gp. A +1 scimitar engraved with the name "Trevor."
61	Piper	Claymore	...with the energy of an overstimulated child...	...who believes their friend might be a **hag**...	...and is wearing a *hag's eye* from a nearby coven.	42 sp. A tub of grease. A *wand of webs*.

62	Poe	Cogturner	...with bangs that everyone agrees do not suit their face...	...who is looking for models for a fashion show...	...and is five months behind on all their bills.	55 gp. A vial of de-aging serum that takes 20 years off a creature's life.
63	Pal	Crysalis	...nervously chewing their upper lip...	...who wants to join the circus...	...and can only tell the truth.	8 sp, 4 gp. A top hat concealing a dozen squirrels.
64	Perrin	Datesi	...blind, but making it work...	...who needs enough incense to bring back their familiar...	...and is immortal.	3 sp. A bottle of milk. An ornate quarterstaff.
65	Quinn	Darksteele	...still sporting the scars from a rogue **owlbear** attack...	...who is looking for some drinking buddies...	...and won't take no for an answer.	An unopened letter challenging them to a duel with a merchant.
66	Quora	Deepstone	...has one of those faces...	...who can't unlock their basement...	...and uses a puppet to talk.	15 cp. A jar capable of storing memories.
67	Quinene	Dwandra	...with a chin that could block out the sun...	...who refuses to bathe and talks to any stray dogs...	...and has a habit of losing their false teeth.	8 cp. A vial labeled "DO NOT OPEN" that contains the expelled gas of a king.
68	Rayyan	Eeaves	...with a whisper-quiet voice...	...looking for the Dream Archive (pg. 24)...	...and can read minds via touch.	90 sp. A liniment that helps with insomnia.
69	Ren	Excellente	...with a cute smile and belt of knives...	...who seeks to kill the town guard who killed their dad...	...and may have made a pact with a demon.	13 cp. Directions to a guard's house. A box of juice.
70	Roux	Emo	...wearing far too many belts and silver jewelry...	...who would rather be listening to heavy lute tunes...	...and is way more apathetic than you.	Sheet music from a bard you've never heard of. A -1 Charisma pinky ring.
71	Rowan	E'tellor	...with the biggest, bushiest beard...	...who wants to learn to fight...	...and is missing their tongue.	13 pp. A jar of beard oil that is also flammable.
72	Samar	Faemoira	...is blessed with lavish curves...	...who enjoys harmless flirting...	...and fears commitment.	29 sp. A small painting of an elven girl.
73	Siya	Firsel	...is a scythe-wielding farmer...	...who spreads propaganda against shapechangers...	...and assumes everyone they meet is a shifter.	35 cp. A colorful piece of chewing taffy that never loses its flavor.
74	Skye	Flintheart	...with armor that shines like the sun...	...en route to the Hall of Many Gods (pg. 50)...	...and is devoid of confidence.	A list of several gods, with at least nine crossed out.
75	Slaine	Frostarm	...with an almost hypnotic voice and air of importance ...	...who needs investors for their pyramid scheme...	...and is a compulsive liar.	14 vials of a potion that smells great but does nothing.
76	Tal	Geasfoot	...who looks like they just woke up...	...who can't find their watch...	...and is never on time.	A watch chain. A pair of fancy hair combs.
77	Tierney	Gigak	...in a tight-fitting, red-scaled jacket...	...who is trying to sell a dragon heart...	...and is particularly awkward.	A note with the location of a dragon's lair.

1d100	First Name	Last Name	Brief Description	Wants and Needs	Secret or Obstacle	Also Carrying
78	Toiv	Gnazbright	...wearing temple robes and a surprised expression...	...who wants to spread the word about their god...	...and is afraid of heights. And depths.	30 sp. A pair of bi-lensed readers. A sack of candies.
79	Tumelo	Goldcask	...with greasy hair and hands to match...	...who is trying to write a love ballad...	...and speaks with wild gestures.	A mourning ring featuring the eye of their mother.
80	Umber	Huneldth	...with a hard, weathered face...	...searching for redemption...	...and once ruled this land.	1 cp, 1 sp, 1 gp, 1 pp. A **deck of many things**.
81	Umut	Hutchrice	...walks with the grace of a dancer...	...who wants to see the next sunrise...	...and is a newly made **vampire**.	390 gp. A sack of grave dirt. A spade. A beret.
82	Urg	Hoover	...wearing a crop top to show off their impressive abs...	...who longs to be the strongest person alive...	...and has crippling arthritis.	42 cp, 71 sp. 3 vials of a tonic that adds +2 to Strength for 1 hour.
83	Val	Honeyeater	...in black leather and a pair of sharp, heeled boots...	...hired to kill a party member...	...and now has cold feet.	62 cp, 21 sp, 92 gp. A gag and hood. 2 vials of *purple worm poison*.
84	Vanja	Iasbex	...has a permanent squint and a stiff upper lip...	...who compulsively judges others' fashion sense...	...and won't listen to human opinions.	3 cp, 9 sp, 21 gp. An opal carved in the shape of a jawbone.
85	Vivian	Igrild	...who appears as if they were struck by lightning...	...who is trying to build a time machine...	...and is absolutely from the future.	5 cp. A sports almanac.
86	Varek	Illynmah	...with a smile that's all teeth and no joy...	...who is on a quest to kill monsters...	...and serves a talking cow.	92 sp. **Manticore** bait. A **griffon** call. Sacks of meat.
87	Wanda	Importan	...with flashy pink hair...	...who is trying to do good...	...and was, until today, a shut-in.	A 20% off coupon for Mage You Look (pg. 34).
88	West	Jarvalsa	...with a smell that is off-putting...	...who is trying to sell some fruit...	...and thinks humans are useless.	18 cp, 4 sp. A stuffed tiger. A tuna sandwich.
89	Weezy	Jaytai	...has bloody, nail-free fingertips...	...who is on the run from a prison...	...and is also a **deva**.	3 cp. A speckled egg. A broken music box.
90	Wooster	Jeffries	...in a droopy robe...	...who needs the blood of 30 crows...	...and is a magic school dropout.	92 gp. A small heart in a smaller cage.
91	Xen	Justice	...in a hat that's as tall as they are...	...who wants to learn Common...	...and is a warlock of The Great Old One.	3 gp. A bag of salt. A bag of pepper. A bag of octopus tentacles.
92	Xuan	Kavius	...with no arms, but two mage hands...	...who wants to go on an adventure...	...and is a total yes-man.	A lyre that's missing all but one string.
93	X'ian	Keystina	...with bare feet and freckled cheeks...	...who is peddling bags of a medicinal root...	...and is a happy-go-lucky necromancer.	A glass orb. A raven's beak. A vial of tiger blood.

94	Yael	Khilltahrn	...dressed in a patch-work coat of dozens of fabrics...	...who needs to spread their father's ashes...	...and is a budding songwriter.	5 cp. A lump of coal. A small box filled with ashes.
95	Yagmur	Koahath	...with one leg, and a hangman's scar on their neck...	...who is hoping to run for public office...	...and was an escaped convict in their youth.	52 sp. An herbalist's kit. A neatly folded poster with their face on it.
96	Yannik	Leagallow	...is deaf and uses gestures to communicate...	...who seeks a new owner for their pet owl...	...and is possessed by the spirit of a god.	5,256 gp. A notebook listing all the things they've done this year.
97	Yuck	Lillyfitz	...has shaggy hair, baggy clothes and a chill attitude...	...who is looking for their dog. Have you seen their dog?...	...and owns a dog that can speak Common.	13 sp, 2 gp. A few gnarled balls of thick cord and cloth.
98	Zein	Lukewill	...has cheekbones that could cut glass and eyes to match...	...who doesn't let anyone get in their way...	...and runs an illegal fighting ring nearby.	81 cp, 3 sp. A list of rules for something called "Brawl Joint."
99	Zeke	Luckdodger	...wearing a hood that covers their gaunt face...	...who is hunting for ancient relics in old forgotten tombs...	...and is an absolute killjoy.	Ink that disappears but can be revealed with a little heat.
100	Zaya	Mavcius	...with a handsome face and sure, kind smile...	...who is looking for inspiration for their new novel...	...and once looked completely different.	A 32-page booklet of so-called "haters"—a few names are crossed out.

RANDOM TAVERN GENERATOR

BECAUSE YOUR PARTY LIKES TO PARTY, ROLL 2D100—ONCE FOR EACH
COLUMN OF THE TABLE BELOW—AND COMBINE THE TWO RESULTS TOGETHER
FOR A SINGULAR NAME SUITABLE FOR A PUB, PARLOR ROOM OR PINT PALACE.
THEN ROLL ON THE VIBE VARIANTS TABLES FOR A LOOK AND FEEL.

1d100	Name 1	Name 2
1	Lively	Flagon
2	Scratchy	Rogue
3	Knobby	Dragon
4	Ruddy	Hag
5	Merry	Pony
6	Sticky	Troll
7	Abandoned	Drunk
8	Courageous	Pint
9	Itchy	Basin
10	Aching	Traveler
11	Handsome	Giant
12	Ornery	Boar
13	Bountiful	Flask
14	Filthy	Drow
15	Quaint	Fairy
16	Drafty	Sow
17	Lanky	Dretch
18	Nasty	Boot
19	Shiny	Serpent
20	Crowded	Lion
21	Reckless	Balor
22	Gleaming	King
23	Winged	Tiefling
24	Jagged	Cauldron
25	Cozy	Goat
26	Harmless	Bard
27	Nifty	Bottle
28	Eager	Pub
29	Pitiful	Shot
30	Deserted	Knight
31	Frosty	Miner

1d100	Name 1	Name 2
32	Soggy	Inn
33	Magnificent	Earl
34	Regal	Duck
35	Rough	Mug
36	Meager	Crevice
37	Embellished	Dagger
38	Proud	Horse
39	Intrepid	Sailor
40	Shoddy	Elf
41	Fair	Chameleon
42	Loud	Nymph
43	Bare	Hall
44	Mysterious	Wench
45	Jaunty	Dump
46	Muddy	Castle
47	Hospitable	Helm
48	Livid	Fox
49	Golden	Throne
50	Salty	Dwarf
51	Knowing	Wyvern
52	Lavish	Haven
53	Silver	Talon
54	Charming	Bar
55	Hairy	Wand
56	Bleak	Den
57	Feisty	House
58	Smoggy	Bear
59	Opulent	Lantern
60	Peaceful	Demon
61	Immaculate	Blade
62	Sleepy	Eunuch
63	Limping	Axe

Tavern Vibe Variants

Every alehouse or wine wasteland has its own energy—whether it's a divey haunt with a few grizzled regulars or a familiar franchise that's somehow the same in every town—and that energy is part of what keeps customers coming back for another round or backing out of the doorway slowly the moment they arrive. Because pubs and lounges are commonly populated with a wide range of patrons from across different walks of life, they are often defined as much by their clientele as their aesthetics.

Roll 1d4 and 1d20 on the tables below to determine the general feel for a bar, beer hall or back alley brew shed.

64	Everlasting	Wagon
65	Wild	Palace
66	Ironclad	Brewery
67	Growling	Minotaur
68	Stale	Wanderer
69	Jovial	Lord
70	Wise	Hideaway
71	Gullible	Cudgel
72	Ample	Tower
73	Rich	Minstrel
74	Cautious	Barrel
75	Wonderful	Tankard
76	Hungry	Bow
77	Wooden	Hearth
78	Yawning	Toad
79	Heavenly	Lodge
80	Rosy	Room
81	Bewitched	Bucket
82	Spirited	Damsel
83	Buzzing	Willow
84	Tasty	Unicorn
85	Snarling	Head
86	Enchanted	Crow
87	Clever	Mead House
88	Pleasant	Cat
89	Deadly	Arrow
90	Tricky	Parlor
91	Treasured	Swamp
92	Antique	Boil
93	Poor	Fool
94	Glorious	Louse
95	Blushing	Hat
96	Ultimate	Cavern
97	Vacant	Winery
98	Dull	Place
99	Weary	Griffin
100	Fickle	Sword

1d4	This place is...
1	...deserted, save for a bartender and one regular...
2	...packed with friendly locals and a few drunk travelers...
3	...oddly quiet, given the number of customers inside...
4	...full of angry, rowdy guests who have all been over-served...

1d20	
1	...with sawdust on the floor and dust in the rafters.
2	...with a wait time of 20 minutes per drink.
3	...and hosting a sing-along night with one of the region's least popular bards.
4	...and featuring a brand ambassador for a new mead.
5	...and hiding an illegal gambling hall through the cellar.
6	...with velvet-lined walls, a dress code and an undeserved air of importance.
7	...with ornamental trophies from beasts and monsters hanging on the walls.
8	...and has no furnishings—only pillows.
9	...and is less of a bar and more of a dance hall, with music so loud it's tough to hear anything else.
10	...with a back patio that's never open.
11	...with an epic collection of classic board games, though most sets are missing a piece or two.
12	...with a large, crater-like hole in the center of the floor that has gone unremarked upon for months.
13	...and is utterly pleasing to the eye, but to those trained in the arcane, is clearly dripping with illusory magic.
14	...and, to those familiar with this sort of thing, clearly has an arrangement with a nearby brothel.
15	...with a tropical theme, with drinks and uniforms to match, and feels like walking through a humid rainforest.
16	...with walls lined with sketches depicting famed adventurers from across the realm enjoying a pint here.
17	...and featuring servers who are enthusiastically invested in their job, wearing several kitschy buttons, and pushily advertising the bar's other locations throughout the realm.
18	...and only serves pitchers.
19	...and has been named best pub in town several times in a row by nobles in the region, a fact its proprietor is quick to remind anyone who enters at least twice.
20	...and features great food at incredible prices, but discriminates against a specific type of customer at GM discretion.

RANDOM CURSE CREATOR

WHETHER BROUGHT ON BY A TREACHEROUS ITEM, A NEFARIOUS SPELL OR A BAD DEAL YOUR GREAT, GREAT GRANDMOTHER MADE TO WIN THE LOTTO, CURSES CAN BE CRIPPLING. ROLL 1D100 BELOW TO FIND OUT WHAT AILS....

1d100	The creature...
1	...must speak in rhyming couplets or take 1d4 +1 psychic damage each time they talk.
2	...believes they are immortal and acts accordingly.
3	...is vulnerable to all damage but feels no pain.
4	...cannot benefit from a long rest if they sleep alone.
5	...is always thirsty.
6	...has carrots where they once had fingers.
7	...can't stop crying.
8	...coughs up 1d4 dragonflies each time they speak.
9	...is allergic to metal and breaks out in leaky sores on contact.
10	...lacks bones and moves as an ooze would.
11	...must use jazz hands when they speak or take 1d6 + 3 psychic damage.
12	...trips and falls flat on their face with every 15 steps they take.
13	...suddenly has rubber-like arms that become twisted and tangled whenever they try to use them.
14	...refuses to be seen without their hat and won't let anyone forget it.
15	...becomes catatonic at the sound of thunder.
16	...finds themselves followed by a hungry stray dog. Another stray will join this growing pack every time the cursed creature takes a long rest.
17	...gets incredibly winded during physical activity and must succeed on a DC 15 Constitution saving throw to avoid passing out.
18	...takes the shape of the world's most notorious criminal.
19	...thinks they are the King on a giant chessboard about to be trapped.
20	...can only eat grass.
21	...can't move their arms or legs.
22	...has an increasingly unignorable hunger for human flesh.
23	...hears cats screaming whenever music is played.
24	...suffers from the delusion they are a time traveler from 300 years in the future.
25	...gains 3d6 pounds per day, rerolling at the end of every long rest.
26	...is compelled to challenge every creature they encounter to a duel.
27	...is suddenly followed by every mouse and rat in the village.
28	...has breath so bad it knocks out anyone who comes within a yard.
29	...weeps blood at the slightest insult.
30	...keeps attracting flies.
31	...can only see the Ethereal Plane.
32	...has their Strength score reduced by half.
33	...has their Dexterity score reduced by half.
34	...has their Constitution score reduced by half.
35	...has their Intelligence score reduced by half.
36	...has their Wisdom score reduced by half.
37	...has their Charisma score reduced by half.
38	...is terrified of water.
39	...has their movement speed reduced by half.
40	...loses 1d4 + 2 hp anytime a creature casts a spell within 60 feet of them.
41	...immediately loses half their max hp.
42	...spreads death wherever they walk, as all plants within a 20-foot radius wither and die in their presence.
43	...smells like last month's fish.
44	...reverts to a childhood state.
45	...loses the ability to learn or make new memories.
46	...must kill a creature with their bare hands every 1d4 days or suffer 50 points of necrotic damage.
47	...has double vision (and disadvantage on all attack rolls and ability checks).
48	...is disgusted by gold.
49	...loses the ability to lie or even omit elements of the truth.

50	...cannot sleep and cannot benefit from a long rest.
51	...loses hp equal to any damage they deal to another creature.
52	...ages 1d10 years each time they take a long rest.
53	...loses 3d6 pounds each time they eat.
54	...glows in the dark, with their light reaching 120 feet.
55	...can only use a total of 20 words per day.
56	...transforms into an overripe watermelon with blindsense. The creature maintains its mental statistics and can communicate telepathically with creatures within 30 feet of it.
57	...has an overwhelming desire to eat (but an aversion to the taste of) sand.
58	...has incredibly flaky skin that starts painfully sloughing off in strips at the slightest touch.
59	...wakes each morning to find they are half as tall as they were the night before.
60	...can only communicate in song titles.
61	...has one of those head colds that just won't quit.
62	...feels their teeth triple in size and their mouth curve into a giant (and agonizing) grin.
63	...turns purple any time they tell a lie.
64	...must walk/run backward or they'll drop to 0 hp.
65	...always looks sopping wet.
66	...completely loses their sense of direction and has disadvantage on all Wisdom (Survival) checks related to travel.
67	...has a permanent mullet that grows back after every long rest.
68	...is vulnerable to cold damage and cannot stop their teeth from chattering at the slightest drop in temperature.
69	...has an 80 percent chance of being struck by lightning in a storm.
70	...forgets how to do basic math. Numbers are meaningless now.
71	...will be pooped on by a bird at least once a day (regardless of location).
72	...is now horribly allergic to pollen and dust.
73	...gets incredibly seasick to the point of collapse when floating on any type of body of water.
74	...no longer has a reflection.
75	...is effectively blind in dim light or darkness.
76	...must ask for permission to enter any dwelling and is barred from entry by un-dispellable magic if they do not receive it from the dwelling's owner.
77	...is anchored to the Material Plane. They cannot travel to other planes, nor can their soul move on after death.
78	...is compelled to give any stranger they meet a high five. If the stranger leaves them hanging, the creature will high five their own hand.
79	...must fend off their own shadow as it tries to strangle them for 1 minute each night at midnight. The shadow has the same statistics as the creature but the only action it can take is to attempt to strangle its creator.
80	...is terribly frightened of the outdoors. They have disadvantage on Wisdom (Nature) skill checks and any rolls made when outside any urban environment.
81	...is called to the endless expanse of the sky. They must make a Wisdom saving throw (DC 12) any time they are near a large drop and will swan dive off the highest ledge available if they fail.
82	...is vulnerable to fire damage and must make a Wisdom saving throw (DC 12) any time they are near an open flame, becoming frightened on a failed save.
83	...is terrified of gnomes and must succeed on a DC 18 Wisdom saving throw any time they see one, becoming paralyzed on a failed save.
84	...cannot stop yawning in an egregious (and fairly disrespectful) way.
85	...becomes incredibly accident prone.
86	...forgets what they were doing and why once per short rest at GM discretion.
87	...loses the ability to modulate the sound and tone of their voice and must speak in a droning, wall-shaking monotone.
88	...passes a curse to every humanoid they touch. Two days after contact, the humanoid will give birth to a fully formed **quasit**.
89	...starts to sink into the ground or floors beneath them if they don't keep moving.
90	...causes all children under the age of 5 in a 30-foot radius (self) to cry uncontrollably.
91	...hears a loud voice in their head that will offer unwarranted criticism of all their combat and social choices.
92	...can communicate with cats but only cats. All other language is lost to them.
93	...grows a cumbersome beard twice as long as they are tall.
94	...is hoarse and all but inaudible.
95	...feels all their skin and hair shedding off their face, exposing their skull.
96	...believes they are friendless, penniless and aimless.
97	...is under the impression every single person they encounter knows their darkest secrets.
98	...dies painfully but is immediately resurrected, with half as much max hp, at the start of each new day.
99	...refuses to wear clothing no matter what decorum might require.
100	...gains a combination of five curses from this table. Roll again five times.

PARTY MAKEUP MAKER

WITH A FEW DICE ROLLS, YOU'LL THINK YOU'VE BEEN CAMPAIGNING TOGETHER FOR AGES.

R oleplaying isn't just about understanding your own backstory—it's about the connections you make with the other players at your table. This table is meant to help players develop an immediate connection with other members of the party. To use it, roll 1d100 with the player to your left and right at the table, then find the corresponding entry on the table. For extra variance, roll 2d100 and use a different entry for the second column. Every player will then have at least one direct connection to another player.

GM NOTE

These relationships are often intentionally vague, so as to give players more room to expand on them as your game unfolds. That said, those that are specific could directly conflict with characters' backstories—and if that's the case, feel free to roll again. And again and again and again until you find something the duo partnering up can agree on.

1d100	Relationship	Detail
1	Parent and child...	...not on speaking terms.
2	Stepparent and stepchild...	...who don't trust each other.
3	Guild ...	...who are enablers.
4	Childhood sweethearts...	...who keep distracting one another.
5	Co-workers...	...who secretly think the other is useless.
6	Coach and trainee...	...who have a not-so-secret handshake.
7	Sponsor and acolyte on a vision quest...	...who have no sense of direction.
8	Beloved comedy duo...	...who can't stand the sight of each other.
9	Old flames...	...who still have the feels.
10	Partners in crime...	...hiding a dark secret.
11	Study buddies...	...who like to cut corners.
12	Former prison cellmates...	...who created their own language.
13	Siblings...	...who love the same person.
14	Stepsiblings...	...who are relentlessly competitive.
15	Half-siblings...	...who never met their dad.
16	Magician and assistant...	...who refuse to be separated.
17	Benefactor and ward...	...on the lam.
18	Knight and squire...	...on a months-long bender.
19	Mogul and hypeman/woman...	...trying to launch a new product.
20	Twins...	...literally attached at the hip.
21	Landlord and tenant...	...who are trying to outlast one another.
22	Cousins...	...who created a controversial new religion.
23	Bartender and patron...	...hexed to repeat the same conversation once a day.
24	Roommates...	...who can never remember each other's name.
25	Amateur athletes...	...who have a bone-deteriorating curse.
26	Actor and director...	...who have publicly stated their hatred for the arts.
27	Neighbors who've lost their homes...	...and can't find their insurance agent anywhere.
28	Teacher and star pupil...	...who are overconfident and underprepared.
29	Subjects of an arranged marriage...	...who speak to each other through other people.
30	Bounty hunter and quarry...	...who pissed off the wrong people.
31	Performer and stunt double...	...who get mobbed by fans wherever they go.
32	Scientist and subject...	...who just lost their funding.
33	Victims of the same criminal...	...and one is a fraud.
34	Explorer and local guide...	...who are carriers of a deadly virus.
35	Traveling fans of the same bard...	...who are fresh out of narcotics.
36	Amatuer sleuths...	...with insomnia.
37	Honey ambassadors...	...deathly allergic to bees.
38	Captain and former first mate...	...who suffer from seasickness.
39	Ghost hunter and client...	...with a healthy fear of bears.
40	Trainer and trainee...	...who love a good high five.
41	Estranged aunt and nephew/niece...	...who constantly argue about money.
42	Poet and muse...	...who gossip about each other incessantly.

#		
43	Addict and sponsor...	...who won't ride wagons for fear of falling off.
44	Historian and part-time assistant...	...who've stolen a prominent author's book idea.
45	Summer camp counselors...	...who despise children.
46	Temple-mates...	..who have lost their faith.
47	Co-conspirators in a would-be coup...	...who are losing their nerve.
48	Longtime family friends...	...who have made a death pact.
49	An alchemist's assistants...	...who always have snacks on hand.
50	Veteran cop and a rookie...	...who are becoming what they hate.
51	Strangers mistaken for one another...	...who simply love a good showtune.
52	Traveling tome sellers...	...who are both behind on rent.
53	Reluctant acolytes on a mission trip...	...who would rather be carousing and carrying on.
54	Roving restaurant reviewers...	...who have been banned from several establishments throughout the realm.
55	Government inspectors...	...who have misplaced their identification.
56	Merchant and hired security...	...with little respect for authority.
57	Brains and the brawn...	...who love a good prank.
58	Fellow orphans...	...seeking their benefactor.
59	Concerned parents...	...trying to stop a dangerous outbreak.
60	Astronomer and astrologer...	...worried about the same comet.
61	Co-authors of a self-help book...	...who are shameless self-promoters.
62	Forbidden lovers...	...who must impress a noble.
63	Strangers linked by a cursed item...	...who lose control of their faculties once every 1d6 days.
64	Town council members...	...who take pleasure in undercutting each other.
65	Robber barons...	...who are strangely anti-capitalism.
66	Archeologists after the same artifact...	...who don't know they're being followed.
67	Spy and handler...	...who are in deeper than they know.
68	Alumni of the same school...	...who know each others' dark secret.
69	Co-chairs of a carnival planning committee...	...who need 1,000 signatures by next month.
70	Prize winners of the same sweepstakes...	...who harbor resentment over a misunderstanding.
71	Legendary adventurer impersonators...	...who don't believe the rules apply to them.
72	Club owner and bouncer...	...who lack scruples.
73	Gambling buddies...	...who refuse to bathe out of superstition.
74	Reporters on the same beat...	...who have uncovered a vast conspiracy.
75	Freelance gravediggers...	...who've lost a skull of great import.
76	Volunteer firefighters...	...who never met a pun they didn't oversell.
77	Subjects of the same demon...	...who need a way out.
78	Sociologists researching a thesis...	...who are dangerously curious.
79	Refugees of the same calamity...	...who bicker to pass the time.
80	Bandmates...	...who are both certain they are the talented one.
81	Terrible hypnotist and lone success story...	...who are gawked at wherever they go.
82	A noble and a pauper who changed places as a bet...	...who are trying to sell the rights to their story.
83	Animal rights activists...	...who are self-righteous.
84	Strangers who saw one another in a dream...	...and are marching toward their doom.
85	Noble and housecarl...	...who refuse to talk about their scars.
86	Bird watchers seeking a rare warbler...	...who are relentlessly positive.
87	Retiree and replacement...	...who are terribly homesick.
88	Thrillseekers with the same guidebook...	...who get antsy when forced to stand still.
89	Strangers indebted to the same crime lord...	...who love a good bribe.
90	Architect and foreman...	...who accidentally destroyed a whole town.
91	Accused of the same crime...	...and one of them is definitely guilty.
92	Competitive eaters...	...who don't care for crowds.
93	Professional grapplers...	...who have three catchphrases each.
94	Undercover cops...	...disguised as pastry chefs.
95	Real estate developers...	...who can't stop flipping property.
96	Debt collectors...	...who constantly trade memories of the good ol' days.
97	The creators of a new ale...	...who know they'll be famous one day.
98	Escapees from the same cult...	...who still have flashbacks.
99	Veterans of the same war...	...who get a new tattoo together every week.
100	A popular charmer and the goofball they bet they could make seem cool...	...who may also be falling in love.

LEGAL INFORMATION

Topix Media Lab
For inquiries, call 646-449-8614

Copyright 2023 Topix Media Lab

Published by Topix Media Lab
14 Wall Street, Suite 3C
New York, NY 10005

Printed in China

ISBN-13: 978-1-956403-39-8
ISBN-10: 1-956403-39-6

ACKNOWLEDGEMENTS

JEFF WOULD LIKE TO OFFER A FAIR AMOUNT OF THANKS...

...to the incredible team at Media Lab Books, without whom these pages would not have been created in any capacity. To Jasmine, for being an incredible collaborator and GM—this project would not have been possible without your inspiration and illustrations. To Liam, for providing material for this title that was so good it forced me to ask you to provide more. To Andrew, for answering all my RPG-related questions at any hour of day. To Paige and the Pretty Six, Jake and the Frothy Frogs, and each member of both the Jimmy Plural Project and the Gathered Company for helping assess (and in some cases truly derail) this material when it was just a bunch of random ideas. Your input and insight, whether intentional or not, helped to make it better. To Nick, Fiona, Buttons née Dijon Mayo, Trousers (R.I.P.), Malbec Whitetail, Zariel and Aemon—may your death saves always be 10 or better. Finally, to my incredible wife. This title would not have been possible without your support (in allowing me to play hours upon hours of games each week), your patience (when I came home late from said games) and overall guiding yet not smothering presence. Every moment with you feels like rolling a natural 20.

JASMINE WOULD LIKE TO THANK...

...my parents, for letting me come back home so I could work on this project. Your support and unconditional love is pretty great, not going to lie. Liam, for introducing me to the world of TTRPGs and for contributing some sweet locations to the book—without you I wouldn't be writing this and the lack of TTRPG content in my life would have left me hollow. My long-term campaign boys: The Drop Ins—Red, Mantl, Elisa, Adelise and Rajaa—I'm still waiting for the day I'll get enough time to have a villain monologue before their untimely death. The incredible parties who helped playtest this content: Seaman, North Sandhole, Yola Bean and Dortaela, as well as Dimitri, Felix, Grandma Hassle and Paerty.

My incredible friends who encourage me every day to keep going: Becky, Natalie, Lauren, Sean, TJ, Shastra, Emma, Kelly, Liisa and Jarred—love you guys.

And, of course, Jeff. I ended up losing count of the times your writing has made me laugh. It's been such an amazing experience collaborating and illustrating your crazy ideas.

Your GMs Are...

JEFF ASHWORTH is a writer, editor and storyteller whose credits include work for Disney, Nickelodeon and World Wrestling Entertainment. When he isn't working on special projects for Media Lab Books, he enjoys playing and designing games with his friends. In his role-playing career he has gambled with giants, sweet-talked succubi and devastated dragons without breaking a sweat. In the real world, after failing a late-night Perception check, he was nearly crippled by a foot-piercing d4. He and his wife live in Richmond, Virginia, with their dogs, Zelda and Lincoln.

JASMINE KALLE is a writer, illustrator and editor hailing from the sunny tropics of Brisbane, Australia. She has a Master of Arts (Writing, Editing and Publishing) and several years of TTRPG experience—though she doesn't tend to put that second part on her CV. In 2018 she embarked on an important quest that led her to the frozen winter tundra of New York and it was there that she first discovered some rather interesting dungeons, went on to fight more than a couple of dragons and hasn't looked back since. When she's not traveling and running games for various friends around the world, she returns home to hang out with her cat, Kiba, and dog, Otto, and regale them with tales of her adventures.

OTHER CONTRIBUTORS

LIAM GALLAGHER is a writer and gamer living in Brisbane, Australia. He has a great love of traveling in worlds both real and imagined. The fact that the latter is usually cheaper is no doubt responsible for his obsession with TTRPGs. Whether daydreaming about some future Antarctic expedition or GMing a crew of friends on a rollicking pirate adventure, his main wish is to have either his mind's eye or his actual fleshy eyeballs pay witness to new and incredible sights.

MICHAEL SHEA is the creator of the wildly popular website Sly Flourish (*slyflourish.com*) and the award-winning author of *The Lazy Dungeon Master, Return of the Lazy Dungeon Master, Fantastic Adventures: Ruins of the Grendleroot* and many other RPG supplements. He has worked with numerous RPG companies including Wizards of the Coast, Kobold Press, Pelgrane Press and Sasquatch Games. Shea lives with his wife, Michelle, in northern Virginia.